WARMAGE: UNDENIABLE

WARMAGE: UNDENIABLE

THE NEVER ENDING WAR™ BOOK FOUR

MARTHA CARR

MICHAEL ANDERLE

DISRUPTIVE IMAGINATION

LMBPN Publishing
PMB 196, 2540 South Maryland Pkwy
Las Vegas, NV 89109

First US edition, May 2020
Version 1.03, June 2020
ebook ISBN: 978-1-64202-934-5
Print ISBN: 978-1-64202-935-2

Thanks to our JIT Readers

Dorothy Lloyd
Debi Sateren
Veronica Stephan-Miller
James Caplan
Jackey Hankard-Brodie
Diane L. Smith
Deb Mader
Kerry Mortimer
John Ashmore
Peter Manis
Paul Westman

Editor

SkyHunter Editing Team

R aven Alby stood at the edge of the stable's roof on the Moss Dragon Ranch. She'd stopped with barely half an inch of boot protruding over the edge and now, she raised her face to the wind, her hands on her hips, and waited.

"But seriously, Raven. I don't know how this is supposed to help either of you." William Moss took a few steps toward her. Years of climbing up onto this roof for either repairs or simply to get away made it easy enough for him to keep his balance. *It's a little harder when a girl like that stands at the edge.* "I'm not even sure this is a good idea to begin with."

Beneath the relatively clean rag she'd tied around her eyes as a blindfold, she smiled. "That's the third time you've said that."

"Well, it's the third time you stepped closer to falling off this roof and breaking an arm. Or your neck."

She laughed. "Is that what your parents used to tell you?"

He stopped, gaped at the back of her head in surprise, and chuckled. "Actually, yeah. I guess it really is that easy to turn out like your parents if you're not careful, huh?"

"I think that depends on whether or not someone wants to be like their parents in the first place. I don't have a problem with it at all."

"I doubt either of your parents were this reckless," he muttered.

Raven turned her head to call partially over her shoulder, "What was that?"

"I said that's fairly obvious." Shaking his head, William took another step toward her, unwilling to take his eyes off her boots. *If she misjudges this, I can be right there to catch her. I'm sure I'm fast enough.*

"Parents aside, William Moss, I thought you promised not to worry about me."

"I did. But you kinda put me in a precarious position when you blindfolded yourself and started talking about how this was only training."

"Precarious position, huh? I didn't make you climb that ladder up here."

After another short pause, he sighed, although he couldn't completely hide a little laugh. "You know what I mean. What if I said I'm not actually worried about you? Only about the bad rap and all the fines that this ranch could expect if you mess up."

"I'd still tell you not to worry." As she listened intently for the sound of her dragon's flight, she tilted her head a little and took a deep breath. "We're not gonna screw this up. Professor Worley's been showing us how to do this for a few weeks now. And if Leander and I don't constantly up the stakes, how are we supposed to get better?"

"Up the stakes? Raven, do you know how many mages in this kingdom's history have even *had* a dragon as a familiar?"

"Well, I know of at least two. Plus the dragon riders."

William snorted. "I don't think the full tally is that much more, honestly. It's incredibly rare. And I've never heard of dragons being able to send thoughts to their mages. I didn't even know that was possible until you arrived and asked to use the stables so you can play dragon roulette."

Raven took a deep breath at the unexpected change in her focus. *Grandpa was a dragon rider* and *a mage with a dragon familiar. I wonder if he ever learned how to send images like this with his dragon.*

She cleared her throat and tried not to laugh at how heavily William breathed behind her. "It's definitely possible. Worley can do it with his familiars, and Headmaster Flynn signed off on him training me to do it. So it's not simply some crazy idea I came up with all on my own."

"I know it's not." He bit his lip and stared at her boots. "But something tells me neither of those guys signed off on you jumping blindfolded off a roof."

With an unconcerned laugh, she stretched her arms out to either side. It made her wobble a little, and he sucked a sharp breath in through his teeth.

"Watch it!"

"I'm fine." She regained her balance and stretched her arms out a little farther. "I got this."

"Uh-huh." His forehead hurt now from frowning in

worry, and he rubbed it quickly before he returned all his attention to the young mage's perch at the edge of the roof.

"And Leander's got this. You'll see."

The minute she said it, an image from Leander entered her mind. He was high above the dragon ranch with a view of the tiny stables ahead. *Wait for the next image and we're good to go.*

"Okay, I know you two have an amazing track record with saying you can do something and actually succeeding with it so I want to believe you. I really do." William took another tentative step forward and chanced a quick look over the edge of the roof beside him. "But if you can't see, that makes this one big shot in the dark, doesn't it? Even for practical purposes. Who's gonna blindfold you in the heat of—Raven!"

He staggered toward her in the same moment that the young mage leapt off the edge of the roof. Of course, he was too late to catch her, but the massive red dragon dropped like a boulder out of the sky much faster.

Raven's boots landed on Leander's back and the treads gripped the thick ridges of his red scales as she sank into a crouch. It only took a second to steady herself before her huge familiar straightened to soar over the ranch and the field scattered with the dozens of Moss Ranch dragons. She uttered a whoop of victory and yanked the rag from over her eyes.

On the roof of the stables, William covered his mouth with a hand and squeezed until his jaw hurt. Finally, he whipped his hat off and scratched his head vigorously, ruffling his shoulder-length blond hair. "That girl's gonna give me a heart attack." A sharp laugh escaped him. "Now I *really* sound like my dad."

He shoved his wide-brimmed hat on again and headed across the roof toward the ladder they'd propped up against the back of the stables. Raven and Leander had already doubled back and landed on the trodden dirt studded with patches of coarse grass by the time his boots touched the ground.

"You saw that, right?" With a grin, she vaulted off Leander's back and spread her arms. "Please tell me you saw that. Because...well, I couldn't see anything."

William leaned back against the stable wall beside the ladder with a thump. "I saw it all right, but I haven't changed my mind about your stunts, though."

For a few seconds, her smile faltered. *He's actually pissed.*

In the next moment, the dragon trainer burst into laughter and didn't stop.

The young mage looked at her dragon familiar, who gazed at her with his glowing yellow eyes narrowed a little in suspicion. "I think we broke him."

"Better that it happens now. Flyboy can't handle the truth." Leander's wings twitched out before they settled slowly against his back again in what she had come to recognize as a dragon's shrug.

"Whew." Doubled over, William slapped his thigh before he straightened and grinned at the two of them with wide eyes.

Yep. He's totally lost his mind.

"You two are full of more surprises than anyone I know." He scratched his jaw and stepped toward them. "I'd be lying if I said that wasn't incredible."

"It would also make you an idiot," Leander added.

"You know what?" The dragon trainer pointed at the dragon and shook his finger. "I'll accept that as proof that you don't think I already am an idiot. That's a good place to start."

Raven chuckled and patted the beast's broad, muscular shoulder. "We're getting better, Leander. Perfect timing on those images."

The dragon snorted. "I know."

William uttered another laugh. "Okay, Raven. I'm convinced. If familiars can actually send images to their mages, a dragon's no exception."

"Huh." She darted Leander a sidelong glance and winked. "I think he found the only thing where a dragon's not an exception."

Her familiar rumbled in agreement and lowered his head to nudge her shoulder.

"Unbelievable." He chuckled and shook his head as he stepped around the end of the stables. His gaze took a wide, sweeping view of the huge, magically penned-in field where the Moss Ranch dragons roamed within the small groupings of different clans. "And no one out there even noticed."

"They noticed," Leander muttered. "Dragons can feel the trust in others. Isn't that something a dragon trainer should already know?"

He turned toward the great red beast and raised an eyebrow. "Of course it is. Which you already know too." They stared challengingly at one another a little longer until William finally spread his arms and inclined his head. "Admittedly, watching Raven jump off buildings blindfolded and riding a dragon without any gear at all is still something I'm trying to wrap my head around."

"Well, thanks for not trying to stop me," she said with a little smirk.

The dragon trainer chuckled and fiddled with the brim of his hat. *I almost did.* "Yeah, well, I'm still working on that too. Even though we all know trying to stop Raven Alby and her dragon familiar is a waste of everyone's time."

"Still." Raven glanced at Leander and put her hands on her hips. "It's good to have friends who let us use their stable as a launching pad."

William stared at her and slowly shook his head. "You know I can't say no to you."

"Which is why we came out here for a little extra practice." Laughing, she stepped toward him. "And thanks for letting us practice here. The Alby Ranch hands wouldn't have recovered so well from watching me jump off a roof. Plus, the goats might've started eating each other or something."

"And the grounds of your magic school weren't an option because…"

The young mage took a deep breath and glanced at the sunset sky with a knowing smile. "This kind of training isn't exactly something I want the whole school to see. There are enough rumors going around about Leander and me already."

"Huh. I wonder why."

She rolled her eyes playfully and moved closer as she extended her hand toward him. "Really, though. Thank you. From both of us."

William snorted at her outstretched hand. "I have no

idea what you're trying to do with that." He pulled her quickly toward him and wrapped his arms around her as he muttered, "I'm glad you didn't jump off a roof for nothing."

After her initial surprise, she laughed and patted his back a few times. "That would've been really stupid of me."

He held onto her a while longer, and she bit her lip and waited for her friend to release her. *Okay, point taken. I scared the crap out of him.*

Finally, he loosened his hold and stepped back, rubbing the back of his neck with a self-conscious smile. "I hope you don't end up having to use that little trick outside training."

Behind them, Leander uttered a few short, quick hisses. Raven wrinkled her nose. "Yeah… Hopefully." *I'm not gonna tell him that we already have.*

The dragon trainer squinted at the uncharacteristically laughing dragon and sniffed warily. "I'm missing something, aren't I?"

"Not at all." Raven clapped a hand on his shoulder and nodded. "We're all good. And Leander and I should get back to Fowler before dark. We gotta wake up and do it all over again tomorrow, you know?"

William's eyes widened. "You plan to come back to jump off my stable again?"

"Well, no. I was talking about the whole day." She chuckled and headed toward her dragon. "You know, wake up with a dragon, go to class, train with Alessandra and then Professor Worley, spend the rest of my free time with a dragon and maybe a friend or two. Rinse and repeat. It's a never-ending cycle, really."

"It sounds like it." William watched in amazement as she took the last few steps to Leander at a jog and leapt onto the beast's huge, wide head for a boost onto his back.

In only a few seconds, she was seated bareback on a huge red dragon and smiled cheerfully at her friend. "We'll be back soon."

"I'm looking forward to it." *I think.* When the two took to the sky, William lifted his hat and waved to them. He lowered his arm when they were out of sight and shook his head. *This town isn't big enough for those two. I only hope she decides to stick around a little longer once she realizes it.*

CHAPTER TWO

Raven lifted her forearm to the gate of Leander's pen on the Fowler Academy grounds. Her access rune glowed a soft orange, the gate mirrored the same light, and the latch popped open with a metallic click.

"We had a productive day overall, huh?" She stepped back, dragged the gate open with her, and smiled as the dragon walked into his enclosure.

"There was some progress."

The young mage chuckled and followed him inside. "I can always count on you to keep me humble."

He turned in a few circles before he lowered himself to the soft, green grass. His gaze settled on her somewhat teasingly and he snorted. "Can you?"

"Well, for some things, anyway." Joining him in the center, Raven stepped closer and rested her hand on his raised snout for a moment before she ran it along the scaly ridges between his eyes. "Like how much work we still have left before we graduate from year one."

"And after that?"

"Well, after that, we're officially Fowler Academy mages for the next three years."

Leander huffed out a quick breath through his nose. "Only you."

"Okay, true. You won't be a mage. But we're in this together and I know I haven't done nearly enough studying for History of Magic. Or Transformations."

"I don't think you need to study anything."

She grinned and ran her hand as far as she could reach down his long neck. "Well, thank you. Honestly, I'm not worried about it. I'm sure we'll pass and move on to year two. I have private training in two different subjects and it's not to help me catch up with the rest of the first-year class. But I still need to put the work in to make sure."

"You're already sure, little girl."

"Hmm. Now I'm not sure if that's supposed to keep me humble too or boost my confidence."

The dragon uttered a short, deep rumble and settled his head onto his forepaws. "It's the truth."

With a smirk, she sank into a crouch in front of her dragon and held his gaze. "You were already too good at knowing what I'm thinking. Once we master this whole mind-connection thing, I don't think I'll be able to keep anything from you."

"Why would you want to?"

"That's a good point." Raven tilted her head and ran her gaze over the long line of his neck, over the ridges of his back, and across the powerful wings tucked tightly against his sides. "Do you need anything before I head off to bed?"

"No."

"Okay, then. I'll see you in the morning."

As she started to stand, Leander raised his snout toward her hand again for another quick pat along his scaly muzzle. When she lowered her hand again, he settled into his usual sleeping position—curled into a tight ball of red scales and translucent wings—and the young mage headed toward the open gate. She paused and looked over her shoulder for one more glance at him, but his eyes were already closed.

It doesn't matter what he says. He's as happy with what we accomplished today as I am.

She slipped quietly out of the pen and shut the gate behind her with a soft click.

When Raven stepped inside her room in the girls' dormitory, Elizabeth sat cross-legged on her own bed, her head lowered over the book in her lap. The girl's long curtain of black hair almost completely obscured her face. "Long day, war mage?"

"Very funny." She shut the door behind her and sighed when the low chatter from the other girls on the third floor vanished completely beneath the sound-proof spell. "You know, you have an uncanny ability to know what's going on around you without looking up from your books."

Her roommate shrugged. "It's a skill highly developed over years of trying to maintain my personal bubble in a house with five siblings running around. It comes in handy when people think you're more focused on reading than listening to conversations." A slow, knowing smile spread across the girl's lips. "I have dirt on them to last a lifetime."

"Ha!" Raven headed toward her bed on the far side of the room and bent to untie the laces of her work boots before she kicked them off. "I didn't know you had so many siblings."

"Yep. And I'm the youngest." Elizabeth snorted. "Brett's twenty. He was the last one to move out before I came here. For a brief summer, I got new clothes and all my parents' attention."

"It sounds nice, actually."

"Not when they're planting six kids' worth of parenting onto only one." The girl closed the book, tossed it onto the comforter beside her, and pulled a few strawberries out of the nightstand drawer to feed to her bat familiar. Iggy poked his head up from where he'd been snuggled in her lap and nibbled at the fruit. "I can say I enjoy having my own clothes far better than hand-me-downs."

Raven sat on the edge of her bed and froze. "Well now I feel really bad about ripping up that dress you let me borrow."

Her friend chuckled and continued to feed her bat. "It's an easy fix. Trust me. My mom went from mending clothes for four boys and two girls to sitting around all day in an empty house. At least, that's the way she talks about it. I sent that dress home, and she sent me this gushing letter about how thrilled she was that someone actually needed her."

"Did you tell her what happened to it?"

"Nope. And she didn't even ask." Elizabeth tossed her dark bangs out of her face but they fell into place over her right eye as they always did. "Maybe I shouldn't have asked her to fix it. That thing might be worth a ton of money someday. You know, worn by Fowler Academy's first-year war mage who destroyed the rest of the Swarm with her dragon."

She laughed and went to her dresser to pull out her pajamas. "Bella and Wesley were there too. I couldn't have done it without them. And if you can make money off a dress I sliced with a knife, go for it."

They both laughed at that, and she returned to the bed to toss her pajamas onto the comforter before she undid the tie in her red braid.

"Hey, speaking of letters, are you staying in the dorms through the rest of the year?"

Raven paused and wrinkled her nose. "What does that have to do with letters?"

"Well…you finally heard from your grandpa."

"Oh." Running her fingers through her hair, the war mage in training sat on her bed again and shrugged. "I got a letter from him, yeah. But I don't think he's coming back anytime soon. He only talked about staying where he is and continuing with his research."

"Where is he?"

"I honestly have no idea." She changed quickly into her pajamas as she spoke. "His letter came from Havendom and that's where Headmaster Flynn sent the letter I wrote in reply. But Connor Alby could be anywhere in the kingdom right now, and I really don't have a better way to find out where that is."

"It must be frustrating."

"A little. But it's definitely better than not hearing from

him for weeks after he disappeared like that."

"Boy." Elizabeth flopped onto her back and stared at the ceiling with a dreamy sigh. "I would love to simply up and leave whenever I wanted, not tell anyone where I'm going, and only send a few letters with vague hints. That's like… the perfect escape."

Raven laughed and pulled her legs onto the bed to cross them beneath her. "I don't think my grandpa was trying to escape anything. But I see how that'd be a big selling point for you. Elizabeth Kinsley's private getaway. No people, no talking, and endless books."

The dark-haired witch snorted. "It's that obvious, huh?"

"It's not like you try to hide it. And for some reason, you still like me."

"Yeah, you're all right."

The room fell silent, and her thoughts drifted to the one and only letter she'd received from Connor. *He thinks magic's coming back and has no way to prove it other than the fact that he has his own magic again. But if he's right…*

She shifted onto her stomach and stretched over the edge of the bed to pull her grandfather's oilskin bag from under it. The crystal ball was tucked away in one of the loose corners, but she finally found it and drew the apple-sized orb out for a quick look. *It's all white again. So for now, at least, there is no danger coming.*

The glass ball thumped into the bag again and she scooted across her bed and folded her arms to rest her chin on her hands and think. *His letter didn't sound panicked, either. Only curious and concerned. At least I have a little more proof that nothing awful's coming.*

Raven pushed off her stomach and began to pull the

comforter down to slip beneath it.

"Are you goin' to bed?"

"Yeah." She turned on her side and smiled as her head sank into the pillow as she closed her eyes. "Like you said. Long day."

"Totally." Elizabeth scooted Iggy aside so she could crawl under her covers too. The bat squeaked and hopped after her before it curled into a ball beside her neck. She stretched her hand toward the orb of light in the middle of the ceiling and muttered, "*Circum inlustro.*"

Even with the light out now, Raven couldn't help but look at the window centered between the beds and the moon rising in the new darkness.

Wherever you really are, Grandpa, I love you more.

In the small town of Heatherwood half a day's ride northeast of Brighton, Jeremy Cathrop walked out onto his front porch and lifted his lantern. The yellow glow only illuminated a small section of the grass beyond his porch, and he shuffled down the steps as he grumbled under his breath.

"These damn sheep. Every night, they find something else to go on about. I'm sick of it."

He reached the pen where his flock had settled for the night. The sheep now bleated uncontrollably and jostled one another as they pushed and crowded together along the fence.

"Why aren't you sleeping, eh? I'm already a grumpy old man. I don't need a flock of wooly animals adding to this —hey!"

A sharp cackle rose from the other side of the pen, followed by the terrified bleating of a lamb held tightly in an elf's spindly arms.

"Oh, no you don't." Jeremy darted around the pen and the intruder scuttled in the same direction. He dragged the lamb with him because the poor animal was too big to slip through the fence while it struggled. "Drop the lamb, you scrawny little vermin!"

"Make me!" The elf hissed a challenge and tightened his hold around the lamb's middle, which made the creature bleat again in sharp little bursts.

"Yeah, you're one of the stupid ones, aren't ya?" The shepherd leapt around the pen again, and the elf ran out of room and tugged his prey with him against the wall of the shelter. "You're in trouble now, you little—"

A rumble like heavy thunder rose directly overhead. The two antagonists looked up seconds before a gust of wind blasted against the sheep pen. It threw Jeremy forward against the rails of the fence, and he shouted in his struggle to maintain his hold on the lantern. Despite his efforts the tiny flame inside was snuffed out instantly. The elf squawked, tumbled sideways, and released the startled lamb, who dropped to the straw with a muted thump.

Another gust of wind buffeted the shepherd's back and pinned him against the fence. "What the—"

With the lantern out, the moon provided sufficient light to see the confused sheep—now startled into silence—and the intruder seated in the grass. The two adversaries looked skyward as another thunderous rumble accompanied a massive black shadow that passed across the moon and blocked out every trace of light in the sky.

Jeremy gulped. The elf squeaked and scrambled to his feet before he sprinted away from the pen and the sheep farm.

Miles away to the east, a grating shriek rose from the Mountains of Jared. The shepherd jumped at the sound, despite the distance, and shivered.

The black shadow vanished from overhead and gave way to the moon and stars once more. He waited and listened intently as his heart pounded in his chest. *Move, you old bastard. Get inside!*

That spurred him into action and he pushed away from the fence. The lantern fell forgotten from his hand and shattered. He staggered over the grass and yelped when his boot kicked an empty pail beside the pen. By the time he made it up the porch steps, he could barely breathe and his arms flailed in front of him to ward off what he couldn't see. He'd forgotten there was nothing on the porch at all but finally reached the door and jiggled the handle with a shaking hand before he finally shoved it open and stumbled into the farmhouse.

His hands still trembled half an hour later. *I never heard anything like that before. And that wasn't a storm passing through. I'd set my life on it.*

Jeremy slapped a hand against his forehead and grunted. "Don't tempt fate, man. Keep that out of your thoughts."

Although he tried to reassure himself with positive thinking, he didn't get any sleep that night. He was too busy listening for the monstrous scream coming from the mountains.

CHAPTER THREE

The next day marked the end of classes for the week, and more than anything, Raven looked forward to two days of only having to focus on war mage training with Alessandra and spending the rest of her time with her dragon.

Before she got there, she had to sit through one final day of classes. Professor Bixby's History of Magic class didn't exactly help with the young mage's jitters.

"Today, we'll talk about the finer points of being a mage and your ability to tap into and use your own magic for various purposes." The vertically challenged professor stood on the platform behind her podium at the front of the room and peered at them from behind the thick lenses magnifying her eyes. "Mainly, we'll discuss that the ability to use magic at all is nothing short of a privilege which must be respected and appreciated above everything else. Because, of course, any mage can run out of the limited supply of magic stored within them from birth."

Raven straightened a little in her chair. *Maybe not.*

MARTHA CARR & MICHAEL ANDERLE

"Now for the history side of this topic, which is in fact where my specialty lies," Bixby continued. "Centuries ago, magic used to be readily available to every Tina, Dan, and Henry."

A few snickers rose at that as the students turned to look at Henry Derks. Grinning, he pointed at his chest with both thumbs and whispered, "Now it's only this Henry."

The young mage smirked at him and rolled her eyes.

"Yes, yes, Mr. Derks. We all know you share a name with a common saying. How lucky for you. As I was saying." Bixby cleared her throat with a high-pitched grumble and continued. "Magic was so prevalent in these long-ago times that it was used for all manner of things—anything and everything in daily life, from household tasks to farm and ranch chores to sewing fancy clothes. Magic was cast willy-nilly all over the place, without any form of consequence to the caster. And, of course, this was long before those of us with magic today were ever called witches or wizards. It was well before the term 'mage' was used to describe a person with a passing mastery of their own skills with magic itself.

"No one can really say for certain exactly why magic diminished over the years to now only appear in strong magical bloodlines while the rest of the world was cut off from using it altogether. But there are a few theories."

The professor lifted her wand above the podium and muttered, "*Illustrare fabulam.*"

A blue circle of light appeared in the air beside her and grew to the size of a window as smoke-like images appeared inside it to illustrate her talking points.

"First is the more widely recognized theory, one accepted the most frequently among non-magical people within Lomberdoon and beyond. Perhaps this seems the best way for most minds who have never felt magic to put reason and logic to its disappearance. Or perhaps they don't much care." A small chuckle escaped the woman, but whatever private joke she shared with herself went completely over her students' heads.

"Most people believe or rationalize that magic is a natural resource of our world like water, timber, gems and minerals, good soil, etcetera. The view is that magic has been used to the extent that there is now only enough to fill the veins of a very select few among us in relation to the total population. Not everyone has magic, as I'm sure you all know. This makes witches and wizards very much the minority."

"But what decides who gets magic and who doesn't?"

"Ah, yes. That leads right into the second theory, Miss Barnaby. Thank you." Bixby pointed her wand at the girl seated in the second row from the front, her lynx nestled in her lap with her face peeking out over the top of the desk. "Of course, this first theory raises many of the same questions as the one posed to us by Miss Barnaby. And this is where the theory of magical bloodlines comes into play."

At the mention of magical bloodlines, Raven couldn't help herself. She turned to look at Bella Chase seated a few seats down in the row in front of her. Bella did the same, caught the redheaded mage's gaze, and raised an eyebrow.

Great minds, I guess.

"*Illustrare fabulam,*" Bixby muttered again. This time, a yellow circle of light bloomed from the tip of her wand

and grew in the air beside her exactly like the first. The blue circle shrank and moved farther toward the wall to make room. "This theory of magical bloodlines proposes that when magic became aware of its own dwindling supply—thanks to the millions of people who had used it for centuries to whatever end they wished—magic itself selected the strongest families with the most inherent magical potential. This is where it funneled itself while the rest of the world lost their ability to so much as conjure a spark. Now, keep in mind, this did not happen overnight. Most historians agree that the process took somewhere between one hundred and fifty and two hundred years to fully weed out those who would never use magic again from those who would continue to pass it on to their progeny through generations to come."

In the back row, Percy folded his arms and smirked. "It's merely survival of the magicalest."

"Most magical, Mr. Alderman." The professor focused on him over the thick frames of her glasses and her frizzy copper hair bounced when she cocked her head. "But yes. The most magical families, if you will, have been selected to keep their magical bloodlines alive and perpetuated into the future."

"That's like luck of the draw too, isn't it?" Bella asked. "We're not destined for magic. It's all about who your family is and whether or not they have a number of witches and wizards."

"Yes, Miss Chase. That is what this theory of magical bloodlines supports. Finally, there's the third theory. And if you're trying to find something to support the idea of destiny, I believe this would be it." The professor cast her spell a third time and a red circle of light expanded in the air. "This theory about the selective existence of magic currently is that magic—as an entity all its own and with something of a sentient view into all timelines—chose to remove itself from the world. Some imagine this was a direct result of too much magic being used by everyone for silly, inconsequential purposes. Or that it became the root cause of jealousy, greed, and petty indiscretions. This theory suggests that those families who retained their magical abilities were chosen on purpose and for a purpose —that each of you are fulfilling your destiny, laid out by magic itself, to become certified and honored mages once you graduate from this school.

"Now, if this were the case, none of us would be aware of what our true purpose is or what we are to do with this privilege so we do the best we can. And perhaps those who put stock in this third theory find some comfort in the belief that magic chose each and every one of us because of who we are and who we will become, perhaps even with the hope that some balance would be restored by magic no longer being accessible to everyone."

"What theory do you believe?" Tessa asked.

Bixby gave the girl a small, tight-lipped smile. "Like politics, Miss Hambridge, I prefer not to discuss that in public."

"Professor?" Raven raised her hand, and the woman actually looked surprised to see any student pose a question in that way.

"Yes, Miss Alby?"

"If that third theory were true, hypothetically, and magic did choose each of us to restore some kind of balance... What happens when everything's finally balanced again?"

The professor uttered a high-pitched chuckle. "I teach History of Magic, Miss Alby. Not prophecy."

A few of the other students snickered and shifted in their seats, which only made their professor smile.

Raven smiled in response and tried again. "What I'm trying to ask is if there's any possibility of magic coming back into the world for everyone. Like it used to be."

The classroom fell completely silent. Bixby's lens-magnified eyes flicked a hasty gaze around the room and her mouth opened and closed as she searched for the words. After a few moments, with a small laugh, she shook her head. "Miss Alby, you have a vivid imagination and a commendable eagerness to dive deeper into so many different topics. Unfortunately, I can't answer that question for you so please take it to someone else."

The young mage frowned and leaned back in her chair. *Dismissed just like that?*

Bixby clapped her hands several times and raised her chin to gaze at the few dozen faces tilted toward her in focus. "Now, to drill my original point home, I want each of you to draw up a summary of a normal day for you in your own lives. This must include one day during the week while you're here at school and one day from week's end. In each, you will detail what an average day would look like if you did not have the use of magic to assist you in whatever it is you use magic for. Hopefully, I won't see very many of these assignments returned with massive gaps of time changed because you've already grown accustomed to frivolous casting."

The woman tilted her head forward over the podium, and when no one laughed or really reacted at all, she sighed. "You'll spend the rest of this class on the assignment, starting now, and if you don't finish today, I expect you all to have completed this by the start of our first class next week. I highly recommend not procrastinating."

She gestured toward the table beside her with the rolled-up scrolls of parchment paper, and each student moved sluggishly from their desks to retrieve one.

Henry slid out of his chair as Raven passed him and stepped into line behind her. He leaned forward to whisper, "It looks like you ruffled someone's curly feathers."

Raven glanced at their professor, who was busy reading something spread out on her podium, and shrugged. "It was an honest question."

"*I* know that but I don't think Bixby understands the difference between questioning the unknown and questioning her."

The young witch turned to frown at him over her shoulder. "If she's gonna teach a class of mages to expand their minds but won't even consider answering an innocent question, what's the point?"

"Hmm." He stroked his hairless chin and squinted at their History of Magic professor before he grinned broadly. "Maybe she's too attached to that little platform. It makes her two feet taller in seconds. Like magic."

She snorted, which made him hiss out a laugh, and Bixby looked up from her reading to fix them both with narrowed eyes above a stern, unamused smile. "Maybe we should save the height jokes for after class, huh, Derks?"

Henry clamped his lips together and shook his head with another shrug.

"Perfect." Raven rolled her eyes playfully and when they reached the table of parchment paper, she took two scrolls and handed one to her best friend. "Since you're not talking, I guess you'll have more time to focus on finishing this super-fun assignment before class is out."

His eyes widened when he took the scroll from her, and she fought back a laugh as she turned to return to her seat. "Wait a minute, Alby," he protested. "No one said anything about not talking at all. I don't think I'd survive that."

CHAPTER FOUR

Once Professor Bixby's class was over, the students stood and exited in record time to hurry to their next class, especially Raven.

"Woah, wait up," Henry called, ducked beneath the strap of his shoulder bag, and half-jogged to catch up with her. Murphy pushed through the other kids into the hall too and joined them outside. "Who lit a fire under you? And you can't use Leander as a default for everything. I definitely would've noticed a dragon in class with us."

Raven gave him an exasperated glance but a small laugh escaped her anyway. "Maybe you didn't notice, but Bixby stared daggers at me for the entire rest of the class. My skin kept tingling, and every time I looked up, bam. Giant bug eyes stared at me." She raised both hands to her eyes in an imitation of their professor's humorously thick lenses.

Henry snorted. The other girl chuckled and adjusted the strap of her knapsack over her shoulder. "I don't think she likes being asked questions she doesn't know the answers to."

"See?" He knocked the back of his hand playfully against Murphy's shoulders. "That's exactly what I said."

"I don't think she likes being questioned at all," Raven muttered. "And now, I've started to think she doesn't like being questioned by me specifically."

"Well, can you blame her?"

Henry looked at Murphy and snickered.

Raven shook her head. "Kind of. Unless I've missed some kind of inside joke between you two."

"Think about it, Alby." He slung his arm around his best friend's shoulders as they headed down the halls of the main building. "Since the beginning of our rich and illustrious careers at Fowler Academy, every time you raise something in Bixby's class, it ends up coming true."

"What? That's not true at all."

"Really? Okay, allow us to lay it out for you. Raven Alby asked about the Swarm ever returning. Bam. The Swarm returned, and you got to fight them."

Murphy pressed her lips together and tried not to laugh as she adopted Henry's sage expression and added to the argument. "Raven Alby asked about the raiders being a real threat to the kingdom. Bam. Raiders scrambled over the great wall, and you got to fight them too."

Raven gaped at them for a moment before she laughed in disbelief and rolled her eyes. "Well, I'll tell you right now I'm not about to pick a fight with magic. And it's not like I can tell the future or anything. I'm only thinking about the possibilities."

"Exactly." Henry pulled his arm back and patted her shoulder. "All the possibilities Professor Bixby never even considered. Or doesn't want to."

Murphy watched her cat familiar Fritz dart away from a few second-years who ran down the stone hall and yelled at each other on their way to their next class. "She probably thinks you have it in for her at this point."

"I don't!" They all laughed. "That's not even my intention. It's genuine curiosity."

"She doesn't know that. I guess you gotta be super careful from here on out, huh? Whatever Alby says in History of Magic will end up in the Future of Magic. Hey!" He nudged her with his shoulder. "Maybe you should teach that class."

"Gimme a break."

The trio of friends skirted a group of third-year girls who conjured fire in intricate animal shapes and made them fight each other in the middle of the next corridor. Murphy grimaced disapprovingly and shook her head. "The only reason they get away with doing that inside is because they're third years. It makes me *really* glad most of these buildings are stone."

Raven peered over her shoulder at the third-year witches, who all laughed as a flaming green alligator bit into a butterfly of blue flames twice its size. "They'd better stay away from the stables."

"Please. With only one puff of fire from Leander, they'll realize how useless their fancy little tricks really are."

"With one puff of fire from Leander, Derks, they won't be laughing anymore at all."

That made the young wizard pause in surprise and his eyes widened as he replayed that image through his mind.

She laughed and Murphy joined her, and the redheaded mage slapped a hand on Henry's shoulder. "That was only partially a joke. Leander would never breathe fire on other students."

He gulped. "What's the partially serious part?"

As they stepped out of the main building and into the courtyard outside the front of the school, she scrunched her nose with a little grimace. "I didn't exactly tell you guys everything about fighting raiders in Azerad."

They stopped at the edge of the courtyard, and Murphy scooped Fritz into her arms when he uttered a distressed mewl at her feet. "Did that actually happen? Dragon fire at actual people?"

Raven nodded. "Actual people, yeah, but they were raiders taking hostages. He did what he thought was best and I don't disagree with him, necessarily. It was only…intense."

Henry's mouth had dropped open. "What was that like?"

"Uh…fast and hot and then a big pile of ash." She shrugged and waited for her friends to say something. "Oh, come on, guys. It was to save the kingdom, remember? Both of you could've ended up killing those raiders you fought—" She lowered her voice and glanced around the courtyard. "The ones you fought literally right here, wasn't it?"

His mouth still hanging open, Henry looked at the roof of the main building and the highest tower at Fowler Academy that housed Headmaster Flynn's office at the top. "Yeah. Almost exactly right here."

"Hey, I don't have anything against bashing a few raiders," Murphy added.

"More like bashing in raider skulls with that ax. Am I right?" He raised his hand toward her for a high five.

"And mean skills with a slingshot." Murphy smacked her hands against his with a little smirk.

Raven smiled at her friends until they turned toward her again. "So you're not totally horrified that Leander burned a few raiders to dust?" *It's probably a good idea not to mention the ones I killed with arrows too. For now.*

Henry leaned forward and raised an eyebrow. "How many is a few?" Murphy smacked his arm and he bounced away from her with a snicker. "Okay, okay. Sorry."

"We're not horrified," the girl added.

"Of course not. Yeah, the idea of being burned alive in two seconds flat by the hottest heat straight from a dragon's mouth is horrifying. But like you said, Alby, he did what he had to do. And you got those hostages out of there —oh. Hey. It's a story of a dragon saving a damsel in distress. That's a new one."

The girls both stared at him, and Raven folded her arms. "Dragon and his mage, Derks. You can't really leave the mage out of this one."

"Oh, my bad." He raised his arms and spread them in a dramatic gesture as he stared into the distance. "The story of a dragon and his mage who's also a dragon rider and training to be a war mage saving the damsel in distress. Yeah. That's so much better. Rolls right off the tongue."

Chuckling, she rolled her eyes and moved around the main building toward the smaller stone building beside it for their Transformation class with Professor Gilliam. "I think you should cross traveling bard mage off your list of possible professions and stick to the slingshot work."

"I second that," Murphy added with a little snort.

"Did you hear that, Maxwell?" Henry glanced at his toad familiar's head where it poked out of the top of his shoulder bag. "They're fans of the slingshot. At least we have their support for something. That's all I ever—"

"Hey, Raven."

She stopped short as Daniel Smith appeared from around the back of the main building. Murphy stopped behind her, and Henry couldn't slow in time to avoid grazing the back of the brown-haired witch's ankle with his boot.

"Ow."

"Sorry, Murph. Unexpected pileup."

"Hi, Daniel." Raven smiled at the second-year student and raised her eyebrows. *We're gonna be seriously late if he doesn't get right to the point.*

Daniel propped his hand against the stone wall beside them, his other shoved loosely into his pants pocket. "How you doin'?"

"Yeesh. I'll see you in there, Alby." Henry stepped around Murphy and jerked his chin at Daniel in a wordless greeting before he strode into the other building.

Murphy pointed after him and shrugged. "I'm gonna..."

"Yeah, okay." Raven gave her friend a quick smile and nodded. *I wouldn't wanna stick around for this either if I were them. Not that this is a bad thing.* She looked at Daniel again and sighed. "I'm doing okay. Trying to get to class, actually."

"Cool, cool." He pressed his lips together and leaned back as he dragged one shoe lazily from side to side across the cobblestone like he had all the time in the world. "I wondered what you're doing for the next few days. You know, no classes and everything."

Despite not wanting to be singled out by Gilliam's disapproval stare, Raven grinned at Daniel and cared less and less about how much of her time he took up. "Oh, you know. Training, training, flying around on a dragon, more training. Sleep and food somewhere in there. The usual."

He chuckled and stepped closer. "It sounds like fun."

"Most of the time, yeah. What about you?" She fought down a grimace once the question popped out. *Great. I gave him an open invitation to keep going.*

"Not much, really. I thought I might stop by at some point to see you. You know, to hang out. That's it."

"Uh-huh." She raised an eyebrow at him and very quickly realized how quiet the main courtyard had become now that all the other students were in their classes again. *Doesn't he have somewhere to be too?* "Well, you're free to stop by whenever you want. I do live here, so…"

"Yeah, I know." Daniel chuckled and his blue eyes glinted over his dimpling cheeks. "I wanted to make sure it was cool with you first."

"It's cool with me."

"Awesome." He continued to stare at her and moved closer by the second.

Does he really think I don't notice? Raven took a deep breath and stepped to the side to neatly avoid him. "I have to get to class, Daniel. Sorry. See you in the next couple of days, I guess. Or whenever."

He turned to watch her power-walk toward the small building ahead and grinned. "I'm looking forward to it."

She turned to give him a quick wave. "Okay!"

As she clutched the straps of her satchel to stop it swinging, she quickened her pace toward the front door of the building that hosted most of Professor Gilliam's classes. *He could've found me later to ask about that. This guy doesn't give up.*

Still, when she jerked the door open and slipped through the halls toward her next class, she couldn't hold back a secret little smile.

CHAPTER FIVE

At the end of the school day, like every day, Raven hurried across the field to the stables and opened the gate of Leander's enclosure. When she stuck her head inside, she found her massive red dragon familiar lying on his side in the tall grass and soaking up the sunshine. His scales glistened under the light and cast glittering, red-tinged reflections over the pen's metal walls.

She grinned. "Guess what time it is."

He grunted. "I don't have to guess."

"Okay, another figure of speech that's now apparently only for humans." With a soft laugh, she leaned against the side of the open gate and folded her arms. "I'm ready when you are."

"I'm coming." With a snort, he rolled onto his belly, rose gracefully to his feet, and shook his head, neck, body, and tail like a wet dog. She tried not to laugh as he scraped a rear claw across the grass a few times before he moved forward to join her out in the field.

Raven pushed the gate enough to leave it open a crack, dusted her hands off, and nodded. "More training. Get excited."

Leander turned to face her and lowered his head. "This is my excited face, little girl."

"Oh. Is that right?" She stroked her chin and tried to look like she was thinking way too hard. "I guess I really have to work on the subtle nuances between your excited face, your hungry face, your bored face, and your trying-not-to-make-a-face face. Don't worry, I'll get there eventually."

The dragon's glowing yellow eyes narrowed and he uttered a rumble of amusement.

Bella and Wesley approached them from the school's main buildings on the other side of the field. The dark-haired mage smiled and jerked her chin at Raven, then stopped to lower her satchel onto the ground against the stable wall. "I'd like to say how great it is that the week's over, but that doesn't really apply to us, does it?"

Raven chuckled. "Not really. But I'd still take training every single day over sitting in a stuffy room trying not to ask all the questions that allegedly tell the future."

As she turned toward her, Bella put her hands on her hips and tilted her head. "Bixby really got to you this morning, huh?"

"Not as much as I apparently got to her first." She shrugged. "But it kinda rubbed me the wrong way, yeah."

"Shrug it off. She's stuck in the past—like, it's literally her job. She doesn't even want to look at what might happen anyway because it's not written down in a collection of old volumes stored in a dusty library somewhere."

Raven did shrug, shook her head, and allowed herself a small sigh.

"I didn't mean literally, but okay."

They both chuckled and looked up when Wesley uttered a little screech and wheeled overhead. The firedrake dipped toward Leander's head but turned away at the last second to dart into another airborne circuit. The dragon raised his head and watched the much smaller familiar intently. When Wesley swooped toward him again, he stretched his neck and barely missed batting the firedrake out of the sky.

She stepped toward Bella and lowered her voice. "Don't look now but I think we might have a case of two reptiles playing a game of tag over there. Or something."

The girl slid a sidelong glance at their familiars and snorted. "I think your dragon has more patience than most people give him credit for."

"And that firedrake doesn't know when to quit." When the girls looked at each other again, they broke into muffled laughter.

They sobered as they saw Alessandra walking quickly toward them from the stone archway from the main courtyard, her arms swinging at her sides. "Here comes War Mage Barnasis."

Raven wiped all trace of emotion off her face and stared straight ahead. "Don't smile."

Bella squared her feet toward their trainer, clasped her hands behind her back, and muttered from the side of her mouth, "Don't move. Don't even breathe."

They both snorted and fortunately, they had sufficient time to recover before the gray-haired woman joined them beyond the stables. She stopped short only a few feet away and studied them warily. Her gaze cut from one young mage to the other. "What happened?"

Raven shook her head a fraction of an inch. "What do you mean?"

"Two of my trainees standing there like they're trying really hard to not look like they're hiding something." Alessandra's eyes narrowed. "So what is it?"

"Our enthusiasm," Bella muttered, her voice completely monotone like their trainers and her face completely expressionless.

Her fellow student barked a laugh and clapped her hand over her mouth to wipe the smile from her face as quickly as she could.

"Uh-huh." The woman turned partially away from them and glanced at Leander before she scrutinized her trainees with an implacable expression. "You know, I put up with more crap from you two than any of the trainees I've had in the last twenty years. And that's only because of what you can already do and what you're capable of, understand?"

"It's an honor," Bella said, inclined her head, and pressed her lips tightly together.

"One might even say a privilege." Raven bit her lip after that and had to stare at the grass at their feet to keep from laughing again.

The veteran war mage grunted. "I think I liked you two better when you were at each other's throats. Let's get started."

The girls watched their trainer stalk farther onto the

field before they followed her slowly. Raven leaned toward Bella and muttered, "I'm fairly sure the day we get her to smile during training will be the day she says there's nothing left for her to teach us."

Her companion smirked. "Now that is a lofty goal."

Alessandra spun neatly, her hands clasped behind her back, and nodded. "You ladies had better pay attention today. We'll dive into some advanced combat magic that's only been approved for higher-level mages—and you, now. You two seem to be the exception to every rule, so I'll simply assume from here on out that nothing's off the table. Listen up."

Raven glanced briefly over her shoulder when she heard Leander approach and he stopped directly behind her with his huge head hovering beside hers. *Yeah, he wants to hear the good stuff too.*

"This spell, in particular, is one of the most difficult to perform," the trainer continued, her voice dry and monotone despite the exciting subject. "It requires both the mage casting the spell and the mage receiving it to be fully versed in its application and in casting it with each other. In turn, this means if you want to cast the Full Appearance to communicate, you *both* have to master this spell."

"What does it do?" Bella muttered.

"I'll get there, Miss Chase. Settle down."

The two young mages shared an exasperated glance but neither of them said a word. Wesley finally swooped from the sky, settled on his mage's shoulder, and curled his long, thin tail around her neck to pay attention with her.

"You know what a calling potion can do," the veteran

war mage continued, her hands still clasped behind her back. "The Full Appearance is a much more advanced version of that potion with the added convenience of not having to carry bulky vials around or running out of resources. Except for your own limited magic, of course."

Raven bit her bottom lip. *That is not a conversation to have right now.*

"Many mages have used this spell during times of danger. The Great War was one such time. And you two have been an active part of what, I imagine, might have become something of the same threat level to this kingdom if you hadn't stepped in when you did." Alessandra raised an eyebrow and glanced skyward. "Yes, that was an actual compliment. Don't let it go to your heads. And you're not as adept at hiding that smirk as you think you are, Miss Chase.

"I'm teaching you this spell to hopefully avoid any of the same close calls we've had in the last few months. When you're separated from your fellow mages—and especially in the heat of battle—the ability to communicate with each other as quickly as possible is imperative. It may even save lives. For instance, take a moment to think about what might have happened if the two of you had been separated in Azerad before the raiders arrived."

"Things would've turned out very differently, that's for sure." Raven patted the side of Leander's scaled muzzle beside her head.

"And I would never have ridden a dragon," Bella muttered.

"I see both of you have threaded out the most important lessons from our little escapade in that city," the woman added dryly. For a few more seconds, she stared at her trainees without any expression at all. "This spell is for your arsenal of magical knowledge only and is to be used when no other options are available. It is not a toy."

"We may be first-years but I think it's very obvious neither one of us thinks magic is a game," Bella quipped.

"I'm merely covering all my bases with this." Alessandra inclined her head toward the young mages and raised her eyebrows. "I know what each of you is capable of achieving and I would fail all of us if I left any important warnings out of this lesson. Such as this next one."

The girls shared another sidelong look with their eyebrows raised.

"Like I said, this is a high-level spell and requires a tremendous amount of concentration and willpower." The instructor's gaze flicked across Leander's face for a brief moment before it settled first on Raven's, then on Bella's. "It also consumes large quantities of your stored magic. The longer the connection is open, the more it will take out of you. Nothing quite like the Magic Meld which, ironically, you two already know quite well. But the Full Appearance most definitely takes a toll on the mage casting it."

Raven took a deep breath. "What if more than two mages know the spell? Can it be cast to speak to more than one person at a time?"

Alessandra tilted her head with a little frown. "Don't get any ideas about using this spell for a group chat over the week's end, Miss Alby. I've only seen the Full Appearance used a handful of times with multiple receiving parties at once. Those were under life-threatening circumstances.

Try that, and you may find yourself in the same condition as after you two dabbled with the Magic Meld."

"It wasn't dabbling," Bella said through clenched teeth.

"Dipping into a highly advanced spell without ever having used it before, even in practice, is most definitely dabbling." The veteran war mage took a deep breath through her nose and exhaled slowly. "If no one can effectively keep two curious, talented, infuriatingly stubborn young mages from somehow discovering and working with magic that has not yet been approved for their use, I might as well be the one to bring this knowledge to you. That way, you'll know what you're getting into, and we'll all understand the consequences once you've had the time to practice under the watchful gaze of someone who actually knows what they're doing. And in case you're wondering, that someone is me. I've done this for decades."

"I'd take you over Professor Bixby any day of the week," Raven responded. Bella snorted, and Alessandra pursed her lips.

"I hope you take this as seriously as I do, Miss Alby."

"I do." Wiping the tiny smile right off her face, Raven nodded and held her trainer's gaze. "I'm serious about this training and learning these new spells. And I'm serious about you being much better than some of our other options. For real."

The veteran war mage narrowed her eyes as she searched for whatever she might have hidden within her words.

She thinks I'm messing around. Why does the truth have to be so serious all the time?

"Well, you can work on improving the way you offer

compliments on your own time, Miss Alby. For now, we'll focus on the Full Appearance. And I'm also very serious when I say that both of you need to be absolutely certain you're not distracted by anything else once we start this."

"I'm ready," Bella said with a curt nod. The amusement had vanished from her face now too.

Before Raven could echo the sentiment, Leander stepped out from behind her and stopped directly between her and Bella. He lowered his belly to the grass and raised his head, staring intently at Alessandra the whole time. Bella was so close, she could have touched him if she wanted to.

And they both know it. How's that for serious?

Raven looked at their trainer and nodded. "We're ready too."

"Good." Alessandra studied them a little longer and the moment was broken when Wesley added his solidarity with a soft screech from Bella's shoulder. "Then buckle up and repeat after me. *Loquimi magus.*"

Both mages took a deep breath and held their hands out. "*Loquimi magus.*"

They said it in unison, and a large circle of air in front of each girl shimmered with a wavering, opalescent light. A shock of powerful magic burst through Raven's chest and spread to her open hand. "Woah."

Bella looked at her and grinned. "You felt that too, huh?"

"Well, I know I'm not imagining it."

Alessandra unclasped her hands to fold her arms across her chest instead. "Actually, that's a fairly good start."

Raven watched the shimmering air in front of her fade away again. "Nothing happened."

"I wouldn't call that nothing. Most people take weeks to even cast that much." Their trainer snorted. "Now, I have two sixteen-year-old witches casting twenty-five-percent of an unlearned spell on the first attempt. Together."

Bella's lips twitched into a small smile. "You can't really be surprised by that at this point, can you?"

"I can be whatever I want to be, Miss Chase. And I want to be impressed. We all know you both are capable of that. So, go impress me." The woman pointed at Bella, then flicked her finger toward the stables. "Behind the stables. You'll cast first and I'll be here to see what happens on Miss Alby's side. Keep the receiver in your mind. Be very intentional about who you want to connect to this spell. Then, you'll switch off until I call it quits, understand?"

"Yep." The girl turned, passed Leander with a small nod, and stopped briefly to lean toward Raven and mutter, "This is gonna be awesome."

"Right there with you," she whispered and glanced away from Alessandra as the woman fixed her with a stern look.

Wesley took off from Bella's shoulder as she headed swiftly around the back of the stables and vanished from view.

"Whenever you're ready, Miss Chase," the trainer called. "Make it quick."

Leander turned his huge head to meet his mage's gaze and uttered a soft rumble of amusement.

Yep. We have the hardass trainer who cares too much to mess around. Lucky us.

A few seconds later, Bella's voice rose softly from behind the stables. "*Loquimi magus.*"

The same circle of opalescent light opened in front of Raven, only she hadn't done anything to put it there. The air seemed to flicker and she caught a brief glance of half of Bella's face floating in front of her before the image blinked out.

"Wow."

"It worked, right?" Bella called.

"For only your second time, it was better than nothing," Alessandra hollered.

"*What?*" The dark-haired mage's impatient protest carried softly from behind the stables.

The veteran war mage turned toward Raven with a nod. "Your turn."

"Right." With a deep breath, she raised her hand again and thought of Bella. "*Loquimi magus.*" The glistening window of light appeared again to reveal as much of Bella's face but this time with a sharp tingle that stretched from Raven's core, down her arms, and to her outstretched fingertips.

Her fellow trainee smiled in the image, which then disappeared as quickly as the last one had.

When it was gone, she drew in a sharp breath and rubbed her chest.

Alessandra leaned toward her and murmured, "It takes its toll, exactly like I said."

"Yeah, but I didn't think I'd actually feel it."

The woman studied her from head to toe, then glanced away. "You felt something when you cast the Magic Meld, I'm sure."

"I went numb. It's not the same thing."

"You overloaded yourself with magic you weren't quite ready for. This time is different."

Raven nodded and shook her hands out. "Fair enough."

She jumped a little when the woman straightened and shouted, "Chase! Again!"

As she glanced at her huge red dragon familiar settled in the grass beside her, Raven shrugged. *Here we go.*

CHAPTER SIX

They only went through two more rounds of practicing the Full Appearance before Alessandra called it quits. "There's only so much you can handle in one day. I'm the one training new war mages, which is why I'm the one calling the shots on how much you can handle."

Raven shook her hands out and stared at them for a few seconds. "Whew. We'll practice this again, right?"

The woman raised an eyebrow and studied her trainees. "I'd say you have a good enough handle on it. Tomorrow, we'll move in a different direction, but we'll circle to casting this one again in the near future. I'll see you two in the morning."

With a brief nod at Leander, the veteran war mage whirled and marched across the field toward the stone archway into the main courtyard.

"I have to admit, that was definitely one of the coolest things we've been taught all year."

Bella looked at her and shrugged. "It was cool, yeah. Next time, why don't you go behind the stables?"

Raven snorted. "She didn't teach me anything special in secret while you were over there if that's what you're wondering."

"No, I wasn't wondering. But still, it's good to know."

Behind them, Leander snorted and stretched his wings. "Sorry you didn't get much of a chance to join in the training."

"Yes, I'm devastated," the dragon replied flatly.

With a smirk, she turned back toward Bella and shook her head. "The sarcasm on this one, huh?"

The girl's smile twitched a little, but she really didn't seem that amused. Wesley fluttered nervously over her head and she stared at her fellow trainee with a tiny frown.

"What?" Raven glanced quickly behind her, but Leander lay in the grass and the rest of the field was empty.

"What do you mean, what?"

"Um…that's a new look. Directed at me." She chuckled and gestured vaguely with her hands. "I can tell when you're about to cut into me for something I may or may not have done, but I'm not sure what's happening right now."

Bella's frown deepened before she brushed past her and headed toward the stable wall and her knapsack that leaned against it. "Nothing's happening right now."

"Okay…" Raven glanced at Leander, but the dragon had closed his eyes. *I won't have help from my familiar, apparently.*

Slinging her knapsack over her shoulders, the other girl turned and approached her with her chin lifted in her normal show of confident superiority. "So, I'm going home now."

Now, she frowned. "It's a free kingdom."

"I know that," Bella snapped. She took a deep breath and her gaze darted around the field for a few seconds before she blurted, "My dad and grandparents wanted me to invite you to dinner at our house tonight. Do you wanna come?"

She gaped in astonishment and fought to keep her jaw from remaining open. "Did you…"

"Yes, Raven. I invited you to my house for dinner." The girl stared at nothing over the other mage's shoulder while Wesley uttered a soft screech overhead. "So are you coming or not?"

"Um…" Raven couldn't help a small burst of surprised laughter. "I think I'd better ask first if this is something your family tried to force you into or if you actually want me to come for dinner too."

"My family doesn't force me into anything." The dark-haired mage readjusted the straps of her pack and gazed at Wesley.

"I thought so." She smiled and waited.

When Bella finally looked at her, she couldn't keep a tiny smirk off her face either. "I wouldn't have asked if I was completely against the idea."

She folded her arms. "Bella, I'm not coming to your house if you don't want me to."

Rolling her eyes, the girl sighed and gestured impatiently. "Okay, fine. I guess I want you to come for dinner —if you want to—and we'll pretend this whole awkward conversation never happened."

Raven's next laugh broke the tension enough for both of them. Bella brushed the hair out of her eyes and shook her head as she continued to chuckle.

"Okay, it sounds good to me." *At least it's not a sleepover.* she glanced at Leander, who acted like he hadn't heard a single word of the conversation. "I assume there wasn't an invitation for a dragon too."

Bella followed her gaze and tilted her head. "Probably not. We don't have that much space as it is. And I wouldn't want to, you know…uh, give my grandma a heart attack or anything."

"Yeah, that wouldn't help any of us."

The girls shared another secret smile, and Bella nodded toward the dragon enclosure at the end of the stables. "I'll wait while you put him in his pen."

"Oh." Raven's gaze darted toward the stone archway into the school's courtyard and she wrinkled her nose. "Actually, I can't go quite yet."

"Why?" Her companion snorted, shifted her weight to one leg, and thrust her hip out. "Do you have a secret school project or something?"

"Well…more like extra training. With Professor Worley."

Another slightly awkward silence passed between them, and Bella's frown returned. "For what?"

"Familiar training." She nodded toward Leander, who still hadn't moved an inch. "Specifically for dragons, I guess, seeing as Leander and I don't have much to do during the regular classes. He offered, and we decided it couldn't hurt." *And it's not like I get invitations to dinner at someone else's house all the time.*

The girl tried to smile again, but her confused frown ruined it. "When did this start?"

"Right after school started again after the spring break."

With wide eyes, Bella leaned forward and lowered her voice. "You've been training with Professor Worley for *two weeks?*"

"Yeah. Not every day. And not at the end of the week when we don't have classes."

"That's... I mean..." She scoffed and stepped away from her. "Why are you the only one who was asked about familiar training? Wesley and I have as strong a connection as you and Leander!"

"I know."

"So why didn't he ask me?"

Raven pressed her lips together and looked at Leander again. *It seems I'm still on my own for this one, huh?* She shook her head and sighed. "Honestly, I think it's because dragons are so different than everyone else's familiars."

Bella scoffed again and turned to face Leander too. "Dragons aren't that different."

Slowly, she turned her head to regard the other mage with a raised eyebrow.

The girl didn't even have to look at her fellow war mage in training to know exactly how she was looking at her. "Okay, there are a *few* exceptions."

Both girls snorted, and Raven brushed a few loose red hairs away from her face. "Only a few. Namely that he can already be farther away from me than any one of the other students' familiars and that he talks. Oh, yeah, and he's bigger than three horses put together. But you're right. Very minor differences."

"I can also think for myself and hear every single word you two are babbling at each other," the dragon added. He opened one yellow eye halfway and rumbled softly.

Bella bit the inside of her cheek. "Okay. Maybe those differences are enough to warrant extra training."

"Yeah. Maybe." Raven pressed her lips together through another tiny smile.

"Still, it would've been nice for him to at least ask if I wanted to get in on this. Wesley and I are already way more advanced in his classes anyway."

"I wonder if he never asked because you've been holding back."

"I've been what?"

"Because you didn't want to hurt anyone's feelings, remember?"

The girls stared at each other before Bella closed her eyes and scrunched her face. "I did say that."

"You totally did."

"Well, then." Bella dropped her knapsack onto the grass and folded her arms. "I'll wait for you, I guess. As soon as you're done with Worley and have put Leander up, we'll leave together."

Raven chuckled. "Are you sure you won't be bored out of your mind watching someone else train with their familiar?"

"Please." The girl dragged her knapsack across the grass, tossed it against the wall of the stables again, and sat beside it with her back against the wood. "Watching you and Leander is never boring. Don't pretend like you don't already know that."

"Thanks." She grinned at the other young mage and when Bella rolled her eyes again, she turned to her red-scaled dragon. "Did you hear that, Leander? Bella Chase complimented us on our foolproof ability to entertain."

"There's nothing wrong with my hearing, little girl."

"Of course not." She turned to watch Professor Worley walking swiftly across the field. His curly black hair and wild black beard fluttered in the slight breeze and bounced with every heavy step. "I guess it's time to show them what we've worked on, huh?"

Leander pushed to his feet, stretched his wings, and exhaled a heavy sigh. "Will there be a stage?"

"A what?"

"This feels like performing, not learning."

Bella uttered a sharp laugh and quickly ended it when Raven looked at her. "What? Much of it *does* look like a performance."

"So this is the day, huh?" Raven shook her head and smirked at her dragon. "When Bella and my familiar start to team up against me?"

"When she's right, she's right." Another rumble of amusement escaped his throat and his head swung from side to side. "And she agrees with me, which most definitely makes her right."

She laughed and threw her hands up in the air. "I guess that's settled. If you'd like me to ask Worley for a stage, I'm sure he can put something together for us."

Leander's tail whispered across the grass as he dragged it to one side, raised it, and thumped it onto the ground again.

"I'll take that as a no." The young mage stepped toward her familiar and pointed at him in a mock warning. "You like showing off too so don't pretend it's all on me."

For a few seconds, the great red dragon held her gaze with his glowing eyes. Then, his head lurched forward and his jaw opened and snapped shut again with an echoing clack an inch away from her finger. Bella gasped and jumped a little at the sound, her eyes wide.

Raven didn't budge.

"Yeah, that's what I thought." She grinned and nudged his head away playfully. The other girl released a long sigh and forced herself to not look so freaked out. When Raven saw the concern on the other girl's face, she tried hard not to laugh. "We're only messing around, Bella. He'd never actually bite me."

"I know…" She shrugged where she sat and let Wesley climb into her lap. "The sound startled me, that's all."

Leander responded with a small rumble and stepped toward his mage, towering high over her. "Never say never, little girl."

"Cut it out." Raven nudged him again and shot the girl a reassuring smile as she muttered, "You're not helping."

The dragon indulged in a few short bursts of hissing laughter before Worley finally reached them beside the stables.

"Sorry I'm late." The man wiped his forehead with the back of a huge hand and huffed a heavy breath. "Alessandra mentioned she'd taught you and Miss Chase the Full Appearance today, and I…well…" He chuckled and tugged on his wiry black beard. "It was more than a mention, honestly. She wouldn't stop talking about it."

Raven wrinkled her nose. "She was complaining, wasn't she?"

"What? Oh, no. Quite the opposite, actually. I've never heard the woman talk so much about anything."

Bella perked up. "We actually impressed her!"

Her interjection surprised him and he turned toward her, entirely confused until he saw her seated on the ground. "Miss Chase. Have you been there the whole time?"

"Yep."

"Huh." He scratched the side of his face through his thick beard and grinned. "I may be a tad more distracted today than I thought."

"Well don't let me distract you." With a tiny smile, Bella gestured toward Raven and Leander. "You have training to do."

The professor glanced from one young mage to the other and his beard fluttered across his chest with every turn of his head. "I suppose that saves me the time of explaining why we're out here, Miss Alby."

"You didn't tell me it was supposed to be a secret."

"No, I suppose I didn't." The man scratched his head in thought, glanced at the clear blue sky, and shrugged. "I didn't expect to have an audience."

The group fell silent, punctuated by a snort from Leander and the muted rip of grass being torn from the earth when he pawed at the ground slowly.

"Well, then. Let's get to work." Worley clapped and strode resolutely toward the center of the field.

Raven darted Bella a curious glance, and the other girl shrugged. *That's right. Bella Chase's passive-aggressive charm. She's gonna wheedle her way into private familiar training too after this.*

CHAPTER SEVEN

"And what about now?" Professor Worley asked.

Raven couldn't see a thing with the man's blindfold on, but Leander's image came through with perfect clarity. Raven paused for barely a second before she pointed up, to her right, and slightly behind her.

He looked at the red dragon who soared effortlessly exactly where his student pointed. "All right, Miss Alby. That's four for four. How much have you two practiced the last few days?"

"Enough." She shrugged and a tiny smile snuck through her attempts to play it off like no big deal. "We're quick studies."

The man chuckled. "I'll say."

Wesley took to the sky and darted toward Leander. He uttered soft, bursting screeches as he fluttered above the red dragon's head.

"Okay." Worley squinted at the blindfold around Raven's eyes and folded his arms. "Now, I want you to let Leander choose where he goes. He must make it somewhere very specific. The next time he sends you an image, you tell me where that is."

"Sure." She hardly had to think about it. *He already has something in mind. I can feel it.* She stood utterly motionless on the field, breathed deeply through her nose, and listened to the birds calling to each other in the woods behind her. When she raised her chin, she smiled at the warmth of the afternoon sunshine on her face. *At least it's getting warmer now.*

The professor gave her three minutes before he cleared his throat. "All right. Where is he now?"

Leander's image popped into her mind with considerably more ease than the others had and she grinned. "Turn around."

"Turn around?" He frowned but did as she said and spun swiftly in the grass. A shout of surprise escaped him when he came face to face with Leander's massive red head and razor-sharp teeth bared in a dragon's grin. He staggered backward, and she ripped the blindfold from her eyes in time to see him stumble toward her. She leapt aside as he regained his bearings and fought to recover from the scare. "Of all the—"

Leander hissed in laughter and lifted his head slowly. Raven covered her mouth to hide her laughter when the man stared at her with wide eyes. Bella chuckled from where she watched them training, and he snorted. "That was—"

A piercing screech ripped through the air and they all looked up to see Gresh wheeling high above them.

One of his familiars checking in on him. She pressed her lips together. *I guess we really did scare him badly.*

Worley lifted his hand in a two-fingered salute at his hawk familiar and Gresh stopped wheeling to soar over the forest behind them. "It's been a long time since I've had a shock like that."

"It was all Leander's idea," she assured him. "I swear."

"Uh-huh."

Another image from her dragon flashed through the young mage's mind—a large, regal-looking doe standing at the edge of the forest, her lean body exposed as she peered at the field from behind a small thicket of bushes. The image was gone as quickly as it had appeared and she turned around to look at the place her dragon had shown her. The deer was gone.

"Professor?"

"Yes, Miss Alby?" Worley cleared his throat and rolled his shoulders before he gave Leander an exasperated glance.

"Is one of your familiars a deer, by any chance?"

The giant, black-haired man turned quickly to face her. "A deer?"

"She was right there in the trees." She pointed and raised her eyebrows. *Because that's exactly what it looked like.*

He studied the forest for a few seconds and sighed. "Did Leander send you that image?"

"Yep."

The man licked his lips, studied the forest again, and gave Raven a knowing smile. "You two are much further along than I thought."

She shrugged and smiled in response, waiting for an answer.

Worley's eyes crinkled at the corners when his smile

widened and he nodded at Leander and put his hands on his hips. "Now I know where you and Leander stand and how much more you've strengthened your bond. I'd say you've about mastered unspoken commands and receiving messages from him."

"He's been very good at sending them for a while." *He's not gonna tell me about that deer. Not with Bella sitting right there.*

"I think that's all we need to cover for today. Good work." He nodded at the dragon, who lowered his head a few inches in reply. "You two enjoy the end of your week. I'll meet you out here again in a few days."

The familiar-training professor turned to return across the field toward Fowler Academy's main buildings. Bella jumped up from where she sat against the stables and hurried after him. "Professor Worley."

The man paused and turned toward her with a small smile, his eyebrows raised.

"When can Wesley and I be a part of this extra training?"

He looked at her in surprise which quickly ended in a rueful chuckle. "I honestly didn't think you'd be interested in this, Miss Chase."

"We're definitely interested." She glanced at Wesley wheeling above them. "And we can handle much more than what you teach us in class, too."

The man nodded and leaned toward her a little. "You do realize that I brought this additional training to Miss Alby's attention because—"

"Because she has a dragon familiar. I know." Brushing aside the thought with a dismissive wave, Bella tossed her head back and gazed intently into her professor's dark eyes. "She told me all that. But I'm ready. Wesley's ready too. We can already do everything you're teaching in class. I want to know more. Faster."

Worley responded with another soft chuckle and pressed his lips together. "I know you're eager. That's a good thing. But to be perfectly honest, I'm not sure additional training outside of class would benefit you and Wesley as much as you think it will."

"What?" She leaned away from him and folded her arms. "Why not? We haven't even shown you everything we can do yet."

"You'll have your moment for that, Miss Chase. In time."

"Can't that time be now?"

The professor took another deep breath and this time, when he smiled, it looked more like he was trying not to grimace instead. "You'll have to put in a request with Headmaster Flynn before I can give you any real answer. Enjoy your days off, Miss Chase."

Without giving her another chance to argue further, Worley turned quickly and strode across the grass. His loose linen clothes whipped about his ankles and his shoulders as he approached the stone archway.

Bella watched him, her mouth open in surprise around the rebuttal she hadn't been allowed to make. After a moment, she exhaled a disgruntled breath and turned. "Unbelievable."

"What did he say?" Raven stood on the other side of the stables beside Leander, patting his broad shoulder.

"That I won't get anything out of extra training, basically. And to put in a request with Headmaster Flynn." The girl rolled her eyes and practically stormed toward the other mage and her dragon. "Why's he so hesitant about it? We're already training to be war mages together. It's not like you have a secret ability I don't."

Only a dragon. She shrugged. "I don't know. It couldn't hurt to talk to Flynn about it, though, right?"

"Except you didn't have to put in a request."

"No. But Worley did. I don't think Flynn would tell you no." Raven blew a few loose hairs away from her face. "It's not like they don't know what you're capable of."

"Oh, they know." Bella folded her arms and shook her head as she glanced in exasperation across the field and the edge of the forest surrounding the school grounds. "I'll keep asking and eventually, they'll give in."

She choked back a laugh. "That's definitely one way to go about it. Or maybe Worley's having a weird day."

"That's not an excuse." The girl stormed past her to snatch her knapsack from against the stable wall.

"Maybe not. But he did seem a little more...avoidant than usual. Especially when I asked him about that deer."

"What deer?"

Raven shook her head. "Never mind."

As she slung her knapsack over her shoulder again, Bella stared at her with wide eyes and raised brows. "So, are you coming with me or not?"

"Oh. Right. Yeah, let me get Leander settled." She gave the other girl a reassuring smile and turned before her classmate could say anything else. *I hope she chills out a little before we sit down for dinner with her family.* She nudged Leander's shoulder and nodded toward his pen. "Shall we?"

The dragon's yellow gaze moved slowly toward Bella but he lowered his head and headed to his enclosure.

Raven stared after him for a few seconds. *The last thing I need is my dragon being pissed at me too.* She hurried to catch up with him and pulled the slightly ajar gate open wide enough for him to slip into his spacious pen. Then, she turned and called to Bella, "Just a sec, okay?"

The girl shrugged like she thought she was asking permission. "Whatever."

She entered the pen behind her dragon and closed the gate most of the way behind her. Leander turned in a few tight circles before he settled in his usual position of either sleeping or waiting for her. She moved quickly toward him and lowered her voice. "Is everything okay?"

"Why wouldn't it be?"

"Well, you... I don't know. You headed in here without saying anything and I'm getting kind of a weird vibe, so..."

Leander snorted and focused on the small crack between the gate and the pen wall. "It's not because of you."

"What's not?"

"The vibe."

Raven glanced over her shoulder at the gate, stepped closer to her dragon, and stroked the side of his scaly muzzle. "That's good to know. Do you wanna tell me what's going on?"

The dragon exhaled a quick, hot puff of air through his nostrils. "Your professor is struggling with something. And your mage friend pushed too hard."

When the realization hit her, she bit back a smile. "You're upset with Bella?"

"Annoyed."

She glanced at the slightly open gate again. "What's wrong with Professor Worley?"

Leander blinked at her. "I can't read minds but I can smell the discomfort. Maybe feel it a little."

"Yeah, I used to think that about Bella too." She trailed her hand along the scaly ridges between his eyes and nodded. "Things might be a little tense after everything that's happened in the last few months. There have been so many changes around here. For all of us."

"I'm very adaptable."

Raven snorted. "Yes, you are. I'm gonna grab your dinner and then I'll go into town with Bella. I'd bring you with me if I could."

"I know."

"Of course you do." After a final pat, she turned away and strode toward the gate. "I won't be gone super-late, though. And I'll come say goodnight when I get back."

Leander lowered his head onto his forepaws and closed his eyes with another little snort.

She slipped through the gate and walked toward the front of the stables. When Bella gave her a confused glance, she shrugged. "I gotta feed the beast, you know?"

She folded her arms, and Wesley came to settle on her shoulder in his usual position.

Whatever tension he smells, it had better not get any worse once we're out of here.

CHAPTER EIGHT

O nce Leander's trough was full of dragon feed and the gate closed securely behind her, Raven stopped beside the stables to retrieve her satchel from where she'd dropped it after the long day of classes and training. "Okay. Now we're ready."

Bella sighed a little dramatically, and they turned together to wander across the field toward the entrance gates to Fowler Academy and the dirt road that would take them southwest and into Brighton's town center.

The first half of the walk into Brighton was quiet and a little awkward. Raven constantly stole quick, sideways looks at her companion, who almost looked like she was doing the same thing.

It's the first time we're doing something together where it wasn't forced on us somehow. That can't be the best common denominator.

By the time they approached the town square and the fountain in the center of it, though, she forgot all about the confusing silence and how the rest of the night would play out. They passed Mrs. Easton's house and the small cottage beside it.

"Hey," she whispered and nudged the other girl with the back of her hand. "Look who's back."

Bella's eyes widened, and she glanced around the boulevard. "I have no idea what you're talking about or why you're whispering."

"Oh." *It's easy to forget we've never made this walk together.* "That veteran wizard sitting on his porch. He's been gone for weeks."

"The crazy guy?"

She darted the other mage a sidelong glance and tilted her head. "He's not crazy. Only...eccentric. Hi, Peter!" She raised a hand to wave and the man's head jerked up from whatever he was studying on the porch in front of him.

"Raven." He scrambled to his feet and his overly large tunic fluttered around his narrow frame. "Raven Alby. Raven."

Before either of the girls could say or do anything else, the veteran mage hurried down the steps of his narrow front porch and practically ran to them. Raven smiled and stepped back a little when he stopped too close. "Hey. I haven't seen you for a while."

"I sent the Endflame." The man's eyes were wide and almost as wild-looking as the day she'd met him. "He saw it, right? The whole kingdom had to have seen my warning."

With a hasty glance at her companion, she shrugged. "About the raiders? Yeah, actually. We had more than enough warning and help. There's nothing to worry about, Peter. Everything was taken care of."

"Raiders?" The man snorted and scratched what little hair was left on the sides of his head. "I didn't raise the Endflame for raiders, girl. Come now. Tell me. What does Connor think?"

"My grandfather?" Peter nodded vigorously, and she could only shake her head. "I don't really know what he thinks about anything right now. He's been gone for almost a month."

"Well, he'd better find something, I tell you what." Shifting from foot to foot, he chewed his bottom lip and clasped his hands together under his chin. "He better find out what's happening or the entire order of the world will unravel right beneath our feet!"

Raven frowned. "What do you mean by that?"

"We won't know what's coming until someone finds the truth!"

Bella tugged on her jacket sleeve and muttered, "We should keep going."

"Ask him what he thinks!" Peter shouted as she turned reluctantly to head across the town center's courtyard. "Ask what he's found. Whatever it takes, it must be done!"

"Next time I see him," she called over her shoulder and caught a final glimpse of the veteran mage hunched in the road opposite his front door. He stared after her. *I know that has to mean something.*

"Don't encourage him," her companion muttered and looked up to smile at a few townsfolk who entered Zeke's tavern for the evening. "What was all that crazy about?"

"I don't think he's crazy." They skirted the fountain in the center of the square, and she studied it with a small frown. *I definitely miss meeting Murphy here every morning.*

"Did you hear the guy?" Bella snorted. "That definitely sounded crazy."

"You know, many people have called me crazy for doing what I know I can do." Raven fixed the other mage a pointed look.

The girl narrowed her eyes in response. "Yeah, but you can actually string together more than one coherent sentence together at a time. The only thing I got out of that was the guy knows your name and your grandfather's name and wants Connor Alby's opinion on something. And those first two are common knowledge at this point."

"Not everyone knows my name." Raven adjusted the strap of her satchel and followed her past the fountain and down the road heading west from the center of town.

"Please. Everyone in Brighton knows about the girl with the dragon familiar. The girl from a long line of mages who eliminated the rest of the Swarm and rescued the governor of Azerad's wife from a raider invasion only a few weeks later."

With a smirk, she leaned away from the other young mage to take a good look at her. "The only part that doesn't apply to you too is having a dragon as a familiar." She glanced at Wesley, who'd flown steadily ahead of them for most of their walk. "And I heard something about fire-drakes being classified as tiny dragons who can't talk. So you're almost there."

Bella shook her head but she couldn't help smiling. "Fine. Maybe everyone in Brighton knows who Bella Chase and Raven Alby are. And everyone knows Connor Alby, our disappearing spent-wizard hermit."

Raven grimaced quickly and stared at the dirt road in

front of each footstep. "Not everyone knows about the disappearing part."

"Well I haven't told anyone in case you were wondering." Her companion's voice had softened now, and she waited for her to look up from the road. It didn't happen. "And I won't tell anyone, either."

"Thanks. There's not really all that much to tell, anyway." *I already told William about Grandpa's first letter and magic maybe coming back. It's better to keep it that way.*

"Still." Bella shrugged. "It's a little weird, though, honestly. That some crazy old—" She sighed and started again. "That a veteran mage like that Peter guy wants your grandpa's opinion so badly. And what the heck is an Endflame, anyway?"

"I have no idea. But I do know that so far, Peter hasn't exactly been wrong. Even if what he says sounds a little off."

They passed between rows of smaller houses on either side of the western road, where older townsfolk sat in rocking chairs on their front porches and children played in the open fields where their parents could see them. Bella frowned and ignored them all. "What do you mean?"

"Well, the day I met him, Peter talked about all the coming dangers and watching for the signs. It was all stuff that didn't make any sense to me when he said it but then we had the rest of the Swarm to deal with."

"It's more like that was a coincidence, Raven. Most of the old veterans from the Great War are spent wizards now too." The girl watched Wesley soar after a few ravens that darted between the treetops and didn't bother to call him. "It's not like this Peter guy has any secret, special way to see into the future or anything. Especially not with all his magic gone."

Maybe it's not gone. Raven shrugged. "Maybe. But I'm not gonna write him off as a crazy old man."

"You can do whatever you want." For a few seconds, they fell completely silent as the two young mages trudged down the packed dirt.

"Thank you very much," she muttered, and they both laughed a little.

"We're right down this road." Bella pointed to a road on their right a few paces ahead. "Only a few properties down past the cornfield."

They turned together onto a much narrower road and headed northwest this time. The sun was beginning to set, the evening still bright and not yet tinged with the softer glow that would settle in about an hour. The houses were spread out there, the properties lined with wooden fences and wiring around barns, stables, pens, and tool sheds. Raven took a deep breath of the fresh spring air and watched the few workers out in the fields finishing their day's work. *This looks an awful lot like southern Brighton. If there were goats in that pen instead of sheep, it could almost be Alby Ranch.*

When she glanced at her companion again, the dark-haired mage stared straight ahead, her lips pursed a little like she wasn't sure she wanted to go home right now. *And she's embarrassed about it.*

Finally, they reached the end of the narrow dirt road, which was nothing more than packed earth that gave way to a few patches of overgrown grass that encroached upon it from the field beyond. There wasn't much else out there beyond the property buildings and a wide river that flowed alongside about an acre of open land behind the last house.

"This is it." Bella exhaled a heavy sigh and wrinkled her nose. "Whatever my family says, don't take it personally. They can be...a lot."

Raven fought back a laugh. "No problem. My skin's about as thick as a—" She stopped short, and her companion flashed her a wide, amused grin.

"You were about to say dragon's, weren't you?"

"No..."

They both laughed, and the other girl nodded toward the huge farmhouse painted white with a red door and red shutters. "You can deny it all you want, Raven Alby. I can see right through you."

"You know, I think the feeling's mutual."

The young mages snickered again—at each other and at themselves—as they headed down the small footpath toward the farmhouse's front porch.

When they were within ten feet of the porch, the front door opened and a gray-haired woman in a bright blue dress and a stained apron tied tightly around her waist stepped swiftly out to greet them. "There you are."

"Here we are." Bella spread her arms with an uncertain smile as Wesley landed on the porch railing and his claws scrabbled against the worn wood for purchase.

The woman put her flour-covered hands on her hips and tried to look serious. A small smile lifted the corners of her mouth, however. "We had begun to think something happened to you."

"That's my fault," Raven said with a little wave. "Bella

didn't know I had extra training after we finished so she waited for me."

"Aha. Well, at least you're here—both of you. I took my time with supper, but as soon as we sit, we're ready to eat."

"Sounds great."

The woman on the porch pursed her lips, tried not to smile, and raised an eyebrow at her granddaughter.

"Okay." Bella rolled her eyes a little and nodded for Raven to continue with her up the stairs and onto the porch. She gestured with a sweeping hand toward the woman who stood near the doorway. "This is my Gram. Gram, this is—"

"Oh, I know who you are." The old woman reached for Raven's hand with both of hers and squeezed it instead of shaking it. "Raven Alby. I've spoken to your grandfather Connor too, once or twice. Betsy Chase, dear. Such a pleasure to meet you."

She smiled and waited to have her hand returned to her. "Nice to meet you too, Mrs. Chase."

"Ha! No, no, no. Betsy's fine. Please." The woman glanced at her hands and quickly removed them. "Oh, look at that. I'm covered in cooking. Come inside, girls. You can wash up and settle in. We'll have supper on the table before you can blink."

With a wink, she waved them inside and shuffled into the house toward the kitchen.

Raven chuckled and wiped her hands on her pants. It then meant she had to dust the flour and whatever else off her clothes.

"Sorry about that," Bella muttered.

"For what? Your Gram seems really nice."

"Some people call it nice. I call it smothering."

With a little frown, she tilted her head and glanced briefly inside the house. "Really?"

"I'm so ready to leave." The girl stepped inside and her guest followed closely.

Raven followed Bella's lead and slipped her satchel off her shoulders to place it inside the doorway beside the girl's knapsack. The house was definitely larger than the small cottage she'd shared with Connor for most of her life. Everything was neat, tidy, and cleanly swept, and a swath of needlepoint designs had been framed and hung along every wall of the main room off the entryway.

Her companion caught her staring at the needlepoint and sighed with exasperation. "Gram's only hobby. She never fails to remind us that leaving all those…pieces on the walls is an honor she earned through hard work and running the property. Which is really only Gram speak for 'I run the house, and I'll decorate it the way I want.'"

As she studied the few dozen needlepoint projects in brilliantly colored thread, she shrugged. "I think it's nice."

"Yeah, okay." Bella snorted and headed toward the other side of the house. "Come on."

She took a few seconds more to look at Betsy Chase's handiwork—the lace doilies over the mantel and the flowered patterns on the upholstered chairs that might have actually been stitched by the woman herself. *At least Bella has another woman with her. I've always had Grandpa and ranch hands.*

"Raven," the other girl whispered harshly from the other side of the front staircase. She gave her visitor an exasperated smile and nodded toward the other end of the house. "Come on. If she catches you staring at those, we won't eat until she's done telling you about every single one."

The girls hurried through the next room, which was set up for sewing and repairs, and made their way into the kitchen at the back of the house. A man in his mid-forties with dark wavy hair like Bella's and the same wide, bright eyes stepped inside from a door onto the back porch.

"I swear if I find out that she's—oh." His gaze fell on the two girls and his face broke into a wide grin. "You actually came home."

Bella rolled her eyes playfully. "It's not like I have anywhere else to go."

"Aw, now. You'll go wherever you want in this world, Bella Bear—"

"Dad." She glanced quickly at Raven and grimaced a little in true teenage embarrassment. "Can we skip the nicknames tonight? Please."

Her dad chuckled and took two long, swift steps across the kitchen toward them. "You must be Raven." He gave her an actual handshake, and she smiled politely.

"That's me."

"So glad you could make it, Raven. Thomas Chase. Bella's dad."

"Nice to meet you too. Thanks for having me over."

"Listen to you." He chuckled again and nodded at his daughter. "I like this friend."

At the large wood-fired stove at the back of the kitchen, Betsy tossed a hand in the air without turning away from the food she served into simple wooden bowls. "So much more polite than that Teresa girl."

"Thanks." Raven started to laugh and stopped herself when she saw the other girl's tightly pressed lips and wide eyes. "The food smells great."

"It'll be ready before you know it. Tom, come help me with these bowls."

Bella's dad hurried across the room to comply and Bella led her visitor outside onto the back porch. "Sorry about that."

"Don't be. Your family's great."

The dark-haired mage took a deep breath and tossed her hair over her shoulders. "Don't get me wrong. I love them and they've done everything they can to help me get to where I am right now. But I don't want to be where I am forever. I think they really don't get that sometimes."

Raven stared out across the open field behind the Chase house. *That was an unexpected confession.* "I can't say I know what that's like. It's only me and my grandpa on the ranch. Or at least it was."

"But your grandpa's not trying to keep you from being more, is he?" Bella stepped around the long wooden table on the porch and sat on the edge, her feet dangling over the sides.

She joined her, still careful not to sit too close, and shrugged. "He doesn't try to stop me, no. But he definitely has his own way to keep me away from things. Like the journals he locked in the basement for sixteen years before he finally decided to show me. I didn't even know that he was a dragon rider or that my mom was an actual war mage until a few months ago."

"It must've been quite a surprise."

Both girls chuckled softly, and Raven swung her legs

back and forth over the edge of the porch. "That's an understatement. I did get a fair amount of, 'You can't tell anyone, Raven,' and, 'I won't teach you how to do that spell,' and, 'I can't talk about this tonight.'"

Bella nodded slowly. "For me, it's mostly, 'Oh, can't that giant report you're scribbling wait another hour, Bella Bear? Come for supper. There's pie.' And then my dad always wants me home to help around the property. It's not like we have a huge ranch or anything, but—" She leaned forward to peer around the end of the porch, glanced behind them at the back door, and whispered, "I think my grandparents are starting to slow down a little, you know? And my dad doesn't get how important it is for me to blow through Fowler Academy with flying colors and get the best mage assignment I can right out the gate. Yeah, whatever I end up doing, part of it will be to help them here. But I have to get out of here, off this little plot of land and out of Brighton. I've always known I was meant for bigger and better things than breaking the town record for the biggest pumpkin or whatever. You know?"

She smirked. "Are they actually trying to break that record?"

"Probably."

The girls watched a few birds swoop into the field to pick at the food they'd found, and Raven brushed her fingers briefly against her mom's red and silver pin on her jacket. "I think I know what you mean."

"It probably sounds like I'm simply complaining." Bella picked at a loose piece of chipped porch between them. "It's not something you have to worry about, huh? You can simply hop on your dragon and fly away wherever you want."

"Ha. Hardly." She blew loose hairs out of her face. "I couldn't fly Leander out here, could I?"

"Very funny."

A little grunt issued around the corner of the porch before an older man with a full head of thick white hair appeared at the bottom of the steps. He smacked his thick work gloves against the corner of the porch as he climbed and exhaled a heavy sigh.

"Hi, Poppy."

The man jumped and steadied himself with a hand against the wall. "Oh-ho! You got me there, girl. Good one."

Bella's smile was more genuine as she pushed to her feet. "You kinda stepped right into that one."

"Well. I didn't see your fancy flying lizard around yet, so I—"

Wesley swooped over the house roof and into view and screeched right on cue.

"And there he is." The man chuckled and hobbled forward across the porch to wrap the girl in a huge hug, grumbling a little as he patted her back with heavy thumps. "It took you a while."

"She was waiting for me," Raven said and stood to join them.

"I see." He grinned, released Bella from his hug, and extended a hand toward their visitor. "Gerald Chase. Bella's Poppy."

She shook his hand. "Raven Alby. Bella's...training partner." Her smile widened to cover her surprise. *I don't even know if she thinks we're friends.*

"Training partner, eh?" Gerald threw his head back and boomed out a laugh much stronger than his slow shuffle would suggest. "That's a good one. It's about time she had some friends as clever as she is. It's good to have you here, Raven. Good to have you—ah." The man hunched and grimaced as he pressed his hand against his lower back.

"Are you okay?" Bella stepped toward him and stretched her hand to help her grandfather.

"Yes, yes, yes. Absolutely…whew." He looked at her and smiled as he waved her off. "There's no need to hover. It's not like I'm an old man who's been out planting crops all day."

"Uh-huh." The girl gave him a warning look, then glanced at Raven.

"What I need now is a heaping plate of your Grams'— aha." The back door opened again. Thomas and Betsy came out with their arms full of platters and trays and bowls. "That's what I call good timing, eh?" He winked at the girls, and Raven crossed the porch quickly to hold the back door open.

"Look at you. Aren't you sweet?" Betsy chuckled and nodded before she hurried toward the long table that had been set an hour before.

Gerald reached toward his wife with slightly crooked hands. "Let me help you with one of those—"

"Don't you dare." She lifted the dishes out of his reach and slipped smoothly around the side of the table to put them on the surface. "I have these balanced perfectly and you've worked enough today."

"Come on, now. Picking up and puttin' down a few bowls isn't work."

"Keep talking like that, Gerald Chase, and you can cook your own supper after you come in from the garden."

Bella's grandpa grabbed the back of the closest chair, leaned on it slightly, and winked at his granddaughter and her friend. "She's been telling me that for fifty years. I know a bluff when I see one."

"You know it's not a bluff." Betsy set the last bowl down and dusted her hands. "That's the only reason you still offer to help set the table."

Her husband gave her a sheepish smile and shrugged. "Got me."

"Yeah, I've been gettin' you for fifty years, too." The woman smiled coyly at him, then pulled out the chair beside him and glanced around the table. "We've waited long enough, haven't we?"

Everyone else took their seats, scooted their chairs in, and passed the bowls of steamed garden vegetables, spring quiche, roast chicken, and salad around. "Grown right in our own garden," Betsy added with a nod.

"Except the chickens." Thomas pulled a drumstick off and passed the platter to his daughter. "I swore I'd never raise animals, no matter what else I had to do, and chickens are no exception."

Wesley swooped from the sky and landed on the porch a few feet away from the table. Bella lowered her head to hide her smile while her dad eyed the firedrake with feigned contempt. After a moment, the man tore off a chunk of chicken meat and tossed it to his daughter's familiar. "Including that one."

The firedrake snatched the meat out of the air and

spread his wings and lowered himself toward Thomas Chase in a little bow.

When Raven burst out laughing, Bella kicked her leg gently under the table to get her attention and handed her the next dish.

CHAPTER NINE

"Now, the way I heard it," Thomas said through a mouthful and waved his fork over his plate, "the two of you are heroes."

"Dad—"

"He's right." Gerald thumped his fists on the table and grinned at the girls. "Our Bella, out to compete in one of the most prestigious competitions for young mages—"

"It's the only one that size, Poppy." Bella pushed her fork around on her plate and tried to hide a smile. "Probably the biggest competition in Lomberdoon. And I didn't even get to compete in a match, so it's not that big a deal."

Raven darted her a sidelong glance and returned to her meal. *She doesn't talk like this around anyone else.*

"Not that big a deal?" The old man huffed and stared around the table. "Oh, sure. I suppose Azerad would have been fine all on its own if you hadn't gone in the first place, huh?"

Thomas took a long drink from his cup and smirked. "I should have gone to Fowler and stopped your headmaster from sending you there. Because it sure did feel like you were gone for four days—"

"Okay, fine. Maybe it's still a big deal that I got to go."

"Damn right it is."

"Gerald." Betsy raised an eyebrow at her husband, and he chuckled.

"Whoops. I must be gettin' too old to remember all your rules, darlin'." He smiled sweetly before he leaned over his plate to fix both girls with a wide-eyed stare. "It is definitely still a big deal."

"And if you hadn't gone," his wife added, "you wouldn't have been there to save all those people when the raiders attacked."

"It wasn't that many, Gram. Only three hostages. And it wasn't all me, either."

Thomas spread butter on another slice of bread and nodded. "That's right. You got to ride on that little dragon too, didn't you?"

Bella's fork clattered onto her plate as she stared at her dad with wide eyes. Raven choked on her sip of water and covered her mouth. "Sorry."

"That's not what happened?"

She shook her head and took another sip of water to keep from choking again. "No, that's definitely what happened. I only, um… Leander's not really *little*."

"Who's Leander?" Betsy asked.

"The dragon, Gram."

"Oh, yes."

The two girls looked at each other and burst out laughing. After a moment, the dark-haired mage looked at her family and sighed. "I wouldn't have been able to do anything if Raven wasn't there. Or Leander. They were incredible."

"And those raiders would've taken the governor's wife right out of the city if Bella hadn't shown up when she did," Raven added. "It was a group effort."

"As is anything worth taking credit for." Gerald narrowed his eyes at the girls and nodded slowly. "And now we get to sit here having dinner with two heroes of Azerad and the entire kingdom."

Her mouth fell open, and she turned to Bella again. The other girl wrinkled her nose. "We're not really heroes, Poppy."

"Sure you are. You worked hard to get into that tournament and instead of fighting a few kids who don't have half your skills, you fought a party of raiders and brought those bastards to justice."

"*Gerald.*"

"Oh, what would you have me call them, Betsy? Bad guys?"

"Scoundrels would work fine."

"It doesn't have nearly the same bite to it."

Thomas laughed and took another bite of bread.

"It's good to find someone who you know will always have your back." Gerald stabbed his fork into his chicken and nodded. "That's very important if you're gonna fly around saving Lomberdoon from all manner of *scoundrels*, eh?"

Raven leaned back in her chair and smirked at Bella. "It's a good thing we were stuck in a guest room together, huh?"

The girl laughed so hard, she leaned dangerously low

over her plate and almost dipped her face into her food. "Not as good as when you finally let me off your dragon. You guys heard about the way Raven and Leander fly, right?"

Gerald glanced across the porch at the sky now lit up with orange and pink and yellow at sunset. "In the air, I assume."

Betsy and Thomas laughed with him.

"Besides that." Bella glanced at her visitor and rolled her eyes playfully. "They don't use a saddle."

Her dad cleared his throat. "Then what the heck do you use to steer?"

"Nothing." Raven grinned.

"How do you...you know. Get on?"

"With a little boost." The minute she said it, she and Bella fell into another fit of laughter. The family looked at each other across the table, and Thomas shrugged.

"Well, I tell you what, girls." Gerald beamed at them and stabbed his fork absently over and over into what was left of his salad. "This whole kingdom should be throwing flowers and garlands and fancy little cookies at your feet for what you did in Azerad."

"You'd better make it gold coins instead of flowers, Dad."

"That too."

Raven took a huge breath through her laughter. *These people are great. Why is she in such a rush to get out of here?*

"Don't worry." Bella wiped tears of laughter from the corners of her eyes and released a long sigh. "When I get my first mage assignment, I'll come home and throw coins at you myself."

Her dad chuckled but the humor seemed to seep out of him. "You still have time before all that, Bella. It's best to keep your head in the now, huh?"

The easy laughter around the table died down, and while Thomas' family watched and waited for him to say something else, the man merely took another mouthful and chewed serenely.

Betsy smiled politely and broke the silence. "So, Raven. How exactly did you manage to get a dragon as your familiar? I imagine it's much harder than connecting with a firedrake, and Bella worked hard enough to get that one."

"It kind of happened." Raven shook her head. "I live near Moss Dragon Ranch. My grandpa and I are friends with the owner and his son. I stopped by one day, and there was this stubborn dragon who no one could train. His only other option was to have his wings clipped before they sent him to this valley in the mountains where all the other untrainable dragons go." She swallowed and glanced at her plate. *Leander would hate talking about this right now.*

"Wings clipped?" Betsy gaped at her. "That actually happens."

"Every once in a while, yeah. I couldn't let that happen. Honestly, Leander didn't want anything to do with me at first. I think the only thing that stopped him from eating me was the fact that I have magic." The family stared at her in mute horror, and she laughed. "That was a joke. He wouldn't have eaten me or anyone."

Gerald chuckled.

"At first, I only wanted to help him save himself. And I wanted a dragon familiar. But I'm sure somewhere, unconsciously, I saw how alike we were and simply followed that."

"Did he see the same in you?" Betsy asked.

"Not at first. It was so much work to get to the point where we both trusted each other." She glanced at Bella and almost laughed again. "There was probably even one point where if someone had told me I could try a firedrake instead, I would have—"

She stopped when an unexpected image entered her mind. It was the same sunset and the same sky behind her off the Chases' porch, only the porch and the building were gone, and around the edges were the metal walls of Leander's pen. A cover of incoming clouds blocked most of the sky directly overhead, but through those darkening clouds, a massive shadow almost blocked out the rest of the light. It was impossible to see exactly what it belonged to, but it was larger than any dragon she'd seen, and the enormous tail that protruded through the clouds was perfectly clear —long, black, glistening with hardened scales, and lined with wickedly sharp barbs along its entire length.

Those clouds are high up. That has to be three times Leander's size at least.

The image faded, and she realized she was staring at the outer wall of the house behind Betsy and Gerald.

"Raven?" Bella nudged her shoulder gently. "Hello?"

"What?" She blinked quickly and shook her head a little. "Sorry."

"Are you feeling all right?" Betsy asked. "You look a little pale."

"Really?" The young mage smiled and forced out a laugh. "I'm fine. I remembered I haven't finished one of the essays we have due next week in class. You know—that summary of our life without magic for Professor Bixby?"

She looked at the other girl for backup, and Bella's eyes narrowed briefly before she nodded. "Yeah. One of her more pointless assignments."

Gerald stroked his chin with a soft hum. "You and Bella really are two peas in a pod, aren't you?"

The girls looked at him and said at the same time, "What?"

"All the studying. Standing out in small towns and big cities. Saving the day together." The man nodded and his smile widened again. "I'm glad you met each other."

His granddaughter tossed her hair out of her face and darted Raven a quick glance as she leaned back in her chair and folded her arms. "We do okay."

"I'll second that." She took a long drink of her water to avoid the family staring at her again. *Note to self. Images from Leander make me stop mid-story.*

Betsy clapped her hands and raised her eyebrows. "Who wants pie?"

"See?" Bella muttered. "Told you."

"I will never pass up a piece of your pie, darlin'." Gerald pushed slowly out of his chair with a little grunt. "I can help you with that, at least."

"All right." His wife smiled at him and headed toward the back door. "Come on, then. Thomas and our two mage heroes can help clear the table."

Bella's grandparents disappeared inside, and Thomas stood to quickly pile as many dishes into his arms as he could. "Do you like pie, Raven?"

"Yeah."

"Just you wait." He nodded and looked way too serious for talking about pie. "Nobody makes 'em like Betsy Chase."

As he headed into the house, the two girls stood together to start clearing what was left on the table. "What was that about?" Bella asked.

"What?"

"You zoning out in the middle of a sentence."

She stacked a few more plates and couldn't bring herself to look at the other girl. *I'm sure she'll know if I'm lying.* "Leander sent me another image."

"All the way from Fowler?" Her companion froze with a plate poised over the bowl in her other arm.

"Yep. Unexpected, right? Hey, at least we know it's impossible to talk and get messages from our familiars at the same time."

"Right." Bella frowned and returned to stacking dishes. "Is everything okay?"

"He's fine. I'm fine. Only surprised, I guess."

"Okay." When they finished clearing the dishes, Bella led her into the kitchen and muttered, "My dad wasn't lying about Gram's pie, by the way."

"Well, now I'm really excited."

CHAPTER TEN

After the pie, Betsy retired to the main room of the house to work on her new needlepoint project and Thomas and Gerald headed to the shed across the property to smoke their pipes.

"That's the only place she lets them do it," Bella explained. The girls sat on the edge of the porch again and watched the men walk slowly across the grass. "They have a couple chairs in there and Poppy's entire stash of special tobacco. The smoke still comes in through the windows sometimes."

Raven laughed. "Does she get on them about it?"

"Nope. Grams merely likes to have everything in its place." With a sigh, she tossed Wesley another piece of chicken she'd stashed from dinner. "It's so boring."

"Boring's not a bad thing sometimes. At least your family's still here together, right?"

"And at least we still have the farmhouse. I can't even imagine what it would be like if the four of us had to live in a super tiny house."

Raven leaned forward and propped her forearms on her thighs. "I bet you'd find a way to make it work."

They sat in silence for a few minutes as the crickets began to chirp a short while before the sun sank completely behind them. Smoke and men's low voices wafted from the shed on the back of the property.

"Hey." She straightened and looked at the other girl with wide eyes. "I know something that's not boring."

"I'm not playing a game with you, Raven."

"Okay, first, I know by now that's only your weird sense of humor. Second, it's not a game. But it's definitely not boring. I'll be right back." She leapt to her feet and headed toward the back door.

"What are you doing?"

"I'm grabbing my satchel. Hold on." She moved quickly through the house toward the front door where they'd placed their school bags.

In an armchair in the main room, Betsy looked up from her needlepoint with a smile. "Heading home?"

"In a while. I need my bag."

"Well, you make sure you come say goodbye before you leave."

With a nod, she returned through the house and did a double-take at the sight of Bella's grandmother sewing pictures into a piece of fabric. *This is so different than working on the ranch until dark. It's kinda nice.*

When she returned to the back porch, Bella hadn't moved. She watched her familiar wheel through the sky, her head tilted in concentration. Her eyes narrowed at Wesley but widened as she gasped. "Yes!"

"Woah."

The girl turned quickly to see her approaching and grinned. "He did it."

"Who did what?" Raven dropped her satchel between them and sat with her legs over the edge of the porch.

"Wesley. He sent me an image!"

"Nice." Unbuckling the straps on her bag, Raven looked up at the wheeling firedrake and nodded. "What was it?"

"Uh…you, actually." Bella snorted. "I didn't hear you step outside so at least I know he's an awesome lookout too."

"Is that the first time?"

"Yeah. I think maybe watching your special extra training with Worley might've rubbed off on us a little."

"You're welcome." They both chuckled before Raven dug in her satchel and pulled out the first of Connor Alby's old journals. "Maybe not as exciting as you and Wesley reaching the next level, but close, right?"

Her companion stared at the old, cracked leather wrapped around so many dusty yellow pages. "Do you really carry those around with you everywhere?"

"No…" She opened the journal to the pages she'd dog-eared and held it over her lap. "Only since we came back from Azerad. You never had a chance to read this while we were there and I haven't taken them out of my bag yet. This feels like a good time if you're up for it."

With her eyes narrowed on the journal, Bella bit her lower lip and took a deep breath. "You opened that to the pages about my mom."

"I did. And I haven't read them at all. I won't until after you do."

"Fine. Why not?" She took it gingerly and placed it in

her lap. After a hasty look at Wesley who flapped over the field, she laughed. "I really hope this isn't a bunch of pages filled with stuff I already know."

Raven shrugged. Her legs swung rhythmically over the edge of the porch again as she leaned back and propped herself up with both hands behind her. "There's only one way to find out."

"Right. I'm a fast reader, so this won't take long."

With a quick laugh, she shook her head. "I don't mind waiting. You guys have an awesome view out here."

Without another word, the girl focused on the pages of Connor Alby's journal dedicated to War Mage Vanessa Chase and chronicled the woman's accomplishments during her service to King Vaughn and Lomberdoon's people.

Raven was content to sit and watch the sky darken slowly while she thought about the image Leander had sent her. *There's no way that was a dragon. It was way too big.*

Bella sniffed beside her, and when she turned to look at her, she saw a tear trickle down her cheek. Wesley settled onto the porch beside his mage and hopped toward her, his claws clicking against the wood. She blinked quickly, sniffed again, and sighed heavily.

"Are you okay?"

"I'm fine." The dark-haired mage swiped quickly at the tear and shook her head. "I had no idea... Raven, have you read any of this?"

"Nope. I stopped at your mom's name 'cause that's what came up after that passage about her and my mom working together."

The girl looked up at her, the tears gone now. "What about the stuff about your mom?"

"Not yet." She shrugged and glanced at the open journal. "I haven't found the right time."

Turning the page again so it fell open at the start of the entry for Sarah Alby, Bella offered it to its owner and nodded. "Well maybe you should make the time. We're... far more connected than you think."

"What?" Raven couldn't decide whether she wanted to stare at the journal and her mom's name written in large cursive letters at the top of the page or at Bella. "Is my mom in what you read?"

"I don't think..." Bella wrinkled her nose and shook the journal gently to indicate that Raven should take it. "If you want to talk about it after you read it, that's fine. But you should read it first."

With a slight pause, she pushed herself through her surprise and took it. Without looking at the pages, she shut it and placed it in her lap. "I will. Eventually."

The two girls sat in silence for a few more minutes and watched the last of the sunlight fade from the sky. "Well, I should get back to Fowler now."

"Yeah, okay."

Raven slipped the journal into her satchel, tightened the buckles, and slung the bag over her shoulder. "Thanks for inviting me over. It was more fun than I expected."

"Ha, ha. Nice compliment." They stood together as the two men headed toward the porch.

"Are you off to that mage school?" Thomas called.

"Yeah. I have a dragon to check in with and a few flights of stairs to climb."

The men chuckled and made their way up the steps. "I can walk you back if you like. Or borrow Bert Olsen's horse. Next house over. He lets me take Whisper out all the time. It's no trouble."

"That's all right, thanks." She nodded and started to turn toward the door. "I made the walk from the ranch to Fowler Academy every morning during my first semester. I'm sure I could get their blindfolded at this point, and it's only half the distance from here."

"All right. Well, we're glad you came to join us for a meal, Raven. You're welcome any time." He extended his hand again, and she shook it.

"Thank you." She stepped toward Gerald and held her hand out toward him. "It was great to meet you all."

Bella's grandfather laughed and scooped her into the same back-thumping hug he'd given his granddaughter. "I say dump the formalities. Any friend of Bella's gets hugs from me."

"Great," she squeaked and took a deep breath when he released her.

"You be safe."

"I will." She almost leapt off the porch but remembered Betsy's request. "Your grandmother told me to make sure I say goodbye."

Bella closed her eyes in mock exasperation. "You don't want to break a promise to Grams."

"I had a feeling it was like that." Raven smiled at the men and opened the back door. "Thanks again."

"I'll come with you." The other girl darted across the porch, and Wesley became airborne to find a place to perch somewhere on the roof. They moved quickly through the house toward the front entryway. "Grams, Raven's heading to Fowler."

"Oh, yes." Betsy set her needlework in her lap and favored Raven with a warm, genuine smile. "So good to meet you, Raven. I'll make that same pie again next time you stop by. I saw how much you liked it."

She swallowed. *That's exactly like the way Grandpa smiles.* "It was the best pie I ever had. Thanks."

Bella opened the front door. "Do you want me to send Wesley with you or something?"

"It's a short walk. You'd better keep the lookout here." Raven stepped out onto the front porch and twisted to look over her shoulder. "I had a good time."

"Yeah, me too." Her companion's gaze darted around the front porch and her shoulders jerked in a quick shrug. "See you tomorrow."

"Training every day of the week." As soon as she stepped onto the thin path off the steps, Bella called her name again. "Yeah?"

"I was serious about the reading." The girl nodded at her satchel. "I don't think it's something you wanna put off for very long."

"Okay. Have a good night." She gave her a quick smile, spun, and hurried toward the side road that would take her into Brighton's town center. The front door closed behind her and she brushed her fingers against Sarah Alby's pin on her jacket. *I simply gotta find the right time.*

It was almost completely dark by the time she reached Fowler Academy's front gates. The temperature had dropped enough to make her breath emerge in little puffs of steam, but her jacket and the walking kept her warm.

She went directly to Leander's pen, bunched her jacket sleeve to flash her access rune, and slipped inside.

"Hey."

His tail moved slowly through the grass as he watched her with his head raised, his eyes fully open. "How did it go?"

"Fairly well, actually. We talked a lot about you."

He snorted and turned his head to fix her with only one eye. "And how much Bella doesn't like riding a dragon."

"That was only mentioned briefly." She waved off his joking comment and approached him. He nudged her outstretched hand with his snout, and she smiled at the invitation to give the scales on his face and neck a good rubdown. "I saw an image. That was you sending it to me, right?"

Leander closed his eyes and rumbled in pleasure under her gentle caress between his eyes. "As far as I know, you don't have another familiar."

She chuckled. "True. It kind of threw me off in the middle of a story."

"What kind of story?"

"About that time so long ago when we butted heads like nobody's business."

The dragon kicked his back legs from beneath him but didn't move his head. "I believe you were the one butting your head against the walls of that pen."

"And you were the one who made that possible. But you're changing the subject."

"From?"

"That image you sent me, Leander. It almost looked like another dragon. A huge one."

He snorted. "And then it looked nothing like a dragon."

"Right. So what was it?"

"I would have told you by now if I knew. But I wanted you to see." The dragon opened his eyes slowly and looked up at her.

"Thank you. That was the right call but I don't know what to do about it."

"Nothing for now. Isn't that right?"

She smiled and ran her fingers down the side of his muzzle and under his chin. "You're really gettin' the hang of this. We should still be careful next time we fly. A giant whatever-it-is flying around while we're up there isn't something we can simply brush off."

"Agreed."

"Good. Do you need anything else before I go?"

"I never do, Raven. You need sleep."

The minute he said it, a huge yawn overtook her. She laughed, shook her head, and rubbed her eyes. "Once again, the dragon nails it perfectly."

He rumbled and lowered his head onto his forepaws. "Goodnight."

"Goodnight, Leander." She slipped through the gate and shut it with a click. In the silence, she couldn't help but glance at the sliver of moon mostly blotted out by the thick clouds still rolling across Brighton.

It's almost exactly what he saw when he sent that image only it's dark now. Really dark. She shuddered and forced herself to look away from the sky as she walked quickly across the field toward the stone archway and the girls' dormitory. *Whatever that thing is, I hope neither one of us sees it again.*

Candy Holloway was dreaming about her grandmother's cinnamon rolls. In the dream, the old lady had forgotten all about the brick oven and left them in for far too long. *That's not right. She's never burned a thing.*

Still, there was no mistaking the smell of smoke.

She woke in the middle of the night to a cry from one of the dragons outside. The smell of heavy smoke only grew stronger, and two more of the dragons at Holloway Ranch cried out.

"Is that—" She leapt from the bed and whisked aside the curtains of her bedroom window. "Warren! Wake up. There's a fire!"

Her husband jolted out of bed and took all the bedding with him. "Are you serious?"

"As a heart attack. Come on."

"What the hell did they get into it about this time?" He turned up the lamp on the table beside their bed and snatched his trousers and shirt from the back of the desk chair.

"I don't know. Orion's been angry at everything lately." She shrugged her jacket on over her night robe and pulled her hair back.

"I told that dragon that if he started anymore issues, I'd have him shipped up north."

"Stop it. Come on."

Warren grasped the lantern and the couple hurried out of their bedroom and toward the front of the house. The screen door slammed shut again behind them, and they raced out to the stables beside the dragon paddock. "Mother of—"

A line of fire raced across the empty field, consumed the grass in a second, and spread quickly.

With a snarl, he stormed toward the stables, where all the Holloway dragons were now awake and raised their voices in concern. "Orion! What the hell do you think you're doing settin' fire to the damn field?"

Two more dragons shrieked.

"Answer me, you good for nothing—"

"It wasn't me!" Orion's high-pitched voice—for a dragon—could be heard above the rising shouts of concern from the others. "There's something out there."

"Yeah, a damn fire. Do you expect me to believe it simply appeared out of nowhere and started all on its own?"

"Warren!" Candy screamed and pointed.

A column of flames as wide as the stables streaked into the ground from the sky. It struck the earth with a roar and threw up clods of dirt and charred grass. A storm kicked up and the wind buffeted the flames to add fuel to the already raging fire.

The dragons in the stable screamed and shrieked as they kicked against the walls of their stalls and tossed their heads.

"Get them out!" She raced toward the stables but stumbling over unseen rocks in the grass before she lifted her nightgown to move faster. She collided with the stable wall in her rush, unlatched the first gate, and threw it open to let Alexander rush out first. "Warren? Warren, what are you doing? The stables are—"

The ground trembled with a mighty rumble as something huge stalked across the paddock toward the building.

"Warren!" Leaving her husband for now, Candy struggled to unlatch each of the stall gates so their ten dragons could get to safety. "Everyone out behind the house."

None of their trained dragons seemed to comprehend the order. They raced from their open stalls and went wild in the field where they bucked and flapped their wings as they ran into each other. The ground rocked beneath her with another deafening thud, and she stumbled into the frame of the last stall before she turned to look for her husband.

Warren's silhouette was perfectly clear against the building flames quickly eating the field.

"Honey, come on. The dragons have lost their minds. Help me get—no..."

A ball of glowing yellow and orange materialized in the center of the field, high above the towering flames.

What is that? She gaped and stared at her husband who seemed frozen in fear directly between that brightening glow of heat and the empty stable.

With a shout, she raced toward him and threw the full weight of her thin body at his back. They landed hard a second before another gargantuan pillar of flames erupted from the glowing ball in the sky. It struck the stables behind them and ignited every inch of the building without moving once in either direction. Wood splintered and cracked and flaming pieces pinwheeled through the sky.

The dragon trainers covered their heads as the debris rained around them. The wind picked up again to blow fire, wood, and dirt against the couple huddled together. Warren's jacket caught fire, and Candy smacked it quickly with her sleeve pulled over her hand before she hauled him to his feet and dragged him toward the house.

Thankfully, the flames hadn't reached that far. All the Holloways could do was to sit on the top porch step and watch the last of the blaze consume every working part of their dragon ranch. The beasts themselves continued to screech and cry out as they ran themselves into exhaustion. They wouldn't leave as they'd been trained to expect severe consequences if they tried.

Candy clenched her jaw and put her arm gently around her husband's shoulders. The man didn't move.

"It came from the sky. Do you see it?"

"I saw it, honey." She rubbed his back and waited for him to say something beyond the same phrases repeated over the last half hour.

"Out of nowhere. Right from the sky. It...from the sky."

She continued to rub his back and looked at the moon and stars muted by the glow of the still-burning fire. The day had been clear, sunny, and with no signs of a storm or foul weather at all, let alone flames and buffeting winds.

So what the hell was it? What took everything from us in an instant?

CHAPTER ELEVEN

"Good morning." Alessandra folded her arms and cocked her head. "You two look as happy to be here as I am."

The two mages in training exchanged a quick glance and shrugged in unison.

"Right. Let's get to it, then. I want you to make another attempt at the Full Appearance. Who will go first?"

"I thought you said we would move on to battle magic," Bella said.

"I changed my mind." The veteran war mage sniffed and stared at the girls for an uncomfortably long time. "I want to make sure that your ability to perform that spell yesterday from the beginning wasn't merely a random fluke."

Raven wrinkled her nose. "It seems kind of unlikely that it would be random for both of us."

"It's also much more unlikely that either of you have the capacity to cast so much as half of the Full Appearance on the very same day you learned it. So you'll do it again. Miss

Chase, you can cast first. Go on." Alessandra shooed them away with both hands.

"I know," she told Bella. "My turn behind the stables."

The girls snickered before she headed toward the long stables at the edge of the field. Leander ambled along behind her and stretched his wings a little in the pale morning light under the clouds that hadn't yet cleared. When they slipped between the back of the stables and the edge of the forest, Raven put her hands on her hips and tilted her head back. "Ready!"

"All right, Miss Chase." Alessandra nodded and stepped back to give her student room to work. "Have at it."

Bella raised her hands and focused on the space between them. "*Loquimi magus.*"

The air shimmered in front of her, and the image of Raven's wide eyes and broad smile appeared a second later. "Nice. I can see your whole face this time."

The other girl's voice came through with a tinny echo, but it was more than clear enough to understand.

Bella's hands started to shake, and as Leander's huge red face appeared over his mage's shoulder in the circle of light, she released the spell. "Woah."

"There it is." Alessandra put a hand on her shoulder and nodded gravely. "That's the drain I was talking about."

"I'm fine." Bella put a hand to her forehead, then lowered it and shook her arms out with a sharp sigh. "Do you still think it's a fluke?"

The woman removed her hand from her shoulder and folded her arms again. "I am as yet still undecided. Miss Alby! You're next."

Raven cast her spell from the other side of the stables.

The same long oval of shimmering light appeared in front of Bella, this one a little farther away than when she'd cast it herself.

"All right." She gritted her teeth and her face rippled in the magic like a reflection in a pond as she looked at her trainer and fellow mage. "Full faces for both of us." Even her tight smile didn't hide the fact that she struggled to hold the spell.

"All right. I'm convinced. You can end it now, Miss Alby." Alessandra nodded.

"I can what?" She squinted at the circle of light. "I can't hear you."

"End the spell, Miss Alby. That's enough."

"I didn't... I can't..." Her eyelids fluttered and the spell ended abruptly.

A piercing shriek was followed by the flap of powerful wings.

"That was too long," the trainer muttered as she raced toward the stables.

"Raven?" Bella shouted.

Before the woman was halfway to the front of the stables, Raven hollered, "I'm fine! I'm—woah."

Alessandra stopped and folded her arms again. The mage staggered out from behind the stables and Leander nudged her lower back with his muzzle to keep her moving forward. "That was pushing it, Alby."

"I didn't mean to." She stumbled forward again when the dragon thumped his snout between her shoulder blades. After a few steps, she turned to pat the top of his head. "Hey, I'm okay. I'm good. I can walk and everything."

"And it looked like you fainted first."

Raven tried to blink her vison into focus so she could at least look like she met her trainer's gaze. "I heard you talking, then I didn't. What happened?"

"Distraction happened, Miss Alby. I told you this spell requires your complete concentration and focus. Do we need to postpone all this for a better time?"

"No. I think I got excited that Bella cast her Full Appearance much stronger than yesterday. And I thought I could too." *Or maybe there's a giant, nasty-looking dragon thing flying around in the back of my mind.*

"Well, you did." The trainer nodded and looked over her shoulder at Bella. "Not a fluke, Miss Chase."

"I know."

"Good. Now that we've covered that, I don't want to see either of you passed out on school grounds from trying to break your own records. Are we clear?"

"Yep." Raven raised her hand again in a little wave. "This headache is warning enough."

"Miss Chase?"

Bella folded her arms and glanced at nothing beside her. "Fine."

Alessandra studied her for a while longer, then muttered to Raven, "The headache should only last another minute or two."

"Awesome."

"All right, mages!" The veteran war mage clapped and Raven groaned. "Take a five-minute break before we move on to practicing how to pull your focus in when you need it the most. I can't have you passing out and falling off the back of your dragon when you're casting a Full Appearance in the midst of a struggle."

She glanced at Leander, who lowered his head and watched the woman stalk toward the center of the field to start some kind of stretching routine. "Sorry about that."

Her dragon pawed the ground and turned away from her. "I didn't enjoy it."

"Me, neither. I won't let it happen again."

"No, you won't."

Still a little shaky, she lowered herself to the ground, crossed her legs, and closed her eyes. *I'll wait for the headache to disappear. Then we're back in business.*

Alessandra hadn't simply been blowing smoke. The two girls did spend the rest of their training that morning seated in the grass, trying to meditate under their trainer's guidance while she intermittently made honking noises, clapped sharply, and cast slightly explosive spells a few feet away to distract them. When she finally released them for the day, she didn't even wait for the questions to start. "Battle magic tomorrow, mages. I highly recommend you keep up with the meditation. You never know when you'll need it."

On that note, the woman left and marched in her usual stiff fashion toward Fowler Academy's main courtyard.

Raven lay back in the grass with a sigh and spread her arms out at her sides. "This is definitely not what I pictured as part of war mage training."

A few feet away, Bella exhaled a long, slow breath. "That was harder than the Full Appearance."

"Seriously?"

"Sitting still and doing absolutely nothing? Are you kidding me?" The girl plucked a handful of grass and tossed it against the slight breeze. "Give me something to read or study or practice, and I'm fine."

"This was practice, Bella."

"Yeah. Practicing boredom. We'll be masters of that in no time."

Raven laughed and rolled onto her side to look at the other young mage. "You are serious."

"It's simply not my favorite. At all." Bella pushed to her feet and brushed the loose blades of grass from her clothes. "I hope she actually gets to the battle magic tomorrow. I was looking forward to that."

"Me too."

"I'm going home. See you tomorrow." She headed toward the main road but turned after a few steps. "Have you read those pages yet?"

She stared at the midday sky that had cleared considerably since morning. "Not yet."

"You might not wanna wait any longer. Plus, once you read about your mom, we get to switch and read the rest of the journal, right?"

With a curious smile, she sat fully. "I finally got you interested, didn't I?"

"You have no idea. Read, Raven. Let me know when you do." Bella waved and hurried toward the road. Wesley screeched in farewell and darted ahead of his mage.

Leander's warm breath fluttered against the back of Raven's neck. "Headache gone?"

"Oh, yeah. Alessandra was right. It only lasted a few minutes."

"You're still concerned."

She turned to look up at him and smiled. "Not about

the headache. I can't stop thinking about that dragon-not-dragon thing. It's really confusing."

"I won't take you out to look for a giant flying creature neither of us has seen before."

"You picked up on my idea to go for a little ride, huh?" Raven stood, brushed her clothes off, and glanced at the sky. "Of course we're not gonna go looking for it, Leander. But I do want to get into that sky. We didn't have time for it yesterday."

He stepped back and spread his massive, translucent wings. "The dragon trainer won't know what to do when he sees us two days in the same week."

"Ha. I think you're right. Let's forget about draining spells and mystery flying things and go make his day, huh?"

The dragon lowered his neck until his head rested beside his front leg and waited to boost her onto his back. "If you can still get on after falling over with a headache."

She grinned, took a few steps back, and pointed at him. "You always know how to motivate me."

Before he could respond, she ran toward him, jumped, and had an extra boost from her dragon familiar's powerful head beneath her boot. The second she reached his back, Leander was already a foot off the ground and headed toward Moss Ranch.

The wind rushed past her face, buffeted her long red braid, and billowed through her open jacket. She spread her arms and savored the feeling of flight, but she found herself quickly opening her eyes again to scan the clear sky.

I'm not paranoid. I only wanna know what the hell that thing really is.

CHAPTER TWELVE

William Moss whooped with excitement when he saw the huge red dragon and his rider glide toward the dragon stables. He snatched his hat off his head and waved it at them, folded his arms, and grinned. By the time they landed outside the fence around the dragon paddock, the trainer had pulled himself together enough to not throw himself at her for a hug.

"Twice in three days, Raven?" His smile faded and his eyes widened at his next thought. "You didn't show up with seriously bad news or something, did you?"

She laughed and patted Leander's long neck appreciatively. "I don't think I've ever shown up here simply to give you bad news."

"Well, you haven't been here this much since you and Leander moved to Fowler, so I had to ask. Are you coming down?"

"I wasn't planning on it." Raven studied the dragons milling around the huge field within the magically enhanced fence. "Do you think Teo might be up for a ride?"

He smirked. "Teo's always up for a ride."

"Great." When she realized her friend hadn't moved, she tilted her head. "I feel like there's a but coming."

"I'm waiting for you to ask if Teo's rider wants to come along too."

Leander lowered his head and hissed twice, which made both young people chuckle.

"I'm sorry. William Moss, would you and Teo care to accompany Leander and me for a ride on this fine spring day?"

"Hey, I like it when you make it sound fancy." He pointed at her. "It almost sounds official."

"I'm guessing the official answer is still yes."

William stuck two fingers in his mouth and leaned toward the fence of the dragon paddock as he emitted a loud, piercing whistle. A few of the dragons out there responded with shrill screeches but only Teo made his way toward the fence and the trainer they both considered his rider.

The lithe silver dragon stopped on the other side of the fence and studied William with his silvery eyes. "You called?"

He smirked. "I saw you running around out there with Isabelle. I had to get your attention somehow."

"Yes." Teo swiveled his head for another glance at the pale-blue dragon in his clan.

"Hi, Teo."

"Hello, Raven Alby. Leander." He inclined his head toward them both. Raven returned the gesture, and Leander spread his wings halfway before he folded them against his back again.

"They wanna go out for a ride," William muttered. "What do you say?"

"I could fly."

"That's what I thought." The trainer walked a couple feet down the fence and unlatched the gate closest to the stables. He held it open for the silver dragon to step through, and the gate shivered a little when he closed it again. He glanced at Raven and Leander and pointed at the stables. "We can't all be fancy and saddle-less, war mage. Give us a few minutes."

She bit back another smart retort and instead, replied, "No problem."

Ten minutes later, he led Teo out of the stables with the full dragon saddle and harness in place. He grinned at Raven still atop the red dragon's back. "Ready when you are, war mage."

Raven grinned. "I'm always ready for this."

"Excellent." William chuckled, gave Teo's bright-silver scales a little pat so the dragon would lower himself to his belly, and stepped into the stirrup to swing his leg over the saddle. "I've missed flying with you two."

Teo dipped his head. "As have I."

"Thanks, guys. Exactly like old times, right?"

The trainer grimaced at Leander's lack of saddle or harness and raised an eyebrow. "Almost."

With another grin, Raven gave them both a little salute before Leander launched skyward with a mighty beat of his wings. Teo followed a second later, and the two dragons wheeled in a wide turn above the dragon field below them. A few of the Moss Ranch dragons raised their heads to watch, but most of them didn't seem to care.

As he eased his dragon alongside Leander and they settled into smooth flight, William returned Raven's salute. She laughed. "Did you guys have anywhere specific in mind?" he asked

"Not really. I thought I'd let Leander take the reins on this one."

"Very funny."

"Thanks."

"Okay, Leander," the trainer called over the buffeting wind that streamed over Teo's gracefully long neck. "Wherever you want. We'll follow your lead."

The red dragon turned his head slightly to look at his counterpart. "I hope your rider will let you keep up."

Teo uttered a short screech that sounded much like a spontaneous laugh. "I don't need him for that."

Raven burst out laughing, and William frowned playfully at the reins in his hand. "Raven Alby, I think you and your dragon are becoming something of a bad influence on Teo."

"All in good fun, dragon trainer. Now, keep up."

The second she said it, Leander beat his wings and hurtled higher above the wisps of clouds left from the day before. The young man only needed to put a little pressure on Teo's reins before the silver dragon streaked after the war mage and her familiar. "You do realize Leander's not exactly trying to lead by example, right?"

They leveled out a few feet below Leander and to the left. Teo turned his head on his long neck and studied the dragon trainer with wide, amused silver eyes. "Of course I do. But Raven might be."

William glanced at her. He could only see her leg over

Leander's back, her outstretched arms, and her profile. But the redheaded mage's eyes were closed, her head thrown back against the wind as she enjoyed the feeling of flight on a dragon without anything to tie her down. "Maybe." *But most of us aren't so lucky to have that kind of a connection with a dragon.*

Leander led them northeast in sweeping patterns that took them over the forest, the small hamlets outside of Brighton, and a few mining sites at the foot of the Mountains of Jordan. She looked at all of it in delight, recognized a few mountain ridges, and patted her dragon's back. "Are you taking us to—"

"Yes." He lowered his head, beat his powerful wings a few times to gain altitude over the peaks of the mountains, and climbed steadily higher the farther north they flew. "It calls to me today. A future I might have had if it weren't for you."

Raven smiled and blinked away a few tears before the wind stole them from her cheeks. *Those are only from the wind. It happens all the time. Mostly.*

"We really are turning this into a blast from the past, aren't we?"

The dragon didn't have to answer.

When the young mage glanced over her shoulder at William and Teo behind them, the dragon trainer gave her a questioning look. She shrugged and her smile widened. *I said I'd let Leander take the reins, didn't I?*

They glided over a wide ridge of jagged stone that rose higher than the other mountain ranges they'd passed. Once on the other side, a broad valley stretched out below them and the long grass and wildflowers provided bursts of color between the hundreds of clipped dragons who called this sanctuary their home now. The voices of so many wild beasts without flight rose to meet them.

Raven swallowed and watched the various clans in the sanctuary move in small groups. Bursts of fire, thick black smoke, and a few columns of glittering dragon frost erupted skyward below them. *They're much more active than last time.*

Finally, Leander descended to land on the other side of the valley on a rounded hill covered in fresh spring grass. Teo and William alighted beside them a few seconds later.

"You're still full of surprises." The trainer waited for the silver dragon to lower himself before he dismounted. "I gotta hand it to you, Leander. This is the last place I expected you to take us."

"Expect the unexpected, flyboy." The red dragon looked at him with narrowed eyes. "Especially from us."

He laughed and ran his fingers through his hair as if to tidy it. "That's where I'm at these days, anyway. Whew. What a ride."

Raven leapt from Leander's back and landed softly in the grass. "It's a perfect day for it, huh?"

"Yes, it is." Her companion patted Teo's side, nodded, and gazed at the long valley of clipped dragons. "They're noisy today."

"I thought the same thing." She stepped toward the edge of the grassy hill. A disorganized circle of dragons on the east side of the valley stamped and snorted and their wings twitched outward in quick flashes of translucent colors. The huge beasts brushed against each other, jostled those beside them, and tossed their heads. "Now I'm starting to think something else."

"Yeah, that doesn't look quite right, does it?" He scratched his chin and watched the odd behavior that played out below them. The other dragons had spread out and moved away from the most agitated beasts to keep a safe distance. "Something doesn't feel right."

"Something's not right," Teo added softly and stretched his neck toward the opposite end of the valley. "Look."

It immediately became apparent what the other clipped dragons were trying to avoid. A massive crater of charred earth, cracked stone, and huge gouges across the mountainside scarred the last highest ridge they'd flown over before landing. Scattered across the devastation were at least four dragon bodies, all torn to shreds.

"How did we miss that?" Raven whispered.

"We flew right over it." William clenched his jaw and scowled at the destruction. "That's what has the others so riled up."

"That's awful." She swallowed uncomfortably, stepped toward Leander, and put a hand on his scaly shoulder to reassure them both. "They didn't...do that to each other, did they?"

"Do you see any dragon here big enough to leave massive furrows like that in the ground?"

Raven looked at him. *He's angry but not at any of us.*

"So what could've done something like this?" she asked.

William sniffed and his jaw clenched with restrained fury. "I have no idea. But it's not something I—"

A series of earsplitting screeches rose from the beasts in the valley. Two of them had begun to fight, any communication they might have exchanged lost beneath the snarls and the endless growls.

"I'll ask what happened." Leander stepped toward the edge of the hill but stopped when he felt Raven's unspoken desire for him to wait.

"Do you think that's a good idea?" she asked tentatively.

The red dragon lowered his head and twisted his long neck to look at her intently. "Do you want to know what happened?"

"Of course I do. But those are *wild* dragons, Leander. Even if they can't fly."

"I have to second that, Leander." William nodded at the red dragon, his brows drawn together in anger and concern. "None have been trained at all. I don't expect any of them to listen to an outsider."

Leander snorted and fixed his gaze on the dragon trainer. "When it comes to everyone but Raven, flyboy, I'm as untrained as they are. Which makes me the best choice to see what they know."

The young man pressed his lips together and looked at her.

"If he can find out what did this, maybe we can stop it from happening again." The young mage nodded. "Leander's right."

Her familiar took that as complete permission and took flight over the edge of the grassy hillside toward the shrieking, snapping, growling beasts below.

William ran his hand through his hair and watched the red dragon land in a clear space yards away from any of the clipped dragons. Some turned to look at him with interest, but most of the others continued to fight and squabble with each other. "I hope he knows what he's doing."

"He does." Raven folded her arms as Leander spread his wings to their full span and stepped toward the closest dragon he thought most likely to tell him anything at all. "Even if he didn't, he'd figure it out."

Teo snorted, pawed the ground, and watched as intently as the riders.

She chewed the inside of her bottom lip. *I have to bring it up.* "William?"

"Yeah."

"Have you ever seen or heard of some other dragon-like thing that's not exactly a dragon?"

He paused before he turned slowly to look at her. "A dragon-like thing?"

"Bigger than three dragons put together. Weird-looking, covered in spikes. That flies."

The dragon trainer gave Teo a confused glance, but the dragon paid no attention to their conversation. "I'm really curious where you got an idea like that, Raven."

"In an image Leander sent me." The young mage puffed her cheeks out in a slow sigh. "Last night. Most of what he saw was only a shadow above the clouds, but whatever it was had a tail. And it was…" She squinted as she tried to come up with the right word. "A little concerning. And yes, it was definitely big enough to leave those kinds of scratches in the ground and do that to other dragons."

William took a deep breath. "There might be a loophole with a familiar sending their mage images from their mind."

"What?"

"Dragons have dreams like everyone else, Raven. When they're asleep *and* when they're awake."

"It wasn't any kind of dream." She frowned at her friend. *He doesn't want to believe me.* "It wasn't a daydream either or some kind of dragon's imagination at work. Leander told me that was exactly what he saw. Besides, a familiar has to concentrate hard to send an image to their mage."

His scowl softened a little and he shook his head. "If that's the case, I have no idea what kind of creature that tail belonged to. Whether or not it's the same thing that scorched the valley and attacked the dragons here, I've never seen it before."

"What about stories? Have you ever heard of giant dragons?"

"No. The only dragons that I know exist are those the trainers help raise, train, and eventually pair with their riders. There were more wild dragons once, a long time ago, but if they're still around, they're somewhere way across the sea. Not here on Threndor and definitely not big enough to do this kind of damage."

Raven studied his profile and the way his jaw clenched and unclenched again. *Wild dragons from across the sea. It sounds like a fairytale but so did being a war mage with a dragon familiar.*

Another round of snarls and screeches rose from the valley, followed by a bellowing roar and the quick snap of razor-sharp dragon's teeth. Teo's wings twitched out from his sides, and he shuffled agitatedly across the grass as he watched the fight below.

Two of the clipped dragons had turned against Leander

and swung their huge heads on long necks to butt the red dragon aside. The others pawed the ground in increasingly aggressive expectation as they added their cries and circled the fighters.

"Leander doesn't seem to be too popular with the locals," William muttered.

"He's fine." Raven couldn't look away from the start of the battle below them.

The larger of the clipped dragons—with mottled brown scales and a large scar running down the length of his flank—spread his wings and reared inches off the ground.

Leander did the same and unleashed a challenging roar. As an unclipped dragon, though, he raised himself onto his rear legs. His wings beat huge gusts of wind against the cantankerous dragons and swatted at the huge brown with a forepaw.

His opponent snarled but stepped back and muttered something that Raven, William, and Teo couldn't hear. Leander launched into flight and left the other startled, agitated, fearful beasts behind him. He flew quickly to the top of the hill and landed gracefully beside Raven before he turned to stand near the edge of the hill overlooking the valley.

She shared a curious glance with William. "Well?"

Leander snorted. "That was interesting."

"What did they say?" William asked.

The red dragon stretched his wings and swiveled his head to look at both riders. "Much of it was nonsense, honestly. They can't seem to agree on anything."

"So we're right back where we started." She looked

down at the clipped dragons, who hadn't settled at all after the newcomer left them.

"Not quite." He pawed the ground and turned. "They agreed on one thing. A monster attacked the clans in the valley."

"A monster." The trainer rubbed his eyes before he stared at the scorched earth across the valley and the scattered remains of the brutally defeated dragons.

"Some beast none of these dragons recognized. And they're all terrified."

Raven approached her familiar and held her hand out, which he bumped with his snout before he lowered his head for a quick pat. "What could scare a dragon, let alone a whole valley of them?" she asked

He exhaled a heavy breath through his nose. "Probably more than you expect if none of them can fly."

"A monster?" William frowned so deeply now that his whole face scrunched. "That doesn't make any sense."

Teo growled softly. "We're not welcome here."

"I had started to pick up on that." Both rider and dragon watched the wild beasts with clipped wings. More of them had turned to stare at the visitors perched on top of the hill. "Raven. Leander. I think it's time for us to go."

"Probably." Raven nodded and leaned toward her dragon. "Are you okay?"

"I'm fine." He rumbled and nudged her hand away. "Their fear makes them useless now. They were more dangerous right after the attack here. But now, they're wary and confused and without any direction."

"What an awful place to be." The young mage sighed a

heavy breath and glanced into the valley again. "Thanks for trying to talk to them, at least."

"It wasn't completely useless."

"All right." William stepped into the stirrup and swung into the saddle. "I'm ready when you are."

"Yeah." With a final glance at the scared, angry dragons without flight, Raven walked along Leander's flank as he lowered himself to his belly for her to climb aboard. *Running and jumping feels like too much right now. He gets it too.*

She stepped onto the base of his tail and walked quickly up the ridges of his back. He rose to his feet again, and when she sat behind his neck, she nodded at her dragon trainer friend. "Ready."

Leander and Teo took flight at the same time and their shadows raced across the valley that was supposed to be the sanctuary of clipped dragons.

Now, it's another dangerous place and they have no way to get out.

CHAPTER THIRTEEN

The excitement over a ride together had all but disappeared when the dragons and their riders returned to Moss Ranch. Raven leapt from Leander's back and brushed her hair out of her face while William dismounted.

"Good work, Teo." The trainer patted the side of his silver dragon's neck and plastered a weak smile on. "You're as fast as ever."

Teo inclined his head toward Raven and Leander. "Thank you for inviting us. I still enjoyed it despite what we found."

"Me too," she replied with a tight smile of her own.

"You did well," Leander added.

Raven, William, and Teo all paused in surprise. *He doesn't usually talk to other dragons, let alone compliment them.* The young mage darted her dragon a sidelong glance, but he was focused on lowering his head toward Teo in return.

"As did you." The green dragon turned toward William. "I would like to return to the field now, William."

"No problem." The trainer deftly unbuckled the saddle girth below Teo's silver belly and slid the saddle onto the ground. He slipped the harness over the dragon's bowed head and dropped that too before he moved quickly toward the gate into the dragon paddock.

Teo began to approach the opening in the fence and paused to mutter, "Don't worry. I won't tell the others what happened."

This time, William's smile wasn't forced at all. "I trust you. Thanks."

Without another word, the green dragon ambled slowly into the field with the other Moss Ranch dragons and disappeared into the throng of beasts who milled around. Two of them backed away when they sensed the silver dragon's distress, but that was the only reaction.

Leander lowered his head until it hovered over Raven's shoulder. "Teo has a better handle on his thoughts than I expected."

"He's holding it together well, isn't he?" The young mage patted the side of her dragon's face. "So are you."

"I don't like what happened to those dragons any more than you do, Raven. But I'm not frightened by a monster no one can describe."

She leaned away from his head to look at him in one glowing yellow eye. "Except for us."

"Perhaps."

William returned from hanging the tack in the stables and dusted his hands off. "I'm with Teo. That was a weird thing to see."

Raven nodded. "Those dragons were really having a hard time. It kind of reminds me of—"

"The dragons in Azerad," Leander finished for her.

I shouldn't even be surprised by now that he can finish my sentences too.

William's eyes widened. "There were clipped dragons in Azerad?"

"No. They could all fly, as far as I know." Raven wrinkled her nose. "Leander was in the stables with a few dozen other dragons. They all seemed as scared as those in the sanctuary today, now that I think about it."

"And empty." The red dragon released a breath and his wings twitched out slightly.

William looked from one to the other, a little perplexed. "I think I missed something."

She glanced quickly at Leander and shrugged. "We think the dragons they stabled there in the city might have been...trained differently. Domesticated, I guess, but to the point where they really didn't act much like dragons at all."

"Until that huge brown ate a raider in a few bites." Her familiar grinned.

"Wow. Actually ate the guy, huh? You don't have to answer that. It was rhetorical."

More than happy to change the subject, Raven tilted her head and added, "I've watched you train the dragons here, William, and you mentioned a standard for training a few times. How strict are those rules, exactly?"

"Well...there are guidelines." The dragon trainer shrugged and frowned as he paused for thought. "Every ranch has their own slightly different methods. Some trainers are extremely heavy-handed with the punishment approach, which I've never enjoyed watching or hearing about. We stay away from that altogether, but a few of those harsher techniques make Leander's small pen here look like a vacation on the beach in comparison."

Raven grimaced. "That's probably what the trainers in Azerad were doing. Or whoever trains the dragons for the city, I suppose."

"It was more uncomfortable there than what we saw at the sanctuary," her familiar added. "The dragons in Azerad had serious problems."

"Are you sure that wasn't simply their reaction to having a snarky red beast show up with his mage?" When the dragon snorted, William stepped back and raised his hands in surrender. "Sorry. That was a joke."

"So were those dragons." Leander's eyes narrowed but he didn't comment again.

"All right. Well, it's not my place to get involved with other trainers' methods. That's up to every ranch, honestly."

Raven shook her head. "William, if you'd seen those dragons, you might have wanted to get involved."

"Hmm." The dragon trainer didn't look convinced. "I'll talk to my dad about it. Maybe he's come across a few of these other trainers or their dragons. He might know more, but please keep in mind that putting dozens of dragons together in the same stable in a busy city tends to dampen everyone's spirits. That might be what you saw too."

"Maybe." *I don't think so.* She shrugged. "If you do talk to your dad, let us know what he says."

"Absolutely." William hooked his thumbs in his belt and watched the Moss Ranch dragons a little longer. "And so you know, I'm still glad you guys stopped by and asked us to fly for a while."

Raven smiled and continued to rub the side of Leander's face over her shoulder. "I have a feeling we'll be back soon for another ride. Somewhere other than the sanctuary next time."

"Yeah, I think that's a good idea. Another chance to clear our heads."

"We'll be back. You can count on that."

"I do." He stepped toward her and Leander, who didn't move from where he hovered over his mage's shoulder. "I wouldn't worry too much about this alleged monster. Honestly, that could simply have been a furious dragon involved in a sneak attack in the middle of the night and staging all that damage to cover it up. They really are smart enough to do that, especially when they're wild."

She nodded. "I know they are. And if that's what happened, we don't have anything to worry about."

"Exactly."

William, Raven, and Leander stood there a moment longer to watch the Moss Ranch dragons who walked, stamped, and lay with their clans in the paddock.

"We should get going. Let Mr. Moss here finish whatever he was working on when we showed up to surprise him." She smirked at her friend and drew her hand along Leander's flank.

"Honestly, it wasn't much of anything. There's much less work now that my dad's not so gung-ho about protecting against raiders."

"Maybe you can take the rest of the day off."

William snorted and snatched up the wide-brimmed

hat he'd hung on the fencepost before their ride. "Probably not. Only a light afternoon."

With a boost from Leander, Raven jumped onto her dragon's back and nodded at her friend. "We'll be back soon. And be careful, okay? If that thing at the sanctuary wasn't a pissed-off dragon in the middle of the night, there's still something out there."

"I have dozens of lookouts with heightened hearing and an even better sense of smell." He gave her a thumbs-up. "If anything is flying around that's not supposed to be, we'll all know."

"Good. See ya, William."

Leander vaulted into flight and the dragon trainer stared after them until they were a spec in the sky heading north toward Fowler Academy.

"See ya, Raven Alby." William sighed, adjusted his hat on his head, and got back to work.

After stopping at the girls' dormitory for a quick meal in the common room, Raven spent the rest of her afternoon in the field at Fowler Academy with Leander.

"No training. No studying. I'm happy to lay out here and wait for the day to end." She leaned against her dragon's side where he had curled in the grass.

"I don't mind this either."

She chuckled and looked at the sky and the small wisps of clouds moving slowly west. "Do you have any more thoughts about what we saw today?"

"Many."

When he didn't say anything else, she laughed and nudged him with her shoulder. "Do you care to share any of them?"

"I don't think that dragon trainer knew what he was talking about at all. Wild dragons are no less capable of sniffing out one of their own than any of flyboy's trained creatures. I smelled something different in that valley, Raven. His sneak-attack theory is foolish and dangerous."

"I know. It didn't seem like William believed his own words either. He simply tried to make us all feel better. Lighten the mood, you know?"

Leander lowered his head onto the ground and his eyelids fluttered against the long green blades of grass that tickled his muzzle. "I prefer a heavy truth to a light lie."

"I'm right there with you. Do you think what you saw last night and the monster that attacked the sanctuary are the same thing?"

"I don't know. I'm not in a hurry to find out, either."

Raven ran her hands over the grass beside her and rested her head against his side. "Because that's when it becomes an issue for us too."

The huge red dragon didn't have to say anything for her to know that he'd had exactly the same thought.

CHAPTER FOURTEEN

After breakfast the next morning, Raven headed out to the field to release Leander from his pen for another day of week's end training with Alessandra. Bella crossed the field from the front gates of the school, and they both slowed when they saw the row of training dummies already set up for them.

"Woah." Raven glanced at her companion, who shrugged in response before she continued her approach. "This is way more dummies than the last time we used them."

"More targets to blast apart with the battle magic we get to learn today." The other girl grinned. "Do you think she'll put them on auto-attack again?"

"I can't even pretend to know what War Mage Barnasis has planned for us. Ever."

Snickering, the girls approached the stables as Alessandra stepped out of the weapons shed and closed the door behind her. "Excellent to see that we're all on time this morning."

"It's a nice change," Bella muttered.

The veteran war mage didn't catch the jibe and focused instead on the two long bo staffs she'd brought with her from the shed. "I hope you're ready to get to work immediately."

She tossed the staffs at her students, and the girls caught the weapons almost at the same time. Bella spun hers in both hands and thumped the butt of it into the ground. "Weapons out means battle magic too, right?"

Alessandra raised an eyebrow.

"Then I'm so ready."

With a smirk, Raven leaned toward the other trainee and held her staff out. "Can you hold this for a sec? I still have to release my dragon."

The dark-haired mage took the weapon and rolled her eyes although she smiled.

Raven darted toward the pen gate, flashed her rune, and poked her head inside the enclosure. "We're up, Leander. And seriously on schedule this morning, apparently."

He rose quickly from where he'd curled after her last visit before dawn and headed toward her. "I hope it's more than watching you meditate today."

"Alessandra pulled the bo staffs out. I think we're stepping it up a notch."

When he emerged fully, she shut the gate and hurried to catch up with his hasty approach to where Bella and Alessandra stood in the center of the field. Wesley swooped overhead and screeched a warning. The dragon looked up and blew a thin stream of light-gray smoke in reply.

The veteran war mage stood in front of the row of

twenty training dummies lined up across the field, her back to the vaguely human-shaped figures made of wood, straw, and burlap. Bella tossed Raven her staff, and the girls settled side by side to start their training.

"Yes, today's the day you'll learn more intense and highly advanced combat spells. Given that I'm not nearly as worried about the two of you casting them on each other as I was only a few weeks ago, I'd venture to say you can handle it."

The young mages snorted but said nothing.

"The first is basically a higher-level version of the minor force spell you squabbled over during the week before the spring break."

Raven darted Bella a sidelong glance. "Awesome."

The girl stared straight ahead, her eyes wide with excitement above a small, eager smile.

"Observe." Alessandra glanced expressionlessly from one young mage to the next, then whirled in the grass and shouted, *"Ecflicto!"*

A burst of white light streaked from her palm and struck the dummy on the end with a sharp crack. The frame exploded and scattered wood splinters, pebbles, frayed burlap, and a puff of loose straw in all directions. When the debris fluttered to the ground, all that remained was the wooden base and a sharp, jagged wooden spike where the center frame had split.

"Yes," Bella muttered.

The woman turned slowly toward her trainees and folded her arms. "I've charmed these training dummies to withstand a much higher strength of magical attack than either of you have practiced with before today. When you can do that to any of them, you'll be ready to learn the next spell. When you can destroy two or more of them at the same time, I'll nod and tell you you've mastered this one. And it goes without saying, but don't use this on any living creature whose life you value even in the slightest. Now, repeat the spell. I need peace of mind knowing neither of you will botch the pronunciation and end up doing something unthinkable."

"*Ecflicto.*" Raven's hands tingled with magic as she said it, despite her very clear intention of not casting the spell.

Bella stared at the dummies behind their trainer. "*Ecflicto.*" A little shiver ran up the girl's back, and her smile grew. "Let's start, huh?"

"Jeeze. It's like having two racehorses snorting behind the starting gate." Alessandra released a long-suffering sigh. "We have all morning, Miss Chase. Do you have any questions?"

"What are the bo staffs for?" Raven lifted hers but stared at the destroyed dummy.

Alessandra frowned at her like that was the dumbest question in the world. "Sparring, Miss Alby."

"So the dummies are gonna fight back like last time," Bella said with a curt nod.

"No. You will spar with each other this morning. The goal is to use this spell correctly, accurately, and with as much force as you can muster while you ward off attacks from an opponent. Got it?"

Raven glanced at her bo staff and smirked. "It's been a while since we've sparred against each other."

"Too long, if you ask me." With a grin, her companion grasped her staff higher with her hand and stepped back in a ready stance. "I look forward to it more than last time, honestly."

"Huh." She glanced at Leander beside her and met the girl's grin with one equally as challenging. "I thought the same thing."

"Just because we're friends doesn't mean we can't fight each other."

"That's probably why we should."

The girls stared at one another, smiled, and waited for their opponent to make the first move. Alessandra scoffed and tossed her hand in the air. "This isn't witty-banter training, mages. Get going!"

Bella lunged forward and brought the staff up for a mighty swing aimed at the other girl's head. Raven blocked with a crack of wood on wood and stepped back again as Wesley swooped from the sky and darted between them. Bella attacked again, brought the staff up from below, and swiped at the other mage's feet before she jabbed toward her stomach, all while Wesley fluttered around Raven's head and screeched.

Sweat built quickly at Raven's hairline, but she managed to duck, parry, and dodge each of the quick strikes. Bella grinned the whole time, her eyes wide and alight with a crazed-looking enthusiasm. *I seriously pity the next person who ends up fighting her for real.*

Raven found an opening for a return strike, and when the other girl lunged out of the way, the redheaded mage extended her hand toward the line of dummies and shouted, "*Ecflicto!*"

A bright white light erupted from her palm, but the attack went wide when Wesley swooped toward her and made her jerk her hand back to avoid his outstretched talons. "Nice trick."

"Wesley's only doing his part." Bella swung again, and the sparring continued.

"That's exactly what you'll have to deal with in battle, Miss Alby. Distractions and attacks from every possible angle. Miss Chase is using every ability at her disposal. What do you have?"

I have a dragon.

Raven parried again, swung into an immediate attack, and pushed the other mage two feet back across the field. Bella empowered her next onslaught with a burst of speed and swung from every direction. She leapt away from Raven's next swipe, ducked, and spun low in the grass before she swung the bo staff in a bold arc toward her opponent's chest.

Wesley fluttered between them and circled again. *Find another opening.*

As soon as she thought it, Leander sent a quick image into her mind—Wesley heading toward the sparring mages from behind her, trying to sneak up on her. She smiled, blocked more attacks, and shifted her bo staff to challenge Bella from the other side.

The girl leapt away and deflected the blow. The red dragon sent another quick, split-second image of Wesley diving toward Raven's upper back. She took a huge step back and tucked the bow staff under her arm as she crouched. Her back knee scraping against the grass. She thrust out toward the dummies with her other hand as Wesley darted without effect over her head and she shouted, *"Ecflicto!"*

This time, her spell didn't miss. The brilliant flash of light exploded against one of the center dummies and it reeled away before the weighted base rocked it into place again.

Leander uttered his own small, triumphant screech.

Bella had stopped her relentless attacks to stare at the slightly charred wood of the dummy's chest.

"That's more like it, Miss Alby." Alessandra's deadpan expression hadn't changed but she inclined her head in acknowledgment. "Using what you have."

Raven straightened and thumped the side of her bo staff lightly against her opponent's shoulder. "You almost made it impossible for me to get a good shot."

Bella turned toward her and lifted her weapon in a defensive position. She smirked and raised her eyebrows. "Almost isn't good enough, Raven. You know that. See if you can almost stop me."

"You're on." She unleashed her own attacks with the sparring weapon and pushed the girl swiftly across the field. Wesley continued to swoop and dive around them while he shrieked and fluttered between them to distract her. "It's bad form to hit a familiar with one of these things, right?"

"In training, very much so," Alessandra muttered.

"I was kidding." Raven pivoted and swung her staff toward her opponent's right side, which made the other girl turn away to block and left her other side wide open.

As the girls moved from one side of the field to the other, Leander stalked alongside them, his gaze focused intently on Bella. When the girl thought she'd found an opening and stretched her hand toward the dummies, the dragon snorted a heavy breath of hot air against her face.

"What—" She ducked away from the huge dragon muzzle less than a foot away and laughed. "This is the kind of training we should've started with."

She jerked her staff in position to block the next attack, and Wesley dove toward Leander but veered away at the last second when the dragon opened his enormous jaws. Both girls chuckled but didn't miss a beat in their sparring.

Alessandra narrowed her eyes and watched her trainees with her arms folded. "This is training, mages. Not a pillow fight." *And I still wouldn't like my chances against these two when it really mattered.*

The girls ignored her and continued their whirlwind attacks with broad strokes, lunges, parries all accompanied by the cracks of staff against staff. Bella swiped at Raven's feet and forced her to jump back. She carried through with the momentum and swung her staff toward Leander's head. The dragon snorted and reared as the dark-haired mage whirled and shouted, "*Ecflicto!*"

The spell streaked from her hand and caught the second dummy from the end to whip it sideways against its neighbor. She pulled her staff up in both hands again barely in time to block her adversary's downward attack.

They grinned at each other, breathing heavily. Bella tossed her hair out of her eyes and stepped back. "Almost."

"You almost hit me," Leander muttered, his head lowered and swaying from side to side as he watched his mage's opponent.

The girl shrugged. "I knew you'd move."

Raven chuckled. "I'd hate to see what would happen if you actually did smack him in the face with that."

"She couldn't." The dragon uttered a low rumble of certainty.

"Is that a personal challenge, dragon?" Bella spun her bo staff again and thrust the butt of it into the ground as she regarded the great red beast that met her stare with amusement.

"Hey!" Alessandra clapped her hands, the sound echoing across the field. "You're sparring with weapons, mages. Not words. Do I have to make you fight each other?"

The young mages glanced at each other, shared a knowing smile, and stepped into ready stances.

"I guess we'll have to turn it up a notch," Bella muttered.

Raven lifted her staff and narrowed her eyes in amused determination. "Bring it."

The trainer made a show of rolling her eyes and shaking her head. The girls returned to their joust and completely ignored her exaggerated reaction. But War Mage Alessandra Barnasis watched them intently and folded her arms again. *So they've finally quit looking at each other as enemies. It took 'em long enough.*

CHAPTER FIFTEEN

The training dummy on the far end of the field crackled and sparked with Bella's final attack. Unfortunately, it didn't explode the way Alessandra had shown them.

"Come *on!*" the girl shouted and thumped the end of her bo staff against the ground.

The veteran war mage clicked her tongue. "I highly doubt that reaction will get the results you want, Miss Chase."

The dark-haired mage sighed in exasperation and shook her head. "I've cast it perfectly. We both have. Those dummies should be in pieces by now!"

Raven wiped a sheen of sweat from her forehead and glanced at her clothes. *Gross. I'm soaked.*

"Advanced battle magic takes time, dedication, and practice," Alessandra replied with a small frown. "It's entirely unrealistic to expect mastery after only one day of sparring, Miss Chase. I don't care how advanced you are or how easily you've mastered your spellcasting thus far."

Bella rolled her eyes. "So what am I missing, then?"

"Time."

The girl scoffed and turned to her companion. "I almost had it."

"I know." Raven tucked her weapon under her arm and looked at the charred, tilting dummies lined up across the field. "We both came really close. If it makes you feel any better, I didn't blow any dummies up, either."

"Yeah, I noticed." Bella raised an eyebrow at her fellow mage, sighed, and gave her a small smile. "It's a tiny consolation, I guess."

She chuckled. "Take 'em where you can get 'em, right?"

The girl pulled her sweat-soaked shirt away from her chest and shoulders, tried to fan it out, and finally gave up. "I don't think we've worked this hard before."

"I have a feeling this is what real training is like."

"It's always been real training," Alessandra interjected. "But you two finally learned how to work together to challenge each other the right way instead of trying to demolish each other however you could."

The girls shared another amused glance and turned toward their trainer.

"That's it for today, mages. It was good work, but it won't be excellent work until each of you obliterates a man-shaped blob of wood and straw. You can try again tomorrow." With that, she spun away and marched across the field toward the stone archway.

Raven stared after her and glanced down at the bo staff in her hand. "What are we supposed to do with these?"

"Do you have access to the weapons shed?"

"Nope."

Bella closed her eyes in exasperation. "Me neither. And there's no way in hell I'll take a sparring weapon home with me."

She choked back a laugh. "I can actually see the looks on your family's faces with that one."

"I don't even want to think about it." The girl twirled her staff a couple of times, grasped it in both hands, and shrugged. "The stables?"

"I believe I can help you with that," Headmaster Flynn said as he approached them from the other side of the barn.

Raven peered at the barn with a little frown. *Where did he come from?*

"You've both made some remarkable improvements," he told them and his long, scraggly gray beard caught the breeze. "I had the opportunity to watch some of your training today and I must say, I'm quite impressed."

She smiled. "Thanks, Headmaster."

Bella shook her head. "It's still not enough. We didn't destroy any of those dummies."

"True. But I wouldn't say it's not enough, Miss Chase. Quite the contrary, actually. You didn't destroy each other, and that's a much better start than at the beginning of the school year."

The young mages shared another glance and the girl finally let herself smile too. "We're working on it."

Raven folded her arms against her damp shirt and chuckled wryly.

"I'm happy to put that away for you, Miss Chase. You're free to go home if you like." Flynn held his hand out and Bella gave him the staff. He nodded and glanced at Raven. "You can put your own staff away, Miss Alby."

He wandered toward the weapons shed between the stables and the barn.

"Huh. It looks like you're the only one getting special favors today."

Bella shook her head. "I can't tell if he took that staff to be nice or to secretly tell me I shouldn't spar with a staff at all."

They watched the headmaster until he disappeared around the end of the stables, then the girl peeled her damp shirt away from her body again and made a face at Raven. "I need a shower."

"Tell me about it." She wiped her forehead again and nodded. "See you tomorrow. We'll blow all those dummies to pieces."

"We'd better." Bella headed to the main road toward Brighton's town center but paused and twisted slightly to look at her. "Have you read those pages yet?"

A laugh of disbelief escaped her. "Wow. Now I know how you felt when I tried to get you to read them."

"So that's a no."

She gave Leander a quick look. The dragon simply stared at her. *I probably shouldn't tell her what we found. Not until we know what we're dealing with.* "I was a little busy last night."

"Well, don't let yourself get too busy every night, Raven. Seriously. Read the journal." With a final wave, the girl hurried across the field. Wesley darted behind her, soared over her head, and wheeled constantly to let her catch up with him.

Raven hefted the bo staff and headed toward the weapons shed. Headmaster Flynn stood beside the open door, waiting for her. He smiled when she stepped into the building to put the weapon away with the others, then closed the door softly and nodded toward the main court-yard and the school's buildings.

"I wasn't merely being polite when I said you and Miss Chase have really made progress over the past few weeks."

"Thanks. How long were you watching us?" They stepped out from between the stables and the barn, where Leander ambled slowly toward them and listened to their conversation.

"Oh, for the last hour or so."

She shrugged. "It would've been more exciting if we'd actually mastered that spell the way we're supposed to. But we'll get there."

"I have no doubt, Miss Alby." Flynn gave her a sidelong glance and his lips twitched in amusement as the afternoon sunlight caught the long scar that stretched down the side of his face. "I was, however, referring to your partnership with Miss Chase."

"Really?"

"Don't act so surprised." The headmaster chuckled. "It wasn't that long ago that you and Miss Chase were repeat-edly brought to my office in the hopes that I would settle some deep-seated dispute between the two of you. I doubt that will happen much more in the future."

Raven glanced at the edge of the field and the road beyond Fowler Academy's front gates. "Probably not."

"I think I may come out here more often during your war-mage training if that's all right with you. It's been some time since I've seen two students who worked so seamlessly together with battle magic."

Surprised by the request, she widened her eyes at the headmaster and nodded. "I don't mind at all. Bella might feel extra pressured, though, if she knows you're watching."

Flynn's smile widened as he looked at the giant red dragon that approached slowly. "I'll remain as silent and invisible as I was this afternoon."

Leander lowered his head toward the headmaster and stopped directly behind Raven.

"I would also like you to join me in my office after lunch, Miss Alby. If you have the time."

The young mage stepped back to run her hand along the side of her dragon's face. "Sure. After lunch. And a shower."

With another chuckle, he nodded at both mage and dragon familiar before he clasped his hands behind his back. "I look forward to it."

He moved swiftly toward the stone archway, and Raven turned toward Leander. "He usually sends someone else to fetch me to his office. It must be important this time."

The dragon stared after Flynn. "I thought it was always important."

"Yeah, but he came out here to ask me himself. I wonder what he wants to talk about. Did you know he was there watching us?"

Leander turned his head enough to focus one yellow eye on his mage. "I did not."

"Huh."

"I don't like it."

Raven couldn't help a laugh. "I can't imagine you would.

Headmaster Flynn's either beaten you in the stealth game, or he worked some serious magic to make sure we didn't see him."

"Of course it was magic."

As she turned toward her dragon's enclosure at the end of the stables, she smirked and let her familiar follow closely behind. "Right. Because no human could ever be as naturally quiet as a dragon."

"Exactly."

She flashed the access rune on her forearm at the gate, opened it for Leander, and waited for him to enter first. "By the way, you really stepped it up a notch with sending those images. It felt like I had eyes in the back of my head."

The dragon rumbled softly as he circled the pen before he settled into the grass. "They're still my eyes, little girl. I suppose I don't mind sharing them with you."

"You're so generous." With a chuckle, she approached him and leaned forward a little to run her hand along the ridges of his snout and up between his eyes. "Seriously, though. There's so much more we can do now with you sending me what you see. Now I have to practice sending images to you and we'll be unstoppable."

Leander snorted, closed his eyes, and enjoyed her light touch. "We're already unstoppable."

"So far. That might have its limits, though. We barely got away with defeating the last of the Swarm, and the raiders didn't put up much of a fight once they saw what you could do."

"They were stupid."

She laughed. "That's one way to put it. Still, I have a

feeling it won't always be that easy. It's not like Bella and I are the most powerful war mages in Lomberdoon."

"Not yet."

Her smile widened, and she patted the side of his face. "You talk a big game, Leander."

"It's not only talk, little girl. We've proven ourselves more than once."

"Yes, we have." With a sigh, Raven peeled her shirt away from her body again and her nostrils flared. "I really do need a shower. And as soon as I'm done talking to Headmaster Flynn about…whatever it is, I'll come tell you."

His only response was to lower his head onto his forepaws and watch her walk across the enclosure toward the open gate.

"Hey, maybe I got another letter from my grandpa. Which might mean he actually got mine too."

The dragon closed his eyes with a small sigh, and she slipped out before she closed the gate and hurried toward the girls' dormitory.

Clean, dry, and in a fresh set of clothes, Raven hurried down the stairs into the common room. "Yes. I made it."

The long banquet tables along the side of the room hadn't been cleared from lunch yet, so she piled a plate with fruit, cheese, buttered bread, and the last chicken thigh on the platter. She took her lunch to the table where Elizabeth sat over another book. Iggy was curled in his mage's lap, apparently asleep.

"What have you been up to?" she asked as she slipped into a chair across the table.

"You're looking at it." Elizabeth didn't look up from her book.

"It must be nice to have all day to read before classes pick up again tomorrow."

The girl shrugged and tossed her black bangs out of her eyes before they fell into place again.

Raven wolfed her food down and followed almost every mouthful with a swig of fresh water from the pitcher. Her roommate looked slowly from her reading and cocked her head. When Raven noticed her friend staring at her, she swallowed her huge mouthful and smiled. "What?"

"Did you forget to eat for the last two days or something?"

Chuckling, she leaned back in her chair and glanced at her almost empty plate. "No. I guess I worked up an appetite training this morning."

Elizabeth smirked and returned to her book.

"Hey, I have a question for you."

"Yeah." The black-haired mage pressed her finger onto the page and looked up again.

"Have you ever read anything about…" Raven wrinkled her nose. *This is gonna sound nuts.* "I don't know. Monsters?"

"Monsters?" The amused smile returned to the girl's face, and she tilted her head quizzically.

"I know, it's a weird thing to ask."

"Not really. But you have to be a little more specific. Some people still think dragons are monsters."

Raven snorted. "Those people should try meeting one.

But it might not be all that far off from what I'm talking about. So more specifically, monsters that might look like dragons. You know—wings, tails, the whole thing. Only bigger and scarier and covered in spikes."

"That's definitely more specific." The girl's eyes narrowed. "But if it looks like a dragon and flies like a dragon…"

"Yeah, most people would say it's a dragon." She sighed in genuine frustration and took another sip of water. "But I really don't think that's what it is."

Elizabeth closed her book and slid it to the side. "Something tells me this isn't a hypothetical question."

"Not really." Raven glanced around the almost empty common room. Two other girls sat at a table behind her, and she stood from the chair to sit again next to her roommate. "You can't tell anyone else about this, okay? Not until I find answers first."

"Now I'm *really* interested." Elizabeth leaned back in her chair and folded her arms. "Sure. I won't tell anyone."

"Okay." She lowered her voice and leaned closer. "Leander saw this…thing flying around two nights ago. It was mostly hidden behind the clouds, so he mainly saw only a giant shadow. But it's tail was…okay, like a dragon's tail but definitely not. All shiny and black and covered in spikes everywhere. It was huge—bigger than any dragon I've seen—and no one seems to know what it is."

"Who have you asked?"

"Well, only William Moss so far. The dragon trainer. He said something about other wild dragons living across the sea, but what Leander saw is here. It flew over the school and everything."

Elizabeth's eyes widened above her growing smile. "That's so cool."

"Um…" Raven chuckled. "I guess I shouldn't be surprised you'd think that. You're always reading something, so I thought I'd ask."

"I've read legends about monsters." The girl glanced at her closed book. "And stories about dragons, but those all come from when people started raising them on ranches. I don't remember reading anything about a monster that's like a dragon but not."

"Right. That's the only way I can describe it."

"Are you sure it wasn't another dragon flying around in the clouds?"

Raven gave her roommate a knowing glance and shook her head. "I know what a dragon in the sky looks like. So does Leander. This was something else."

"Awesome." Elizabeth ran a few fingers down Iggy's curled back in her lap and nodded. "When you do find out, let me know. I might be able to find even more books about it if I know what I'm looking for."

"That would be helpful. Thanks."

"What?" The other mage laughed and straightened in her chair. "I was talking about books for me to read but if you want to borrow them, I guess that's cool too."

"Still helpful." Raven stood and stretched across the table to gather her plate and cup. "I'll let you know."

"Where are you going now?"

"Flynn's office." She gestured with her arms and stepped backward toward the tray for used plates beside the banquet tables. "I've been summoned again."

"Not surprising. Good luck."

Before she could thank her, Elizabeth had already opened her book again and was immersed in the pages. She deposited her plate and cup on the cart, braided her hair, and tied it back quickly before she hurried to Headmaster Flynn's office. *It feels like I'm in there all the time. This had better be good.*

CHAPTER SIXTEEN

When she reached the top of the tower's winding staircase, the door to Headmaster Flynn's office was wide open. *That's new.*

Raven stepped through the doorway and knocked lightly on the open door. "Headmaster Flynn?"

"Miss Alby." The headmaster looked up from his desk with a smile and set his quill in front of him. "That was faster than I expected."

"Do you want me to come back later?"

"No, no. Now works perfectly. Please, come in."

She proceeded into the man's office that also doubled as his living quarters. Flynn's massive wolf familiar Rider lay on the floor beside the wall, his head raised to look at her. "Hi, Rider."

The wolf's mouth opened and his tongue peeked out over his sharp teeth as he panted.

"I'll only be a moment." Flynn stood from his chair and dripped melted silver wax onto the four rolls of parchment paper on the desk before he stamped them with the Fowler

Academy seal on his ring. With a nod at his handiwork, he looked at her and smiled. "I'd like to ask a favor of you and Leander, Miss Alby."

"Oh. Okay." She glanced at the papers on his desk. *Nothing from the capital and no new letters. Bummer.*

"I have a few messages that need to be delivered." He brushed the scrolls together into a neat pile on his desk. "And to be perfectly honest, the novelty of having a student at this school with a dragon familiar hasn't quite worn off, even this far into the year. This is why I'm asking you and Leander to deliver these messages for me."

Raven's eyes widened. "You want us to deliver your letters?"

"Yes." The headmaster cleared this throat before he broke into a wide grin. "Of course, I can use another messenger on horseback if I must. But these are rather time-sensitive letters, and I thought you both might appreciate getting out of Brighton with more of a purpose beyond flying as far as Leander wishes to. Unless Azerad was enough for you."

The young mage perked up and nodded. "We can handle it."

"That's what I assumed."

She smirked. "As long as Leander and I don't become the go-to messenger for Fowler."

"Oh, ha." Flynn chuckled and gathered the narrow scrolls into one hand as he stepped out from behind his desk. "That is one condition I can most certainly agree to, Miss Alby. Correct me if I'm wrong, but I believe you have the rest of the day to yourself."

"That's right."

"Excellent. Then I would very much appreciate it if you and Leander could use this afternoon to deliver these for me. Preferably as soon as you leave this tower."

Raven took the scrolls and started to read the names written across the outside above the wax seals before the headmaster handed her another piece of parchment paper.

"This is a list of the people who need to receive those letters. Please be sure to deliver them only to the people whose names you see here and not to anyone else. Certain letters have a tendency to be delayed when they change hands multiple times. And I've included something of a crude map to help you orient yourself." The man chuckled and pointed at the list when the young mage took it. "These are all larger towns around Brighton. You'll only go as far as Bluredge, which isn't nearly as far as Azerad. On a dragon, I should think you'll find it easy enough to reach all four towns and return to school grounds before dark. Or a little after."

"That shouldn't be a problem."

"Yes, I know how fast that dragon of yours really is." He turned toward his desk, opened a drawer, and pulled out a vial of premade calling potion and a coin purse. "But if you find yourself in a situation where time is working against you, be sure to let me know."

She had to shift the scrolls she held to make room for the vial and the coin purse, which clinked heavily in her hand. "I get an allowance for this?"

The headmaster nodded at the purse and raised an eyebrow. "For emergencies only. Otherwise, I would very much appreciate the return of both potion and coin."

"Of course." Raven grinned at him and waited for the rest of his instructions.

"That is all, Miss Alby. Thank you for agreeing to do this. It saves me considerable time, which I'm already running low on as it is."

"Thanks for trusting us with your letters." She lifted her armful of items and nodded. "We'll be back before you know it."

"Excellent." Flynn returned to his chair and picked his quill up again.

Raven turned quickly and ran down the stairs. When she burst through the front doors of the main building, she almost raced through the archway into the field before she skidded to a halt on the cobblestones. "Bag. I need a bag."

She laughed at herself and went to retrieve her satchel from her room. *Headmaster Flynn's sending us on special errands now. It seems simple enough. I bet it's some kind of test.*

With the items stowed safely in her satchel, she raced across the field toward Leander's pen. He snorted in greeting before she pushed her jacket sleeve up to expose her access rune, she poked her head into the enclosure, and grinned. "We have a job, Leander. Straight from Head-master Flynn."

The dragon turned his head to regard her with a steady stare. "What?"

"Yeah. Come on." She opened the gate and waited for her familiar to emerge from his special temporary home.

"And what, exactly, is our job?"

Raven closed the gate and checked the straps of her satchel to make sure it was secure. "We're running errands, now."

"I see. I hope he doesn't plan to make this a regular occurrence. I'm not a messenger dragon."

"You know, that's basically what I told him." She chuckled. "He didn't exactly say he'd never ask us to do this again, but it feels like a one-time thing."

"How far?"

"Four towns right outside Brighton. He says we could get to all of them and back before dark, so this'll be a piece of cake." Raven frowned thoughtfully as they headed out into the field. "I have a feeling it's not only about delivering letters, though. That's easy enough. I bet he wants us to see something."

"Or perhaps he wants to show us off to these smaller towns."

Raven looked at him and smirked. "I didn't think about that, but it's definitely a possibility."

Leander's low rumble made her laugh, and he turned his head to lower it beside his shoulder. "Let's go do our job then, war-mage messenger."

She ran toward him and jumped, helped by a boost of his scaly head beneath her foot, and laughed when he took flight seconds before she'd sat fully behind his long neck. As always, the moment when he accelerated skyward was exhilarating.

Moments later, she took the folded list out of her jacket pocket and made sure she held it tightly enough that the wind wouldn't whip it away. Her eyes watered a little with the rush of air, but that faded quickly as she studied the map. It was drawn in the same black ink as the list of towns and names, but a small red dot had appeared above the words 'Fowler Academy' and it was moving.

Something of a crude map? Yeah, right.

Smiling, she located the town of Canterdown, and Leander instantly changed course to head west away from the school. *It's so easy. Simply follow the moving map and hand over some letters. At least they're all new towns we haven't seen yet.*

It took them half an hour to reach the outskirts of Canterdown. She leaned forward on her dragon's back and tried to get a better view. "Is that smoke?"

"Yes. More smoke than I'd expect."

"That doesn't look right." The young mage didn't have to instruct her dragon to fly a little lower toward the farmhouse and the property buildings that stood along the eastern edge of Canterdown. The closer they got, the more her heart sank.

The farmhouse and all the outbuildings had been burned to the ground and most of the blackened remains still sent up heavy plumes of black smoke. The entire field between the buildings had been scorched, and the brittle, curled grass lifted in a puff of ash and soot beneath the next beat of Leander's wings.

"That's considerable damage," Raven muttered.

"Buildings burn. Fields burn."

"But a natural fire doesn't do that." She pointed to the left, where two huge furrows of upturned earth were now visible behind the charred farmhouse.

He took them higher again and turned his head to look at her. "That seemed familiar."

"It sure did. Maybe someone in Canterdown can tell us what happened."

The small wall around the town came into view and as

they passed high above it, she frowned. "I guess we didn't think far enough ahead about where to land."

The townspeople going about their business in the center square looked up when Leander's huge shadow passed over them. Two men unloading supplies from a cart pointed, and the horse hitched to the cart tossed its head with a nervous snort.

"Not in the town." Raven patted Leander's neck. "How about an open field where no one's gonna freak out about a dragon and his rider coming in for a landing?"

"I'll find it." He banked and turned in a wide circle, careful to stay outside the edge of the low wall built more for aesthetics around the settlement than real defense. The nervous, curious shouts from the people followed them.

They ended up landing half a mile beyond the main road in a clearing without any people, livestock, or buildings. She squinted at the rider on horseback who galloped toward them. "That was fast."

"They knew we were here."

"And they only sent one rider." She took a deep breath. "At least they left the torches and pitchforks behind."

Leander swiveled his head around to face her and narrowed his eyes in a dragon's frown. "Why would they bring those?"

"Never mind."

The rider pulled his horse to an abrupt halt on the road and fought with the reins to hold his mount steady. He'd left at least a dozen yards between his horse and the young mage on a dragon's back, but they were both still clearly nervous.

Raven raised her hand in greeting, and the man cupped

his mouth to shout, "What's that dragon doing outside Canterdown?"

She glanced at the list in her hand before she pocketed it again. "We have a letter for Bo Pierson."

"What?"

"A letter for—" With a sigh, she pulled her leg up to slip off Leander's back and dropped to the grass. "I'm not yelling a conversation. I'll be right back."

Leander nodded and watched her intently as she stepped onto the road and toward the uneasy rider and his horse.

"I have a letter for Bo Pierson," she said once she was close enough to the rider to not have to yell. The man pulled back on the reins to keep his horse from bolting, but he stared at the dragon. "From Headmaster Flynn at Fowler Academy."

"What?" Finally, he looked at her, surprised that she'd appeared so suddenly in front of him.

"A letter for Bo Pierson from Headmaster Flynn at Fowler Academy." Raven fought not to shout it again at such close range.

"And who are you?"

"Raven Alby. I'm a student at—"

"I'll take the letter, miss. That dragon's not getting into Canterdown." The man extended his hand.

"Sorry. Headmaster Flynn wants me to deliver this to Bo Pierson directly."

He frowned, glanced at Leander again, and waved her forward. "I'll take you into town to speak to him. The dragon stays here."

Raven scrunched her nose. "I can't leave him here either."

"Well. it's one or the other, miss. But that dragon's not coming any closer to the town center. Things are rough enough today and people won't take too kindly to something like that walking around our home."

"His name's Leander." She started to fold her arms, then forced them down to her sides. *I'm only the messenger and this guy obviously doesn't know anything about dragons.*

"Well, whatever his name is, he stays here. We have enough people scared and confused as it is."

"Because of the fire?"

The rider swallowed and studied her warily. "I s'pose you saw that on your way in, comin' from the sky."

"We did. Is everyone okay?"

Her concerned question surprised him out of his stoicism. He fumbled absently with his tunic and shrugged. "Well, the family got out in the nick of time last night when their field started burning. They lost the livestock, although we can't rightly say if that was from the fire or...whatever started it." His gaze traveled slowly toward Leander but settled quickly on the redheaded mage again when the dragon snorted.

"I'm glad no one was hurt. Is there anything we can do to help?"

He cleared his throat. "Not likely. Did you and that dragon come out here to help or to deliver a message?"

"Sometimes it's the same thing, right?" Raven spread her arms and smiled in an effort to be non-threatening, but the man's frown only deepened.

"Not today. I gotta get back to doin' my part in town,

miss. And I gotta go tell the rest of them what a girl and a dragon are doin' flying over Canterdown. So what'll it be?"

There's always another way, isn't there? She put on her best air of dignified politeness and lowered her head. "Would Bo Pierson come out here to take this letter from me himself?"

"Well, I—" The man sputtered as he reined his mount in again when the horse stamped and stepped sideways across the road. "I suppose you'll wait for me to go ask him, won't you?"

"I'll wait. Headmaster Flynn said these letters were time-sensitive, so we won't go anywhere. If you don't mind."

"Nah. I don't mind." He darted another nervous glance at the huge red dragon that hadn't moved before he turned his horse to face Canterdown again. "I can't promise Bo Pierson will want to come out here."

"It would be great if you could still ask. Tell him who the letter's from. And you can give him my name too, if it helps."

"Uh-huh." He tapped his heels against his mount's sides, and the horse was more than happy to race away. They galloped down the road toward the town center and disappeared behind the low walls.

Raven bit her lip and went to Leander. "That was one of the weirder conversations I've had in a while."

"You handled it well."

She chuckled. "You mean compared to how you would've handled it?"

He lowered his head toward her and narrowed his yellow eyes. "I find the threat of dragon fire or a few bitten-off fingers is especially effective."

"I bet." He nudged her hand away playfully and she couldn't help but laugh. "It's a good thing Flynn didn't send you on this trip alone. And let's try to keep the dragon threats to a minimum while we're doing this, okay?"

"Are you worried about tainting our reputation, war mage?"

She fixed him with a mock-stern expression and tried not to smirk. "Elizabeth told me that some people still think dragons are monsters. I merely don't want to give anyone a reason to believe that kind of lie."

Leander rumbled softly and lowered himself to his belly in the grassy clearing beside the road. Raven stood beside him and faced the center of Canterdown, her arms folded. "I guess this isn't as easy as I thought it would be."

Twenty minutes later, four riders on horseback thundered down the road from the settlement.

"Finally." Raven straightened from where she'd leaned against her dragon's side and pushed to her feet. He did the same. "I hope one of those riders is Bo Pierson."

The horses stopped at the same distance from the clearing, and she strode toward them, the rolled and sealed letter held loosely in her hand.

"Raven Alby?" A man with a shock of bright-white hair growing almost like a mop on the top of his head turned sideways to look at her as he fought to stop his horse from shying away.

"Yes." She held the scroll out. "I have a letter for Bo Pierson from—"

"Headmaster Flynn, yes. I heard." The man glanced at the first rider, who nodded solemnly. "I'm curious to know why Aiden Flynn would send a girl on a dragon to deliver a letter."

"It's time-sensitive." Raven shrugged. "I'm a student at Fowler Academy and living on the grounds for the year, so I happened to be in the right place at the right time. And no offense to horses, but dragons are faster."

"Indeed." The man dismounted and handed the reins to the rider beside him before he approached the young mage who stood in the middle of the road. "And he chose to send his message with a student who won't take no for an answer. It wasn't my first choice to come out and meet you, Miss Alby, but Charles assured me you insisted on delivering that in person." He nodded at the scroll, and she fought not to clench it tighter in her hand.

"Are you Bo Pierson?"

He smirked. "In the flesh, young dragon rider. And believe me when I say the people of Canterdown have far too much to discuss, plan for, and repair today. None of us have the time to pretend to be someone we're not."

"Fair enough." She handed the scroll to him and he nodded curtly in thanks. "We saw the farm on the east side of town. What happened?"

The man blinked and pressed his lips together. "We don't know, to be perfectly honest. Fortunately, the owner and his family got to safety before the worst of it, but it left them in something of a bind, as you can imagine. And the people I'm responsible for protecting want answers I simply can't give them. I don't suppose a letter from your headmaster might also come with insight as to what we might expect?"

"Sorry. I'm only delivering letters."

"Yes." Bo Pierson glanced briefly over his shoulder at the three other riders who waited patiently for this meeting to end, though the horses weren't nearly as willing. He leaned toward her and lowered his voice. "I knew I recognized your name when I heard it. I'm sure you know by now that word's spread of what you managed with the…the Swarm a few months ago. I can't help but wonder if—"

"I can give you insight there. The Swarm's gone. Completely this time."

"Is that a reassurance from you or from the headmaster of Fowler Academy?"

"Both." *Probably.* Raven gave the man a reassuring nod, and he straightened. "Whatever happened to that farm has nothing to do with the Swarm. But if I find an explanation for it, I promise Leander and I will make another trip out here to let you know."

"And Leander is…"

"My dragon familiar. Sir." She gestured behind her with a polite smile without breaking away from his gaze.

"Yes. I would appreciate that, Miss Alby. And I'll hold you to your promise. The next time I see a dragon and a young mage student flying over my town, I'll be sure to come out here myself the first time."

"Okay. We'll move on now. I have a few more letters to deliver, so…"

"Of course. Thank you for your time." The man glanced at the sealed letter in his hand and slipped his fingernail carefully beneath the edge of the stamped wax. He unrolled the parchment paper, recognized Aiden Flynn's scrolling handwriting, and paused. "Did Headmaster Flynn say anything about sending a reply with—"

The flap of broad, powerful wings cut him off and scattered leaves and dust blew across the road. He sighed and looked up to see the young dragon rider and the great red beast soar over the trees, headed west. After a moment, he turned to look at his men—who also stared at the disappearing messengers—and cleared his throat. "If anyone asks more questions about next steps, be sure to tell them Canterdown has a dragon rider as a friend. At the very least, it might spread some peace of mind."

CHAPTER SEVENTEEN

The next town on Flynn's list was called Dresdel, farther northwest than Canterdown and almost twice as far away. When they reached the outer farms and ranches around the town—which were much smaller than those outside Brighton or even Canterdown—the mage wondered if they'd have to send a rider into town again so she could deliver the next letter.

"Hey, look at that. Dresdel has their own dragon ranch. It's the best place to land a dragon."

Leander lowered his wing and banked left to head in that direction. "As long as they don't expect me to wear a lead."

She patted his neck. "We've handled that before. A dragon ranch in a small town down south can't be nearly as stingy with the rules as a few stables in Azerad."

This new ranch had its own landing strip of trampled dirt that ran parallel to the long, fenced-in paddock much like Moss Ranch's. Some of the ranch hands looked up and waved a greeting as Leander passed overhead. The group headed toward the landing area to greet the newcomers.

A handful of dragons inside the paddock looked marginally interested in the unexpected arrival, but only two of them screeched a call. Leander didn't reply.

"Hey, there." A woman with a long brown ponytail swinging against her back jogged toward them and slowed to leave the red dragon enough room to turn. "Welcome to Haverson Dragon Ranch. I don't believe we've—" The woman stared in awe as Raven dismounted. "Did you fly in without a saddle?"

"No harness, either." With a broad smile, she approached the woman and extended her hand. "Raven Alby. And this is Leander."

"Janice Haverson." The woman shook her hand, stepped back, and stared at Leander with wide eyes. "Nice to meet you, Leander."

The red dragon's wings twitched, and he looked away from the dragon trainer to gaze at the other beasts in the paddock.

"Huh. He has an attitude on him, doesn't he?"

Raven chuckled. "That's his tame version."

"And you have a dragon with an attitude who lets you ride him. Bareback." Janice shook her head and put her hands on her hips. "I can't quite—oh, wait. Are you the girl from that magic school?"

"Fowler Academy. Yep."

"That's right! We've heard about you and Leander. I can't believe I didn't recognize the names. Hey, Harold! Jim! It's the mage girl with her dragon."

Two ranch hands in their early twenties jogged toward

them, grinning from ear to ear. "Well I'll be..." one of them said. "Jim Magress. How do you do?"

"Raven Alby." She shook his hand and the minute he released it, the other man snatched it and pumped it up and down between both of his.

"Harold Boster. Nice to meetcha. Can I say that everything I've heard about you and that dragon of yours completely changed the way I thought things were supposed to run around here?"

The other woman rolled her eyes. "Here we go again."

Raven chuckled and tried not to shake her hand out when he released it from his crushing grip. "Having an open mind isn't such a bad thing."

"It's not an open mind he's talkin' about." Janice pointed at the man with a playful scowl. "This chatterbox who calls himself a working man wants to start training all our dragons to answer to hand signals instead of a harness."

Leander snorted and the ranch hands burst out laughing.

"Ain't that how you do it?" Harold asked.

Jim punched him in the shoulder. "Man, how's a dragon supposed to see a hand signal when you're flying on its back?"

"Well...then some kinda voice command, right?"

"It's called having a conversation, Harold." Janice chuckled and shook her head again slowly. "You've had all kinds of bad ideas, but you still haven't thought this one through."

"I'll get there." He gave Raven a lopsided smile and leaned closer. "So how do you do it, then? No saddle, no harness. Fine, no hand signals, either. You ain't talkin' to that dragon the whole time up in the sky, are ya?"

"No, actually." She stepped aside to look at Leander but he intentionally blocked out the entire conversation. "He's my familiar."

"Uh-huh." Harold nodded slowly, his mouth open in excitement. "Your familiar what?"

"You bonehead. She goes to that magic school."

"They take dragons at magic school?"

Janice rolled her eyes. "Every day. The man can get any dragon in the whole damn ranch to follow him around like a lost puppy but beyond that, he can't put two and two together."

"I'm a mage," Raven said calmly and gave Harold a reassuring smile. "Every mage has a familiar. Leander happens to be my familiar and a dragon."

"Well, I'll be…" He scratched his head. "How does someone manage a thing like that?"

Jim scoffed. "You gotta have magic first, man. I think you're out on that one."

"Well, shit. Oh, 'scuse my language, miss." He lowered his head. "I get mouthy sometimes."

"I've heard worse." Raven slid a hand under the strap of her satchel and glanced around the large, clean, well-maintained dragon ranch. *I wonder if William's ever stopped by this one.*

"That's enough talking about useless things," Janet added with a smirk. "What brings you out here, miss mage?"

"Just Raven."

"Sure." All three workers smiled at her expectantly.

"Actually, we're delivering letters. I have to get one to Magister Verdeel in town, and we were relieved to see this dragon ranch here."

"Oh, yeah." Jim chuckled. "Not much dragon-friendly parking in a town without a dragon ranch."

"That's one of the things we found out today." She gestured toward Leander. "I hoped you might have space here for Leander to wait for me while I make the delivery. I can pay you to rent a stall—"

"Please." Janice stepped toward her and clapped a hand on the young mage's shoulder. "I won't charge Raven Alby a single copper. Are you kidding? After everything you've done for this kingdom already? How old are you, girl? Nineteen? Twenty?"

"Sixteen."

"Six—" The woman jerked her hand back and squeaked in surprise.

Jim and Harold burst out laughing.

"Did she say sixteen?"

"Yes, ma'am."

"That's what I heard too."

"My stars." Janice laughed. "That's even better. You go on and do your business in town, Raven. Leander will be fine here with us."

"Thank you."

"All right." Jim turned away with a thoughtful glance at the red dragon. "I'll go get the lead."

Leander spread his wings halfway and took a step toward Raven. "No lead."

"No..." The baffled man pointed at the dragon, turned toward the young mage, and let his jaw fall open.

"That's part of it too," Raven added. "He doesn't do leads."

"How in the world…"

"But a stall in your stables would be fine, if you have room."

"Go on and shut that mouth, Jim." Janice snickered and Harold leaned sideways to shut the other man's mouth for him. "Leander, you're more than welcome to wait for your rider in the stables. But I wonder if you'd prefer to go out into that field and take a load off until she gets back."

Leander studied the Haverson Ranch dragons and snorted. "The field."

"The field it is. Right this way." Janice marched down the fence toward the gate and waited for the red dragon to turn and follow.

Raven reached her first. "Leander hasn't exactly been trained like most others."

"Yeah, we hear that often. Every ranch has their own trainers with their own methods, Raven. I promise he'll be fine."

"Well, he wasn't trained by a dragon-trainer, either."

The woman stared at her and pressed her lips together until they practically disappeared. "Say what, now?"

"He wasn't trained by a—"

"I heard you, girl." The woman's laughter was sharp and skeptical. "If a trainer didn't get that big red of yours to take a rider in the first place, then who did?"

"I did."

Janice threw her head back and howled with laughter. "Are you pullin' my yarn, mage girl?"

"Not even a little tug."

"If that isn't the most... I mean..." The woman scratched her head and laughed again. "You sure are full of surprises, Raven. Both of you. A sixteen-year-old girl in magic school trains a dragon like that with no lead, no saddle, no—whew! So tell me why you think that's gonna be a problem for him in our field here."

"We've seen some other dragons recently who didn't really know what to do with him," she muttered. Leander had paused beside the fence again and gave them the appearance of privacy for the conversation. Still, he allowed himself an amused rumble as he watched the other dragon clans move around the field. "I'm not worried about him in there."

"But you're wondering if my beasts are gonna turn on one who shows up a little differently, huh?" Janice patted her arm and grinned. "Don't you worry about that one, girl. Haverson dragons don't have a problem with different. They know what he is. As long as he doesn't step in there and try to start a fight, we're all good."

"I'll finish one if I have to," Leander interjected and swung his head away from the fence to stare at the ranch owner.

"Ha! Consider me warned, Leander." The woman gestured dramatically but her grin remained in place. "If any of mine give you trouble, you have my permission to beat their dragon asses back in line."

Raven lowered her head and choked back a laugh. Her dragon stepped quickly toward Janice as she opened the gate and paused beside Raven to position his head close to her ear. "She's okay."

"You hear that, Jim?" Janice called. "I have approval

from the saddle-less dragon himself. Now you know you won't find a better job than the one you got right here."

Jim chuckled and shook his head. Harold pumped a fist in the air. "Haverson for life!"

The woman scoffed. "Jim's tryin' to squeeze me for higher pay, makin' empty threats to leave, and Harold wouldn't dip outta this place if I made him work for free. Go on in there, Leander. Make yourself at home and holler or somethin' if you need anything."

"I won't."

She glanced at Raven as she shut the gate behind the visitor. "He won't holler?"

"He won't need anything." She smiled and held her hand out. "Thanks for letting him stay for a while."

"It's my pleasure, girl. My pleasure!" The woman gave her hand an enthusiastic shake.

"I won't be very long. Half an hour or an hour. Then we'll head out of here."

"Whenever you want, Raven. We're glad to have him here." Janice nodded at them both before she strode toward her ranch hands, who both leaned against the metal bars of an open pen, their elbows slung over the top rung behind them. "Didn't we already break for lunch? What are you doing standing there? Go on."

The men pushed themselves off the bars, chuckled, and threw the newcomers last-minute glances before they returned to work.

Raven turned to her dragon and widened her eyes. "This sure is a change of pace from Canterdown, huh?"

Leander shook and stretched his wings. "Our reputation precedes us."

"Apparently so. I'll try not to take too long. Hopefully, the people in this town have less going on."

"I'll wait."

"I know." She stretched over the top of the fence and ran her hand along the side of his face. "Have fun."

He snorted and turned away from her to focus on a small, curious yellow dragon pacing close by as it stared at the newcomer. "Hello."

The yellow dragon darted away, and Leander swiveled his head toward Raven. "Fun."

"Well, it's something." Chuckling, she waved goodbye and headed across the ranch toward the road. She slipped the folded list out of her pocket to double-check the name and nodded. *It should still be easy. This time, I can leave him where I know he'll be all right.*

CHAPTER EIGHTEEN

R aven sat on the steps outside Dresdel's Town Hall, stared at the huge clocktower in the center of town, and sighed in frustration. *That guy behind the desk told me ten minutes. It's been forty-five.*

The door behind her at the top of the steps swung open, and a man wearing a long, bright red robe darted down the stairs with scrolls and a few huge tomes tucked under his arms.

"Excuse me." She stood as he descended. "Can you tell me how long—"

The man brushed past her and disappeared into the busy throng of Dresdel's people going about their lives.

"Thanks, anyway," she muttered and let her hand fall against her thigh. "This is ridiculous."

The young mage headed up the stairs and pulled the huge wooden door open. Her work boots clicked against the polished stone floors when she stepped inside. Once the door shut, it took her a moment to adjust to the much darker room before she walked down the long hallway at the front of the building toward the man seated behind that desk.

"Excuse me."

"Yes?" His quill scratched furiously across his parchment paper, but he didn't look up.

"Raven Alby again. Waiting for Magister Verdeel. I think it's been a little longer than ten minutes, which is what you told me the second time."

The man's head whipped up and he pushed his thin-framed spectacles up onto the bridge of his nose with a sigh. "Raven Alby. Yes. I apologize, Miss Alby. Again. But Magister Verdeel has been in meetings all morning."

"I know. It's three-thirty in the afternoon."

"It's—" He cocked his head and frowned. "Are you sure?"

"I was outside watching the clocktower."

"Hmm. Well, the best I can do is to tell you to sit once more and wait. It shouldn't be more than another—"

"That's okay. Don't try to guess the time again. Can I sit in one of these chairs?"

"Of course."

Raven turned and strode toward the long row of chairs on her right along the hallway. Three men and a woman were waiting there as well. One of the men had his eyes closed, his head propped against the wall. The other two men spoke to each other in low voices, and the woman had pulled some yarn and knitting needles out to pass the time.

I bet that's more to keep from dying of boredom than to hang on her wall later. The thought made her smirk, and she took an empty seat between her and the men deep in conversation. On the other side of the woman, the sleeping man grunted, shifted his position, and began to snore.

"How long have you been waiting?" Raven whispered and leaned slightly toward the woman.

"I have no idea." The needles moved rhythmically and their wielder looked up with a gentle smile. "Did you bring something with you?"

"No. I didn't think I'd be here this long."

The woman chuckled. "You're not from Dresdel, are you?"

"What gave it away?"

"The fact that you stepped into the Town Hall without anything to keep you busy." The woman nodded toward the large cloth bag at her feet. "I brought an extra pair of needles."

"Oh, no thanks." She shrugged. "I wouldn't know what to do with those anyway."

"Really? Your mother never taught you to knit?"

"Nope."

"Crochet? Needlepoint? Anything?"

Raven slid her hands along her thighs and shook her head.

"Your grandmother didn't pass any of that down, either?"

"We're not really a knitting kind of family." *And that's as much as I can say without making her feel bad.* Still, the brief image of Connor Alby sitting by the fire with a pair of giant needles like these made her chuckle.

"Suit yourself. It's a great way to pass the time."

"I bet." Raven leaned forward and studied the man

behind the desk, who hadn't once looked up from his writing. *I wasn't supposed to need anything to pass the time.*

It felt like an eternity in that silent hallway while everyone in the chairs waited for the man behind the desk to call the next person there to see Magister Verdeel.

Finally, two large double doors burst open at the end of the hallway, and two men walked out swiftly. "I'm telling you, Roger, it's something we most certainly need to be concerned about."

"It was a fire, Matthew. That's it. I've wasted my entire day following you around on some wild goose chase and now, I'm finished. Go home. Hug your wife. Stop overreacting."

The men's footsteps echoed through the hall. "You're not listening to me. This wasn't only a—"

The door closed with a soft thump behind them and cut their voices off. Raven leaned back in her chair and sighed.

"Some people value their time way too much, don't you think?" The man seated on the other side of the young mage turned toward her and winked. "He should know better. Trying to get a meeting with Magister Verdeel is one of those things that takes all day. If you're lucky."

"Oh, great." Raven chuckled wryly. "That would've been nice to know before I was sent to run errands. This is only my stop number two."

The second man puffed out a sigh and twirled the end of his dark mustache. "It should've been your first."

"I realize that now." she leaned her head back against the wall and stared at the chairs along the opposite side of the hallway. The men beside her resumed their conversation again.

"Hey, you think those two yuppies were talking about the same fire?"

"How am I supposed to know? We came here for our business, not theirs."

"Well, sure. But there's been more talk the last few days than I like to hear. I tell you what, Don. Strange things are happening again 'round here."

Raven straightened in the chair and turned to face them. "What kind of strange things?"

The man beside her laughed. "Caught your interest, huh?"

She smirked and gestured at the mostly empty hall. "Anything's better than sitting here doing absolutely nothing."

"No truer words, miss." He chuckled and nudged his friend's shoulder. "You wanna tell her or should I?"

The mustached man sighed and closed his eyes. "Be my guest."

"Right." Her neighbor turned toward her again, nodded, and wiggled his eyebrows. "Now, I can't say I know the whole of it, which is why we're here in the first place. I've seen different farms and homesteads burned to the ground in the last week. Three. Unless there's some kinda new sickness rolling around that makes people burn their own homes and livelihoods, I'm apt to think we have trouble on our hands."

Beside him, Don snorted.

"Oh, don't you go blowin' me off like that, man."

Don leaned forward so he could meet Raven's gaze. His mustache twitched when he sniffed. "Reggie thinks there's a witch out in the mountains hexing everyone's farms and burning the fields."

"That's an awfully simplistic way to put it, but yeah. That's close."

Raven frowned. "Have you seen any magic coming from the mountains?"

"Well, I…" Reggie gaped at her and leaned back in his chair. "No. I can't say I have."

"Ha. See? There's one thing your crazy theory doesn't cover." The second man leaned forward again. "He doesn't live anywhere near the mountains."

"Well, neither do you. And it's not simply a crazy theory, man. There's something unnatural going around. Witches. Powers of the darkness. Could be anything, really."

"Is anyone telling stories about monsters?" Raven asked.

Don twirled his mustache again and raised his eyebrows. "Oh, there are always tales of monsters somewhere."

"Now monsters, I haven't heard a thing about," Reggie added. "Oh, except for that dragon trainer who rode through from Delton's Crossing the other day, remember?"

"The bald one?"

Reggie rolled his eyes. "The only dragon trainer we've talked to in the last few months. Unless you went out to Nadine or something and didn't bother to tell your business partner about it."

Don shrugged and leaned back in his chair again.

"Did the dragon trainer say something about monsters?" Raven tugged her satchel slightly where she'd set it between her feet.

"Not exactly." Reggie scratched his head. "But he went on and on about a dragon ranch way out east by the mountains that had some trouble with a huge fire. It came outta nowhere, you know?"

"That could have as easily been the dragons, though, right?" She leaned away when the man stretched his neck over the armrests and widened his eyes.

"But something else spooked the dragons. As far as I know, those beasts aren't afraid of the kind of fire they can make all on their own."

Don clicked his tongue. "What do you know about dragons? You haven't seen one in person closer than twenty feet."

"That doesn't mean anything. Dragons breathe fire. They fight. I've heard the stories. They don't spook each other. Anything that scares a dragon that much is something the rest of us need to keep a lookout for, if you ask me."

The other man shook his head and closed his eyes.

"Thanks for the tip." Raven tried to smile while she thought through the new information. *A burned-down ranch near the Mountains of Jared and terrified dragons. It's close enough to the dragon sanctuary to be more than simply another fire.*

The doors at the end of the hall opened again, and the man seated behind the desk looked up at someone she couldn't see. He nodded and called, "Raven Alby. Right this way, please."

"Finally." She scooped her satchel up and slung it over her shoulder. "I'll be fast, I promise. Good luck with your meeting."

"You too." Reggie smiled. Don gave her a little salute and the two men fell into hushed conversation again.

"Through those doors, Miss Alby. Thank you for your patience."

I wasn't really that patient, but okay. She smiled at him and stepped into the next room. The man pulled the doors shut behind her and she paused to take in the interior. She stood on the door side of a gigantic table in the middle of another massive room. This one looked more like a study with books crammed into shelves along either wall, and the man seated at the head of the table on her right gave her a curt nod.

"What can I do for you, Miss…"

"Raven Alby." She stepped forward and extended her hand. "You're Magister Verdeel?"

The middle-aged man with dark circles under his eyes looked at her in surprise and shook her hand. "Yes, I am. You must have come from far away to see me if you didn't already know my face."

"Only from Brighton."

"*Only.*" He chuckled and ran a hand through his light-blond hair. "That's quite a ride. It takes most of the morning, as I remember it."

"Not on a dragon."

Magister Verdeel cleared his throat. "Excuse me?"

Here we go again. "I'm a student at Fowler Academy with a dragon familiar. Headmaster Flynn sent me to bring you a letter. Here." She thunked her satchel onto the table and rummaged inside to retrieve the sealed scroll with the man's name on it. "That's all I came for."

The man took the scroll gently but didn't open it.

"You're the young mage who fought on a dragon at the Tournament of Mages."

"Yes."

"And singlehandedly saved the governor's wife from raider abduction."

"No. Not singlehandedly. I had Leander, Bella Chase, and her familiar Wesley with me too. It was a team effort."

"Interesting." Magister Verdeel raised his chin and studied her curiously. "I must have heard vastly changed versions of the same story."

"Probably. Whoever said I did all that on my own doesn't really know what they're talking about." That comment made the man laugh, and she smiled. "Bella was the other first-year at the tournament. She deserves as much credit for helping the governor's wife as I do."

"Indeed. I must say, I'm quite impressed, Miss Alby. The stories don't quite do you justice."

Raven buckled her satchel and slung it over her shoulders. "Thanks."

"Hmm. Headmaster Flynn certainly has a flair for the dramatic, sending you all the way to Dresdel on a dragon. Is there anything else you wanted to discuss with me?"

"Not really. I have a few other letters to deliver, so I should be on my way. Thanks for your time."

"Thank you, Miss Alby." The man smiled and nodded once before he returned his attention to the sealed scroll.

Raven spun and headed quickly to the double doors. When she pushed them open and stepped into the hall, three more people were seated in the chairs lined up against the walls. Don and Reggie watched her with confused frowns as she passed them.

"Only a super quick meeting," she muttered and gave them a thumbs-up. "Good luck."

She forced herself to walk down the hall although she wanted to run, and the man behind the desk called out someone else's name. *I seriously hope there aren't any holdups at the next two towns.*

The front door to the town hall opened smoothly, and Raven stepped out onto the top step. The sky glowed with the orange and pink rays of sunset, and she looked at the clocktower in the center of the square. "Are you kidding me? How was I in there for over three hours?"

The young mage raced down the steps and across the center of Dresdel toward the road to the Haverson Dragon Ranch. *I hope Leander's okay. If he wasn't, he would've sent me some kind of image but I think we ran out of time.*

CHAPTER NINETEEN

The sun had almost completely set by the time Raven could see the outbuildings of Haverson Dragon Ranch. *There's no way we'll make it to the other towns and back to Fowler before dark. Not even slightly after.*

She paused beside the small inn on her right and sighed. "I guess this counts as an emergency."

The door creaked open when she stepped inside the inn, and a woman with a head of tight copper curls looked up from behind the bar. "Hello."

"Hi." She approached cautiously and lowering her satchel slowly from her shoulders. "I hope you have a room open. Only for the night."

"We have more than enough rooms, miss. The fine location of this inn makes sure of that."

"I'm sorry?"

The woman chuckled and wiped her hands on her apron. "Being so close to Haverson Ranch down the way. My grandfather thought it would be a swell place to open an inn, and the family never left. Some people don't mind being this close to dragons overnight. Most people do."

"Oh." Raven laughed and nodded. "I know what you mean. And I definitely don't have a problem with being this close to dragons." *I'd prefer to be closer, but this isn't turning out to be my day.* "I'd still like to rent a room."

"Brave girl. It's two silver for the night. A third'll get you supper and breakfast in the morning."

"Great. Let's do that." The young mage propped her satchel on her knee and opened it to take Headmaster Flynn's coin purse out. When she opened the drawstring, her eyes widened. *This is more gold than I've ever seen all in one place. What was he thinking?* "Sorry. I gotta find them."

"Take your time." The woman smiled and watched the girl dig around in a plain brown coin purse.

"Here." She set the three silver on the counter and nodded. "Thank you."

"I should thank you, miss. We haven't had a new face around here in months." The woman peered over her shoulder toward the room in the back, then leaned forward and whispered, "Honestly, I'm very tired of seeing the same old faces week after week."

"I'm happy to help."

Laughing, her hostess took a large key from under the bar and nodded toward the staircase on the other side of the inn. "Right this way."

Raven followed her up the stairs and down a short hallway. They stopped at the first door on the left and her guide opened it and handed her the key. "Return this in the morning before you leave. It's the only one."

"No problem."

"And Clive'll whip somethin' up for you as soon as you're hungry. Are you hungry?"

"Not yet. I have to make one more stop first but it shouldn't take too long."

"That's fine. You come let me know when you're ready." The woman paused at the stairs. "Oh, my name's Celeste. Don't hesitate to shout for me if I'm not where you can see me."

"Thanks."

With another happy nod, Celeste descended the staircase and resumed her post behind the bar.

Raven peered into the room and sighed. *This is good enough for one night. I can't believe I actually have to do this.* She lowered her satchel to the floor beside the door, then locked up and hurried down the stairs.

It only took her five minutes at a powerwalk to reach her destination, and the last of the sunlight was fading quickly. Jim stepped out of the stables and gave a low whistle. "That was one long hour, Raven Alby."

"You're telling me. Is everything okay here?"

He chuckled. "Oh, yeah. That dragon of yours is settling in just fine."

"Thanks." She raced along the fence and scanned the dragons out in the field. *I never thought I'd try to identify him in the dark.* She cupped her hands around her mouth and took a deep breath, but the screech of greeting she recognized cut her off. "There you are."

She ran the rest of the way toward Leander, who practically skipped toward the fence, his wings stretched wide and fluttering at her approach. "Raven—"

"I'm so sorry, Leander. The people at the Town Hall made me wait forever."

"It's not—"

"They didn't have any clocks or windows or anything, and I didn't know what time it was until I got outside. Flynn didn't say anything about having to wait in line to deliver a few letters—"

"Stop talking." Leander snorted and lowered his head toward her. "I'm fine."

"Right." She chuckled and stroked his muzzle affectionately. "I thought you would be but I got back here as fast as I could. I'm sorry it took me so long."

"I hardly noticed you were gone." He hissed in laughter and swished his powerful tail across the grass.

"Thanks."

Janice approached from the far corner of the paddock with a wave. "I never thought I'd say this about a dragon," she shouted, "but Leander's been a real peach."

Raven laughed and rubbed her hand down her dragon's neck. "Is that right?"

"Everyone's favorite." The woman stopped beside the young mage and put a hand on her hip as she grinned at Leander. "Even with Ignatius, and that's saying something."

"You made friends with Ignatius?"

"No." Leander nudged her hand again. "But I didn't make any enemies."

"And that's sayin' something." Janice chuckled. "Ignatius is the big golden-brown one trottin' along after Harold out there."

"So you didn't make enemies with the biggest dragon on the ranch." Raven smirked. "Good work, Leander."

"I didn't even try."

"We've started putting everyone up for the night," Janice added. "I was about to call Leander over here for a little conversation about giving him his own stall until you got back. It looks like that wasn't necessary."

"Actually, I think it might be." She wrinkled her nose at Leander with a shrug. "Sorry. That stupid waiting room took all the time we had. Do you mind staying here?"

"For one night?" The dragon snorted. "How will I survive?"

"Ha!" Janice slapped her thigh. "How indeed. He's more than welcome to stay here, Raven. Leander, why don't you meet us at the gate outside the stables? I'll show you both where you'll put up for the night."

"Thanks, Janice."

"Anytime, Raven Alby. And I mean that, girl. Absolutely any time. Your dragon familiar is the life of the party, I'll say that much." The woman jerked her head in the direction the fence ran. "I'll meet you over there."

Raven watched Leander stare after the dragon trainer and folded her arms. "Life of the party, huh?"

"I can be charming."

"When you want to be." They headed toward the stables with the fence between them. "I'm glad you actually did have fun."

"It's a new experience. I have fun with you, of course."

"But these are other dragons. I get it. Haverson Ranch seems like a good place with good people."

"I agree."

"Right on over here, Leander." Janice gestured toward an open stall on the end. "We cleaned it yesterday."

"What about you, Raven?" Her dragon spoke calmly but she sensed his concern for her.

She pointed east toward the inn, which was now only a dark shadow in the fading light. "I have a room and I'll be back here first thing in the morning to get you."

"All right." He sniffed the air and raised his head toward Janice. "Food. Good night, Raven."

"I hope it's good." Chuckling, she returned to the road and waved at Janice and her ranch hands on the way. *It's a little weird that he's so okay with all this. But I'll take it over a repeat of Azerad any day.*

After a surprisingly delicious dinner as the only patron present at the inn, Raven wished Celeste and Clive—a short, squat man with no facial hair and a shiny, bald head —good night and headed to her room. She took her satchel off the floor and brought it with her to the bed. "A ridiculous amount of money for emergencies and a calling potion. At least Flynn makes sure his messengers are prepared."

She pulled out the bright-purple calling potion and uncorked before she drew her arm back and muttered, "*Tractoria* Aiden Flynn," and tossed the potion out of the vial. The wave of purple liquid sloshed and hovered in mid-air in front of her. It opened into a much less detailed view than the Full Appearance spell afforded. *That's definitely his office.*

"Headmaster?"

Flynn looked up quickly from his desk and seemed

startled. He removed the spectacles resting on his nose and chuckled. "Good evening, Miss Alby."

"Hi. I'm, uh…using the potion to tell you Leander and I won't be back at Fowler tonight. It's already dark and we're only outside Dresdel."

"Is that so? I hope you didn't run into too much trouble."

She rolled her eyes. "No. Only incredibly long wait times to see Magister Verdeel. Like, almost five hours."

"Oh, dear." The headmaster tugged his beard and leaned back in his chair. "I had no idea it would take you that long."

"Yeah, me neither. That's why we haven't finished getting your letters out there. I have two more left, and we'll get to them tomorrow. You gave me the calling potion, so I thought I should probably use it. And I already booked a room for the night. I'm at the inn near Haverson Dragon Ranch."

Flynn raised his eyebrows and laughed again. "That's fine. I'll make sure your professors are aware of why you'll be absent in the morning. And before I forget, Mr. Smith came by during dinner a few hours ago asking for you. Should I deliver any messages for you, Miss Alby?"

Crap. I totally forgot about Daniel. "Uh, no thanks, Headmaster. I'll tell him what happened when I get back."

"Very well. I appreciate the update, Miss Alby. I'll watch for your return around mid-morning tomorrow. Good night." Flynn waved his hand through the image.

"Good ni—" Raven sighed and her shoulders slumped. "I guess he didn't need a response."

She watched the shimmering circle of the calling potion

fade into nothing, recorked the vial, and tossed it into her satchel. "It's easy cleanup for a potion you have to throw."

The young mage kicked her boots off and climbed under the covers of the small but immensely comfortable bed in her rented room. Once she'd turned down the lantern on the table beside her bed, she pulled the sheets up over her shoulders and sank into the pillow.

We'll start over in the morning. And I'll make sure I don't wait five hours again simply to hand over a letter.

CHAPTER TWENTY

R aven slept dreamlessly for the first half of the night, and when the first dream came to her, it didn't last long. Everything was burning, engulfed in flames, and terrified dragons darted in all directions as they leapt, flew, swooped, and screeched at the sky.

She bolted upright in her bed at the inn and gasped. "Woah. Where the hell did that come from?"

Fighting to slow her racing heart, she took slow, deep breaths and paused.

Somewhere outside, more than one dragon screeched. In the next moment, dozens of dragon voices rose in the darkness, soft over the distance but unmistakable. "Leander."

Alarmed, she tossed the covers off and leapt out of bed to thrust her feet into her work boots. She tied the laces quickly to keep them from falling off before she snatched her satchel up and sprinted out of the room. Her running footsteps pounded down the staircase, and she stumbled blindly across the inn's main room before her eyes adjusted to the darkness.

The front door of the inn thwacked against the wall when she threw it open, and the young mage didn't even consider the other guests or the inn's proprietors she might have awakened with all the noise.

As soon as she turned down the road toward Haverson Ranch, she saw the flames. Thick black smoke rose in columns against the night sky, clearly visible even in the darkness. The dark shapes of the Haverson dragons were scattered across the field as they shrieked at each other and their trainers and whatever had riled them up like this.

That wasn't a dream. It came from Leander!

By the time she reached the stables, she could hardly see a thing through the smoke. She coughed, waved it out of her face, and tried to ignore the chaos around her as she headed to her dragon's stall.

"Leander!"

"Raven! I'm here!" He snorted and poked his head out of the open window.

"Are you okay?"

"Yes."

"Why are you still in there? The stables are on fire."

He glanced at the flames that consumed the ceiling above him and lowered his head. "I was waiting for you. Stand back."

She stopped short and jogged to a safe distance as he pounded his bulk through the burning frame of his stall. Flaming splinters of wood scattered in all directions, and the young mage turned and ducked to cover her face. His muzzle nudged her shoulder, his scales warmed by the heat of the flames he'd endured until she reached him.

Raven spun and threw both arms around his head in a tight hug. "I'm glad you waited, but I'm not sure waiting in the fire was the smartest option."

"I breathe fire, Raven. Obviously, it doesn't burn me."

"Right." She released him and turned to take in the destruction all around them. Huge swaths of the dragon paddock were on fire and the air was still filled with smoke and so many different voices that shrieked and called in confusion and fear.

Halfway across the field, Harold raised his hands in front of the slender yellow dragon and tried to calm her as she screamed and stamped and tossed her head. Two other dragons barreled into each other head-on, cried out as they fell together, and scrambled on top of each other to be the first one back on their feet.

"Have you seen Jim and Janice?" she asked as she struggled to see through the flames.

"No."

"I hope they got out okay. I can't see if their houses was struck by the fire—"

"Raven." He said it so sharply that she stopped and looked at him with wide eyes.

"What's wrong?"

"I can smell it."

"Smell what?" *I only smell smoke.*

Leander lowered his head and scanned the burning dragon paddock. A low, terrifying growl of warning rose from his throat. "Hatred and fury."

Raven swallowed. "From the dragons?"

"No. Something…else."

She stepped closer to reassure herself with her hand on his warm shoulder. "Do you think it's the—"

A high-pitched dragon's scream ripped through the air, followed quickly by two more. The other beasts shrieked, bellowed, and called, but the single-voiced screams seared through all of it.

"She needs help," Leander muttered and curved his long neck to lower his head beside his shoulder.

"Right." Raven took a few steps back, ran toward him, and leapt. His boost up was as effortless as ever, and the red dragon was airborne before she'd had a chance to sit. What was left of the burning stables crumbled beneath a gust of wind that sprayed sparks and smoke in his wake.

The young mage crouched low atop her dragon's back, ready to steady herself with her hands against his neck if she had to. She stepped a little farther back with one foot to improve her balance and quickly scanned the chaos beneath them. *We're looking for a dragon who needs help. That might be all of them at this point.*

"There." Leander dove and she did have to press her hands against his scaly hide to avoid being blown off his back.

They landed at the other edge of the paddock and inside the fence, where a small, dirty-white female screamed repetitively. The toolshed on the other side of the fence had fallen on her and pinned down her splayed wing and most of her tail. *What could knock a whole building down like this?*

She leapt from Leander's back and raised her hands as

she approached the terrified dragon slowly. "We're here to help you out of here, okay?"

The beast screamed again and bucked beneath the weight of the shed. In the flickering light of the fire, Raven saw the coiled wire that had wound around the dragon's leg and now squeezed tighter and tighter the harder she struggled.

"Stop kicking. That only makes it worse." She took another cautious step forward. "We can get you out of here, but I need you to—"

The young dragon screamed again and fought even harder to escape. A clan of Haverson dragons stampeded across the field behind Raven and Leander. They collided with each other and breathed their own bursts of fire in their confusion. *That's really not helping.*

"I'll try to lift this…shed off you, okay?"

The dragon stopped flailing for a moment and stared at Raven with wide silver eyes. Her sides heaved and nostrils flared as she snorted with each rapid breath. She opened her mouth again for another cry, but Leander stepped forward quickly and lowered his huge red head to hers until their muzzles almost touched.

"Be still." He snorted in her face, and the young dragon closed her eyes against his hot breath. Her head trembled at the end of her long, stretched-out neck, but she let him nudge her gently and finally found enough comfort to do as she was told.

"Thank you." Raven meant it for both dragons, and she stepped around the small white beast toward the crushed wing. The fallen building groaned and shuddered when she tried to lift the corner. "It's too heavy. Leander, can you—"

"Yes." The second he stepped away from the trapped dragon, the smaller creature began to scream again.

"Never mind!" she shouted. "Keep her still. I'll find a way."

Leander knocked his head against the young female's, his nudge both a comfort and a warning now. "Don't make it worse."

She fell still, and Raven took a step back and reached toward the heavy beams that pinned the young dragon's wing. "This might be a little loud. *Ecflicto!*"

The brilliant white streak darted from her hand, impacted with the fallen debris, and shattered it into dozens of smaller fragments in an instant. *Alessandra doubled up the magical armor on those dummies!*

The young female shrieked and lifted her wing free of the debris. It fluttered limply at her side as she kicked and struggled to escape from the wreckage.

"Wait, wait! Slow down!" Raven raised her hands to get the dragon's attention, but the screaming started again. "You're still caught—woah!" The mage ducked beneath the quickly strengthening wing as it whipped through the air over her head. "Leander, don't let her—"

"Be *still*!" Leander roared and swung his powerful neck against the little female's shoulders. He stepped closer and loomed over her to almost pin her beneath him.

"Okay. Good." Raven stepped lightly behind the dragon and bent toward the rear leg wound tightly in wire. Somewhere across the paddock, another burning building caved in and the dragons renewed their terrified uproar. *I didn't know dragons could lose their minds like this. It doesn't matter if they are trained or wild.*

She found the thin wire quickly and grimaced. It had coiled so tightly that it pierced the tough scales. Dark rivulets of blood dribbled down the dragon's leg. Raven sighed heavily and drew her dagger from her boot. *It's worth a try.*

The blade was useless until she remembered one of Connor Alby's minor tricks. She lifted the dagger to her lips and muttered, *"Acuite."*

It flashed a silver light and the young mage lowered it to the wire again. She only had to saw back and forth twice before the wire snapped. "There! You got—"

A dirty-white tail thumped against her shoulder and she tumbled back. Leander reared to check on her, and the young female screamed again as she scrabbled to find purchase in the grass. She leapt and darted forward to drag herself free from the rest of the debris before she stumbled across the field and right into a massive wall of smoke.

"Did she hurt you?" The red dragon prodded the back of Raven's shoulder with his snout.

"Not really." She eyed the magically sharpened dagger in her hand before she slid it into her boot. "It's a good thing I had a tight grip."

"That dragon is a fool."

"That's what happens when people let themselves freak out. And dragons. Come on, let's see if anyone else needs help."

Leander gave her a boost onto his back again before he launched once more into the smoke-filled sky.

Raven coughed and squinted through the heavy smoke.

The heat of the fire below them rose on either side of her dragon. "I can't see down here—" She coughed again.

He responded to her thought by ascending in an effort to put more space between them and the destruction below for a better view.

One more point for a mage's connection with their familiar in case talking's impossible.

Leander made a wide turn around the far side of Haverson Ranch and she scanned the beasts that darted through the flames and the destroyed buildings. A group of dragons huddled below, looked at them, and screeched as they spread their wings and stumbled around in fear.

They're not looking at us. "Leander, I think we need to be really careful."

"They're confusing us for what they thought they saw."

"Maybe. But it's a good idea to—look out!"

The massive black shadow barreled toward them out of the sky too quickly and came upon them too suddenly. Leander turned his head to look seconds before the huge being knocked him sideways. The red dragon roared and Raven gasped as she fell. Her hands flailed to catch his outstretched wing that was already too far out of reach.

He screamed as he dove toward her but the entire sky— all the glittering stars and the columns of smoke that blotted them out—disappeared beneath that enormous black shadow. The young mage's back thumped against something cold and firm. The impact threw her head back hard and pain burst through her skull. Her eyes fluttered, her vision went blurry, and the last thing she saw was more of the same glistening black shadow enclosing her.

CHAPTER TWENTY-ONE

W hen Raven woke next, the only thing she was aware of was the agonizing pain that throbbed in her head. She groaned and tried to roll over, then took a sharp breath through her teeth. *Moving makes it worse. Awesome. I'll lie here for a while, then.*

She gave herself what felt like a few minutes and tried to steady her breathing. *Don't hyperventilate and pass out again, Raven. Just breathe. You're obviously not dead.*

When she finally managed to open her eyes, she stared at a curved ceiling of stone. A large crevasse split the ceiling down the middle to expose the brightest stars still twinkling in the pre-dawn sky. In the next moment, the smell hit her.

Ugh. It smells like rotten meat and smoke. Or maybe that last one's only me.

After a few more attempts, she finally pushed off the cold stone floor beneath her and blinked in the dim light. "*Circum inlustro.*"

A small orb of soft yellow light bloomed at her fingertip

and separated to float close by. She held her head with both hands and groaned again. "What a headache. Leander? Are you in here?"

Her voice echoed repeatedly but she didn't get a reply.

Raven looked up and narrowed her eyes against the brightness of her light spell. Her gaze fell on the pile of bones a stone's throw away and she swallowed thickly. "That explains the smell."

It hurt considerably to turn her head in any direction, but she forced herself through it to make a thorough study of her surroundings. *A giant cave. Alone. With—oh, good, more piles of bones. What the hell?*

A small pressure tickled at the back of her mind like a memory she couldn't quite grasp. It was followed by a fuzzy image of Leander's pen at Fowler Academy, the field still dark in the gray-blue before dawn. Her heart raced again with a renewed anxiety, and she took more deep breaths. *That's coming from Leander. He has no idea where I am.*

She closed her eyes again and took more deep breaths. "Think positive, reassuring thoughts," she whispered. "It's kinda hard given the circumstances."

The anxious concern that didn't belong to her faded and she sighed. "Maybe he felt me. Maybe not. But at least now I can think clearly."

The young mage gazed around the enormous stone cavern again and winced at the pain that seared through the back of her head when she looked at the sliver of sky through the crevasse in the ceiling. She touched the back of her head and sighed. "I'll take a huge bump over blood any day."

Raven rolled her shoulders and groaned as she slipped the straps of her satchel off and set it gently beside her, careful not to move her head too much. *It's a good thing I don't pack any sharp objects in there. Now what?*

Alessandra's words from two days before spun through her mind. *"It consumes large quantities of your stored magic. The longer the connection is open, the more it will take out of you."*

"Right." Raising her hands, Raven wiggled her fingers and tried to focus. "I'm gonna need serious brainpower for this. I only hope I didn't hit my head too hard." It took longer than she had hoped, but she managed to do the spell—not perfectly, but it would hopefully be enough.

"Bella. Come on, Bella. Wake up. This is important."

The girl rolled over in bed and slapped her hand at nothing. "Huh?"

"Yes! Wake up!"

Frowning, the dark-haired mage propped herself on her elbow and blinked groggily. When her vision finally focused, she jerked away and almost fell over the edge of her bed. "Raven! What are you doing here?"

"Oh, man. I'm so glad this worked. I'm not in your room, Bella. It's the Full Appearance. I don't think I can keep it open much longer so listen, okay?"

Bella's gaze traveled over the image of Raven's face and half her torso floating in the air beside the bed. "It's really clear this time."

"We can talk about that later. Right now, I think I'm in trouble."

"What? Where are you?" The girl shoved her tangled hair out of her face and straightened.

"I...don't know. A super creepy cave somewhere that smells like rotting meat. So—"

"What the hell?"

"Bella! I'm serious. Listen. When you get to school, make sure Leander's okay. He's there. I can't reach out to him so I cast this to tell you. It looks like Alessandra had perfect timing with our training."

"What do you want me to do?"

"After you tell Leander I'm still alive and that you talked to me? Go tell Headmaster Flynn and make sure you relay everything I tell you. I don't know where I am on a map, but I'm in a huge cave so I assume the mountains. Probably. But there's a giant crack in the ceiling, so I can at least see the sky."

"Can't you climb out?" the girl asked.

Raven glanced at the top of the cave the other mage couldn't see. "Not from this one. I'm fine for now, but I don't know how long that'll last. I only hope I wasn't brought here as someone's mid-morning snack."

"What?"

"There are piles of bones in here, Bella. Did you pay attention to the more important stuff I said?"

The girl tossed her head and nodded. "Of course I paid attention. I'll talk to Leander and then Headmaster Flynn. Got it."

"Good. I..." The image of her face started to shudder. "...next time...when they..."

The Full Appearance spell winked out, and Bella sighed in frustration and stared at the opposite side of her room. "This was not the way I thought I'd start my week off. And it's not even light out yet. Jeez."

She kicked the blankets off and scurried around her room to get dressed and ready for the day.

With her knapsack slung over her shoulder, she darted down the creaking staircase and ran into the kitchen.

"Morning, sweetheart." Betsy Chase shuffled into the room with a yawn. "You're up early."

"I've only been out of bed for a few moments. I have to get to school early to finish a few projects."

Her grandmother turned toward her and studied her suspiciously. "You have last-minute schoolwork to finish on the first day of the week?"

"Yeah, Grams. We're coming up on our finals and I will pass those tests no matter what." She removed the cloth covering the basket of rolls on the counter and took two. "So I gotta go. I'll see you tonight." She leaned closer to give to the old lady a quick kiss on the cheek before she turned to head toward the front of the house.

"Are you sure you don't want something more than a few rolls?"

"I'm sure. Love you, Grams!" The girl raised a hand but didn't turn.

The front door opened and shut with a bang, and Betsy shook her head with a sleepy chuckle. "Even brilliant mages have to eat. That girl's burning the candle at both ends, not that she'll listen to anything I have to say about it."

Out front, Bella leapt off the porch and walked as fast as

she could down the side road leading to Brighton's town center. Wesley screeched, launched off the roof, and swooped toward her to flutter around her head.

"I know. It's important so I'm going, okay?" The young mage bit into the first roll and frowned. "I honestly never expected I'd be the one who has to save Raven Alby from... whatever she got herself into. This had better not be some kind of joke."

When the Fowler Academy grounds came into view, she was almost out of breath and her calves ached from walking so quickly. *I should have run here.*

The sun had risen enough to illuminate the field beside the school, but she didn't have to see anything to know that the agitated screeches that rose from beside the stables came from Leander. "Raven wasn't kidding."

She broke into a run while Wesley dove and swooped ahead of her.

Beside the dragon pen, Professor Worley stood in front of Leander in his night robe, his hands raised cautiously as he tried to talk sense into the panicked dragon. "Leander, I can't help either of you if you don't tell me what happened."

"I don't know!" The dragon roared again and lashed his tail against the wall of his enclosure with a metallic clang. "I don't know where she is. We were together and then we weren't."

"Where were you last?"

"The fire. And the—" Leander shuffled back and screeched again, his yellow eyes wide and blazing. "Where is she?"

"That's what I'm trying to find out, Leander." The

professor took a step toward him. "I need you to calm and walk me through it so we can work together on this one."

"Don't tell me to calm!" The dragon reared and vented a column of fire into the air.

Worley ducked anyway, then caught sight of Bella Chase and Wesley hurrying toward them. "Stay back. This isn't a good time—"

"She's okay!" The girl skidded to a halt in the grass and raised her hands automatically when the huge dragon turned to fix her with his intense gaze. "I talked to Raven. She's—"

"*Where?*" he roared. "Where is she?"

"I don't know. She doesn't know. But she—"

Leander's wings extended out to their full span and he charged forward. Bella threw herself out of the way, and Wesley fluttered around Leander's face to catch his attention. "Raven!" the dragon bellowed and dug his claws deep into the earth.

"She told me to talk to you first thing, Leander," the girl shouted. He whirled again and snorted. Two plumes of dark, thick smoke burst from his nostrils. *I can't believe I'm doing this.* "She cast a spell that let her talk to me. Raven's in a cave somewhere. That's all she knows. But she felt you and she saw that you're here at Fowler. She wanted me to tell you she knows. You got through to her, okay? Raven's all right. We'll help you find her."

The dragon's nostrils flared as he snorted again. His wings twitched before they settled slowly against his back and he lowered his head. "Raven said all that."

"Come on. I'm more than smart enough to not make this up." She glanced at Wesley, who soared in tight circles over Leander's head. *The dragon's calm now. We're good.*

Leander stepped toward her, kept his head at eye level, and stopped with nothing more than a foot between them. His hot breath blew the air away from her face but the young mage stood her ground. "I can smell a human lie, girl."

"Good." She pressed her lips together and raised her chin. *Don't blink.* "Then you know I'm not lying."

He stared at her for a moment longer and when she didn't budge, he grunted and jerked away from her to stalk across the field. "Find her."

"Yeah, that's the plan." Running a hand through her hair, Bella turned around to face Professor Worley.

The man stared at her, his mouth slightly open, and cleared this throat. "Miss Chase, that was…um…"

"You're welcome. I guess riding a dragon for five minutes in the middle of a battle gives me special negotiating abilities or something. How long has he been out here?"

The man scratched the side of his mouth and glanced at the dragon, who paced across the field. "I came out maybe fifteen minutes ago. He was making all that noise a long time before my wakeup call."

"So Headmaster Flynn's probably awake too, right?"

"Probably, yeah."

"I need to talk to him." Bella hurried toward the stone archway.

"Miss Chase! Wait!" He strode after her. "I don't like the idea of leaving Leander out here on his own—"

"He's not going anywhere, Professor. He's waiting for his mage."

Worley stopped in his tracks as the young mage maintained a purposeful pace toward the school's main courtyard. He glanced at the fuming dragon now under some semblance of control and nodded. "He sure is. I'm coming with you, Miss Chase. The headmaster's more likely to open his door this early in the morning if I'm on the other side of it."

CHAPTER TWENTY-TWO

Ten minutes into the History of Magic class that morning, Professor Gilliam stepped into the room with a gentle knock on the door. "Excuse me, Professor Bixby. I'm sorry to interrupt after you've barely started, but I would like a word with Mr. Derks and Miss Murphy, if you don't mind."

Bixby's gaze shot right toward the named pair, her magnified eyes even wider as she blinked at them. "I don't mind at all, Professor Gilliam. Go ahead."

Henry and Murphy exchanged confused glances.

"Quickly, please," Gilliam added.

The students gathered their things and stood from their seats. His desk screeched across the floor when he knocked into it.

"Sorry. I just...my bad." He returned the desk to its place, elicited another screech, then shrugged and hurried toward the door. "Murphy, wait up."

Snickers and whispered conversations filled the room as the two disappeared down the hall. Bixby clapped sharply and leaned over her podium. "Did Professor Gilliam address any of you? I don't think so. That's none of our business, and after the two days you had to yourselves, I should think you're all quite rested enough to focus. So, focus. Please and thank you."

Gilliam set a brisk pace through the stone hallway of Fowler's main building. Fritz darted between their legs, and Henry had to pay extra attention to his feet as he leaned toward his friend. "What's going on?"

"How would I know?" Murphy stared at the tight bun on the back of Professor Gilliam's head. "Did you do something I should know about?"

"Did I— Come on, Murphy. No way. Even if I did, I wouldn't set you up to get in trouble for it."

She gave him a sidelong glance and smirked. "Well, I appreciate that hypothetical chivalry, but it doesn't change the fact that we were pulled out of class for no reason."

"What if it's about Raven?"

Professor Gilliam stopped at the bottom of the winding staircase that led into the tower and the headmaster's quarters. She studied them both for a moment, her lips pressed firmly together, then walked ahead of them and simply expected them to follow. They did.

"Henry, for the bajillionth time, I don't know where Raven is. She's more likely to tell you if something happened."

"I dunno." He scratched his head and followed her up the stairs. "What if it's something more for...you know. Girl talk or whatever."

"Really? You think either of us are super into girl talk?"

"You're girls. And you talk."

Murphy exhaled a sharp sigh. "Unless she suddenly decided she hates both of us and cooked something up to get us in trouble, I really don't think this has anything to do with Raven."

"She wouldn't do that."

"I know." Henry almost knocked into her when she stopped below Professor Gilliam at the top of the staircase.

The woman knocked quickly on the door, and Headmaster Flynn's voice came through with perfect clarity. "Come in."

Gilliam opened the door, stood on the second-to-last stair, and gestured for the two young people to enter. Murphy took a deep breath and walked into the study. Behind her, Henry gulped and glanced at Maxwell's head peeking over the top of his messenger bag. "We'll be fine, Maxwell. Don't worry."

The professor stepped into the room, stopped beside the door, and closed it behind her. Headmaster Flynn stood behind his desk. On the other side of it, three chairs had been placed in a half-circle. In one of them, Bella Chase turned to look at them with wide eyes. Wesley perched on her shoulder with his tail wound tightly around her neck.

Henry frowned. "What's she doing here?"

"Miss Chase is the one who asked me to pull you both from class and have you brought here to join us, Mr. Derks." Flynn's long beard jerked oddly against his chest as his jaw clenched and unclenched. "I wanted to wait but Miss Chase was more insistent than usual. She has already spent considerable time with Leander and I was unavailable when she first arrived at my office. Given the nature of the problem, she is understandably impatient."

"We didn't do anything," Murphy added. "Whatever it is, it wasn't us."

He glanced at Gilliam with a small frown, then gestured toward the open chairs beside Bella. "You're not here for punishment, Miss Murphy. Please take a seat. You won't want to be standing when you hear what we have to say."

The girl rubbed her forehead slowly and headed toward the chair beside Bella, who watched her with a concerned frown and glanced at Henry.

"Aw...fine." He sighed heavily and shuffled toward the last chair. "This doesn't sound good."

"It's not." Bella bit her lip and leaned back in her chair. "But it could be worse."

"Oh, yeah? How?"

Headmaster Flynn stared at his desk as he lowered himself slowly into his own chair. He folded his hands neatly on his desk and gazed at each of the missing mage's friends. "This morning, Miss Chase brought to my attention a certain development regarding Raven Alby, and we both agreed it was the right thing to let you know what's happened."

All the skepticism drained out of Henry—along with all the color from his face—and the armrests of the chair creaked beneath his tightening grasp.

"We have reason to believe that Miss Alby was abducted during the early hours of the morning—"

"Abducted?" The young man lurched forward in his chair. "You mean like kidnapped?"

"Perhaps."

Murphy paled too. "By whom?"

"We have yet to discover that missing piece of the puzzle, Miss Murphy." Flynn's upper lip twitched in discomfort. "As of this moment, Miss Chase has confirmed that your friend is still very much alive and so far unharmed. We're now doing everything we can to find her and bring her safely back to Fowler Academy."

Henry cleared his throat. "What about Leander?"

"He is outside on the field."

He folded his arms and slumped in the chair again. "I call bull."

"Mr. Derks—"

"Nope. No way. If Raven really was kidnapped or abducted or whatever, that dragon would be out there getting her back."

"Please lower your—"

"If anyone even tried to put a hand on her, Leander would rip them to pieces. You know that. What's really going—"

"We're not making this up, Henry," Bella shouted and twisted in her chair so she could face him. "Raven contacted me this morning with basically a calling potion, okay? She told me everything."

"Then why's her dragon here?"

"They were separated," the headmaster interjected. "Professor Worley has spent the last few hours this morning getting as much information as he can from Leander. Who, I might add, is incredibly distressed by this turn of events."

"So am I!" The young man gestured wildly, then settled his hand on his head and rubbed his hair vigorously.

Beside him, Murphy sat rigidly in her chair and stared at the edge of the desk. When she blinked, a tear rolled down her cheek, and she looked at Headmaster Flynn. "What can we do?"

Henry perked up a little. "Yeah. Tell us what needs to happen, and we're on it."

The man took a deep, heavy breath. "I admire your dedication to Miss Alby and your willingness to step in during a crisis. I really do. But as of now, the responsibility falls onto this school and its staff, not it's students."

"What are you saying?" Henry leaned forward.

"I'm saying there is nothing you can do, Mr. Derks." Flynn's eyebrows drew together in pain and sympathy. "Let us take care of it. And when we know more, we'll tell you."

"Are you serious?"

"Quite."

He stared at Murphy and Bella, his eyes wide and pleading. "Did he tell us to do nothing?"

Bella folded her arms. "He's been telling me that all morning."

"We can't just *do nothing*," he shouted. "My best friend's been kidnapped, we don't know where she is, and the only person who can really protect her isn't actually a person and is here instead of with her!"

"Mr. Derks—"

"We helped with the raiders." Murphy's voice was low and soft but it held steady as she looked up to meet Flynn's gaze. "Should we have *done nothing* that day, too?"

The headmaster's lips parted to reply, but he glanced at Professor Gilliam instead. She didn't have anything to say, either. "Miss Murphy, protecting this school and your professors by being in the right place at the right time is one thing. Intentionally putting yourself in harm's way to find and rescue your friend, wherever she may be, is something else entirely."

"No, it's not. You said we helped save the kingdom after the raider attack. All of us. Finding Raven and bringing her back *is* saving the kingdom."

"Yeah!" Henry pointed at his friend. "That's exactly what I was gonna say next."

"We're Raven's friends," the girl added. "If anyone should help to find her right now, it's us."

"Until we know more about the situation, Miss Murphy, I can't allow any of you to—"

"We'll help you find out more," Henry interjected and pushed to his feet. "We'll talk to everyone, talk to Leander, ask if anyone saw what happened—"

"Sit *down*, Mr. Derks!" Headmaster Flynn's voice cracked through his circular office despite the fact that he hadn't left his chair and didn't move. On the far side of the room, Rider snorted.

The young man stumbled toward his chair and dropped into it.

"I'm sorry to have to take these measures. The three of you have done more than your fair share for Fowler Academy, Brighton, and the kingdom. But I will not endanger any more of my students, and I will not allow you three to endanger yourselves. I expect to see you all in your classes, studying diligently to pass your finals at the end of the year —which is coming up rather quickly. And it is my fervent hope that each of you passes your first year to continue your schooling at this academy."

The three young mages stared blankly at their headmaster.

Professor Gilliam cleared her throat. "You're excused from the rest of your classes for the day. But tomorrow, you're to return to your regular schedules and attend every class. That is how you can help Raven the most. Keep taking care of yourselves and uphold your responsibilities until we bring her safely back to Fowler."

"Thank you, Professor Gilliam." Flynn nodded at her, flustered by his inability to do anything else. His gaze drifted over the three students. "You may go."

"Yeah." Henry lurched to his feet and jerked his shoulder bag toward him when it caught on the armrest. "Raven can't go anywhere, though, can she?"

Flynn held the boy's gaze until Henry whirled and headed toward the door. Bella and Murphy pushed to their feet silently and followed. "Let me make this clear, young mages."

Henry stiffened and didn't turn to face the headmaster. The girls gave him wide-eyed glances over their shoulders.

"If I see or hear or even suspect any of you are looking into this on your own, you *will* be removed from this school. This is not a game."

The young wizard thumped his hand against the door and shoved it open. Murphy and Bella followed him into the winding staircase, and Professor Gilliam pulled the door shut, leaving her and Headmaster Flynn alone in his office.

"I can't believe this," Henry muttered as he stamped down the steps. "He wants us to do absolutely nothing. It's not like this is some other kid we met at the beginning of the year. This is Raven."

"What are we gonna do?" Murphy stopped on the stairs to scoop Fritz into her arms and held him close to her chest.

"Not nothing, Murph. I'll tell you that much."

"You heard him, though. We'll be expelled if he thinks we're doing anything but sitting like good little students through all our classes." The girl sighed despondently. "Do they seriously think we can simply forget about Raven and focus on school like nothing happened?"

"That's why he wanted to wait until the end of the day to tell you," Bella said.

"Oh, but you wanted to bring us in first thing in the morning and ruin our entire day." He waved his hand dismissively but didn't turn to look at her. "Real thoughtful of you, Bella."

"Hey, *my* day started with Raven waking me up way too early with that spell and telling me to get over here and handle everything for her."

"Poor Bella Chase." He snorted. "Here's what I wanna know. Why the hell did Raven use a calling potion to talk to you? I've been her best friend since before we could walk. And you… Do you guys even like each other?"

Wesley screeched as they reached the bottom of the staircase. Henry ducked his head as the sharp sound echoed against the walls and he stormed into the hallway.

"Henry!" Bella shouted.

His shoulders slumped before he turned slowly to face her. "What?"

"I get that you're upset, okay?"

"Oh, yeah. Good. Then we're on the same page—"

"Will you please—" Bella glanced up and down the hall and lowered her voice. "Listen to me for two minutes. That's it."

He shoved his hands into his pockets and fixed her with a deadpan stare. Murphy stepped quietly beside them to form a small triangle of mage students in the empty hallway.

"First of all, Raven and I do like each other, actually. And yeah, I'd even say we're friends. She'd probably say the same thing."

"Congratulations."

Murphy elbowed him in the side and shook her head.

"Look, if I didn't care about what happens to her, I could've simply forgotten about the whole thing, gone back to sleep, and left everybody else to figure this out on their own. But I do care. And I'm the person she called, so I'm a part of this too."

"And you still haven't answered my question about that. Why did she call you?"

Bella took a deep breath and closed her eyes. *I can't keep secrets now.* "Because the spell she cast to do it only works if the person you're trying to contact knows the same spell and can use it too."

Henry snorted. "That's a lame excuse."

"It's the truth, Henry. Alessandra taught us the spell only a few days ago. It's a good thing Raven and I are as skilled with magic as we are. Otherwise, no one would know a thing beyond what her terrified dragon can spit out between his attempts to tear the stables down."

The two friends shared a glance, and Murphy clutched

Fritz a little tighter before she asked, "You talked to Leander?"

"Yeah. I guess he likes me too or something. I don't know. But that's…" She shrugged and glanced at the front doors of the main building. "Actually, I have an idea."

"Good for you. I'll take a walk." Henry whirled and stormed toward the front doors.

"Come on, Murphy." Bella nodded and hurried after Henry.

The other girl watched her and muttered, "My friends call me Murphy."

"Well, if we're not friends after we save Raven together, I'll stick with calling you Anne Marie, okay?"

The mages headed outside into the warm morning. Henry glanced over his shoulder and snorted. "I didn't ask if you wanted to come with me."

"I don't care."

"Wait a minute." Murphy hurried to catch up. "You said after we save Raven. Are you serious?"

"Of course she's not serious, Murph." He spun and gave Bella a disparaging look. "She cares more about graduating at the top of the class than anything else. Even Raven. She's not gonna throw that away and risk being expelled."

Bella folded her arms and shifted her weight to one side. "You really think you have me all figured out, don't you?"

"It wasn't very hard."

"Guys, can we please cool it for two seconds?" Murphy stepped between them and Fritz leapt from her arms. "Seriously. Bella said she had an idea and she wants to help."

"I do." The other girl nodded. "And for your information, Henry Derks, the only thing I really wanted before this morning was to graduate first in our class and get out of Brighton with the best mage assignment I could find. That's been my dream for longer than I can remember."

"So you're not gonna help us."

"No." She glanced at Murphy. "Is he always this thickheaded?"

The brown-haired mage shrugged.

"Whatever. The point is, I still won't risk being expelled from Fowler Academy by being stupid and flailing around trying to do this on my own."

"Yeah." He sneered at her. "That's what I thought."

She lowered her chin and returned his look with a steady stare. "And I won't risk leaving Raven in whatever danger she's in and not do anything about it."

Murphy shook her head. "Bella, you heard Headmaster Flynn. We can't do both—"

"Oh yes, we can." Bella glanced around the empty courtyard and nodded. "We merely have to be *very* good at covering our tracks. So are you in or not?"

The two friends looked at each other, and the frown Henry gave her held more pain than she'd seen in him.

"I'm in," Murphy said with a firm nod.

"*Murph.*"

"This is for Raven, Henry. That's it. So get rid of whatever you have against Bella and suck it up already."

Bella and Henry stared at the brown-haired mage who'd been nothing but quiet, shy, and easygoing since they met at orientation. He gave her a tight smile and nodded. "I like this side of you, Murphy."

"Yeah, well, it's the only side I have right now." She turned toward Bella. "You said you have an idea."

"I do. And it'll make things much easier for us to help find Raven without anyone knowing what we're doing."

"Great." Murphy stuck her hands on her hips. "So let's hear it."

"Not here." She turned in a tight circle and scanned the empty courtyard and the various buildings around them. "Come on."

She led them across the paving and through the stone archway into the field. Leander still paced beside the stables while he stretched his wings and snorted but he no longer made all the noise. Professor Worley sat in the grass in front of the agitated dragon, his legs crossed and his back to the three young mages who sneaked past the wall during class.

The next time Leander turned to pace toward Worley, he caught sight of the students and paused to raise his head.

Bella crouched beside the wall and stared at him. *He can see me. I hope he can trust me to do this.*

She nodded once, and on the other side of the field, Leander snorted before he turned again to pace in the other direction.

Relieved, she turned toward her companions and whispered, "Come on. Hurry."

They slunk around the back corner of the wall and thankfully, no one at Fowler Academy saw anything.

CHAPTER TWENTY-THREE

William Moss swung his leg over Teo's saddle to dismount and patted the silver dragon's long neck. "Good work this morning, Teo. I know it was a lot."

"It was necessary." The dragon turned his head to look at him and his silver eyes narrowed in concern. "Are you all right?"

"Honestly, I don't know. But I will be. As soon as we—" He turned at the sound of pounding hooves coming toward them from the main road into town.

The rider was in his teens, his face flushed and eyes wide as he pulled his horse up at the front gates of Moss Dragon Ranch. The animal shied away from the gates, as nervous to be around dragons as the young boy. "I have a message for Mr. Moss!"

"Which one?" William shouted back.

"Uh…" The boy whipped a folded sheet of parchment paper from his pocket and scanned the address. "Ernie."

"Yeah, hold on." He looked at Teo and shrugged. "I gotta go get Dad."

"I believe he's already heard the call." The dragon lowered his head and focused his gaze on the narrow road that cut across the ranch toward the Moss family's home.

Ernie Moss jogged down the path, lifted his cap, and waved at the rider. "Ernie Moss. Give me a moment."

"Dad." William caught Teo's harness as the dragon slipped his head through it in a practiced move so he could be led from the front instead of at the saddle. Dragon and trainer met Ernie Moss where the footpath joined the main road inside the gates.

"Keep Teo ready to ride, Will." Ernie pointed at him and situated the newsboy cap on his head. "I have a feeling we'll take off again."

"We just got back. I don't know what else we can do."

"Well, it looks like someone has something for us, doesn't it? I'll take care of it. Just…wait until I know more." Ernie walked swiftly down the wide dirt road until he reached the gates.

He watched his dad and pressed his lips together. *Telling me to wait today is like telling me not to breathe.*

The man exchanged a few words with the messenger on horseback before the boy turned his horse and left off at a gallop in the direction from which they'd come. The owner of Moss Ranch took longer than William liked to read the letter in his hand, looked at his son, and walked up the road. "It's a message from Fowler Academy."

"Shit, I didn't even think about that." He clapped a hand onto his head and stared at the clear blue sky.

His dad cast him a sharp glance and shook the message. "From Headmaster Flynn himself."

"They have to know by now, right?"

"Of course they know. Raven Alby's gone missing, and her dragon's at that school without her."

William ran his hand through his long blond hair and sighed. "So why did he send you a message?"

"It's for both of us, more or less." Ernie handed him the letter and waited for him to read the short, succinct message.

"He wants us to go there?"

"Apparently, the fact that we're dragon trainers holds some importance." The senior Moss shrugged, took the letter, and slipped it into his pocket. "It's turned a long morning into an even longer day, huh? We'd better go."

"But what if Nadine sends words while we're gone? Someone needs to be here to—"

"Michael and Romeo will be here, son. They'll keep things running, and if anyone sends word—from Nadine or otherwise—we'll hear about it when we return. That's what ranch hands are for." Ernie clapped a hand on his son's shoulder, nodded, and hurried toward the stables. "I'll get the tack out. Go call Renaldo for me."

"Renaldo's off rotation for the next week."

The older man paused, glanced over his shoulder, and nodded. "Right. I knew that. What about Calista?"

"Under different circumstances, she'd be thrilled."

"Excellent. Pull her out." He pointed at William with a distracted smile. "It's a good thing I keep you around, huh?" Without waiting for a reply, Ernie continued to the stables.

William pressed his lips together and led Teo toward the fence lining the dragon paddock. The dragon lowered his head toward his rider and breathed softly. "He's not doing very well, is he?"

"What gave it away?"

Teo clicked in the back of his throat, and William glanced at him.

"Sorry, Teo. I shouldn't take it out on you."

"You aren't. I imagine it's difficult to hide Ernie's condition."

"Yeah. It gets harder every day." They stopped at the fence and he looped the harness over the top of the post. "And now with Raven missing and he wants to be involved... This isn't the day I expected to have."

"It's not the day anyone expected to have, William."

"You're right about that." Shaking his head, the dragon trainer walked down the fence toward the closest gate. "Wait here a minute, Teo. Dad wants Calista."

"As you wish."

He forced himself to breathe steadily as he reached the entrance and unhooked the coiled lead hanging over the post. Then, he unlatched the gate, slipped through it, and closed it again behind him. With the lead slung over his arm, he stuck two fingers in his mouth for a loud whistle that rang across the paddock. "Calista! Time to ride!"

The clans gathered in loose groups around the field looked up at his call. The paddock quieted for a moment before a blue-gray dragon rose from where she'd been lying in the grass and stretched her wings. As soon as she moved toward the fence, the other Moss dragons returned to their usual lounging about in the sunshine, playing with their clan members, or milling around in groups of two or three.

William slipped the lead off his arm and smiled at

Calista's approach. *It's another normal day for them. And why would they care? Raven spent all her time with Leander.*

"I'm ready to fly," she said, her voice low and oddly calming.

"Good. Thank you."

The gray-blue dragon with bright blue eyes glanced from William to Teo and back again. "And Teo?"

"Teo's with me, Calista. Ernie asked for you specifically."

"Ah." With the lead around her neck, the female dragon followed him toward the gate and waited patiently for him to open it again. "I'll be gentle, then."

William chuckled. "I think that's exactly why he asked for you."

I can keep the rest of Brighton from seeing how much he's changed but I can't hide anything from a dragon. Definitely not a whole ranch of them.

"Come on, Teo." The dragon trainer removed the lead from the fencepost with his other hand and led both dragons steadily toward the stables. "We're off for another meeting."

"Where are we going this time?" Calista asked.

"Uh…Fowler Academy, actually."

The blue-gray female snorted. "I did not think a school for mages accommodated dragons."

"Actually, they're already accommodating one full-time. You remember Leander."

"Of course."

"He's been there for a few months. Hey, Teo, when we get there, maybe you could—"

"I will try, William." The silver dragon inclined his head. "It depends on whether he's willing to listen."

"Right. And who knows how that'll turn out without Raven around. Hey, Dad. We're ready for you."

A loud grunt and the thump of heavy dragon tack rose from inside the stable. Ernie Moss emerged with his worn saddle slung over his shoulder, the harness dangling from his hand. "Thank you, Will. Calista." The man grinned at her. "I'm glad to see you're up for the challenge."

"With you, Ernie? Always." She lowered her head so William could slip the lead off and Ernie dismissed his son with a nod.

"All right, girl. Come down a little there so I can...ah. There we go." Twice, the man missed sliding the wide harness over the female dragon's head but he didn't seem to notice. Finally, he managed to slide it on and slung the straps over her back. Calista turned her head slightly to look at William and Teo.

I can't tell if he's trying to fake it or really doesn't notice anymore.

"Now, we get this saddle..." The man swung the saddle up but clearly couldn't have reached if Calista hadn't lowered herself to her belly for him. When she stood, he ducked beneath her to catch the saddle girths and buckle them together. "Well this is...huh. I need a little more —damnit."

"Dad?"

Ernie sucked in a sharp breath through his teeth and backed out from beneath the dragon, rubbing his fingers. "I can't get a grip on the damn buckle. Who decided to make those things so small in the first place, huh? That's what I wanna know."

"Here." He handed Teo's harness to his dad and stepped toward Calista. "I got it."

"That's fine. I'll keep Teo right here. Once the weather warms up, this arthritis'll cut me a break again. Not too much longer now, I should think."

"I know." He buckled and cinched the girths beneath Calista's belly and gritted his teeth. *The arthritis isn't the problem and everyone knows it.* "All right. You're good to go." He patted Calista's side and she lowered herself to the ground again for Ernie to mount. "Thanks, Calista."

"Of course."

They shared a glance before William took Teo's harness from his dad and nodded. "You good gettin' up there?"

"Boy, I've trained and ridden dragons since before I knew your mama. Don't ask if I need help climbin' up like some kid wantin' a ride on a birthday pony." Ernie grunted and threw an arm up over the female dragon's back as he tried more than once to get his foot into the stirrup. When he kicked himself up at last, he only managed to get halfway over.

Teo stepped toward him, but William tugged gently on the halter and held him back. *He's gotta be able to do this on his own at the very least. Only a little more time.*

Finally, Ernie Moss heaved himself over the saddle, slid his other boot into the far stirrup, and cleared his throat. "Slow and steady, eh?"

"That'll do it, yeah." The young man met Teo's gaze before he climbed into the saddle. When Teo stood, both dragons headed down the wide avenue of trampled dirt and sprouting grass between the stables and the paddock fence. "Go ahead, Dad. We're right behind you."

"You watch, Will. Your old man will show you how it's done." Ernie patted Calista's neck and clicked his tongue. "Nice and easy, Calista."

"You're the one who trained me, Ernie. I know what to do."

He chuckled as the blue-gray dragon began a steady run down the length of the fence. She spread her wings, ducked her head, and became airborne in a smooth, gentle arc a few moments before they reached the corner of the paddock.

Teo turned his head to look at William. "Renaldo isn't really out of rotation."

"No, but he takes off like a cannon. Let's go." The dragon trainer lifted the harness lightly, and Teo launched skyward to quickly gain up speed and come abreast of Ernie Moss on the gentle Calista. Together, they headed northeast toward Fowler Academy.

Professor Worley watched Leander pace across the field and took a deep breath. "How long can you keep that up?"

The dragon snorted and eyed the mage warily before he swung to walk away. "Until either she's back here with me or I hear where she is and go get her myself."

"When was the last time you ate, Leander?"

"I don't need to eat."

"Everyone needs to eat."

"You expect me to—"

A shadow passed across the field, followed swiftly by a second. Both dragon and professor looked up as two dragons and their riders turned above them in effortless flight. Ten seconds later, Teo and Calista landed softly in the grass. Both William and Ernie Moss looked grim and tired already, even though it was before midday.

"Mr. Moss." The professor pushed to his feet and dusted his loose-fitting clothes off. "Both of you, I suppose."

"We received a letter from Headmaster Flynn asking us to come," Ernie said as he dismounted swiftly and easily from Calista's lowered back. He fumbled with her harness as she ducked beneath it to let him lead her from the front. "We took off as soon as the messenger left Moss Ranch."

Worley rubbed his chin covered in the thick, wiry black beard and frowned. "Did his letter mention what's happened?"

"It didn't have to." William dismounted from Teo's saddle and adjusted the harness with practiced ease. "Leander already told us everything."

"I'm sorry?" The professor glanced at the red dragon, who'd stopped pacing and now faced Teo and Calista, his head lowered so much it almost touched the ground. "I've been out here with him since dawn."

"And I was outside with him at Moss Ranch before dawn." The young trainer nodded at Leander, and the red dragon snorted, his head swaying from side to side.

"That would have been nice to know beforehand," Worley told the dragon familiar.

Leander glanced quickly at him and narrowed his eyes. "You never asked."

"I…" He clenched his eyes shut and took a deep breath.

"I didn't consider having to ask every question imaginable to get all pieces of the story."

"Well, you're talking to a dragon." William handed Teo's harness to his father, who took them with brisk movements and a quick nod. *Dad certainly pulled himself together for this little visit.* "Do you mind if I have a few words with Leander myself?"

"It's not really up to me." Worley gestured toward the red dragon.

"I was being polite. Leander? Do you mind?"

Leander studied him for a moment, then snorted and turned away to stalk across the field.

I'll take that as a yes.

"I'll be right back."

"The headmaster's waiting for us, Will."

"It'll only take a second." The young man raised a hand toward his dad and nodded. "I assume this chat with Flynn might take a while. Do you have room to stable a few extra dragons for a couple of hours?"

Worley grimaced and ran a hand over his curly mop of black hair. "We have room in the pen, but…" He chuckled dryly. "Raven's the only one who can open it. We didn't think we'd be worried about dragons trying to get into the enclosure when we set all that up."

"What about leads?"

"Sure. We have rope."

William nodded. "Dad, why don't you show the professor how to unsaddle a dragon? I'm sure he'll find it interesting."

"Oh, sure. Come on, Mr…"

"Worley."

"Worley." Ernie waved him toward Calista. "It's real simple, now. Much like a horse, only the horse is three times the size with wings and an even worse bite, eh?"

With the two older men occupied, he headed toward Leander, who'd stopped on the far side of the field beside the forest to watch him approach. *As long as Dad has something to keep him busy, he'll be all right.*

He stopped a good ten feet from the red dragon and spread his arms in a placating gesture. "I only want to make sure you're okay."

"I am not." He snorted and began to pace along the tree line.

"Have you heard anything from her? Or felt anything?"

"I know she's alive. For now." Leander's gaze shifted from side to side with his sweeping head, but he didn't look at the trainer.

"We're doing the only thing we know how, Leander." William stepped closer. "Asking for help wherever people are willing to give it. We'll find Raven and we'll bring her back."

"*You* will find her, William Moss. *I* will bring her back."

"Okay." The dragon trainer nodded and raised his hand. "I know it's a lot to ask right now and we haven't had this conversation in a long time. But I have to ask today. Do you trust me, Leander?"

The dragon stopped pacing and raised his head slowly to study him. "Raven trusts you."

"She does."

"And you care about her."

William exhaled a slow, heavy sigh. "More than she knows."

Leander stepped toward him, met his gaze, and extended his head slowly on his long, muscular neck toward William's outstretched hand. He hovered there, two inches out of reach, and snorted. Finally, the dragon nudged his palm with his snout and turned away. "Get to work, flyboy. Find my mage."

"I will. That's a promise."

When he reached his dad and Professor Worley, the men had unsaddled both dragons and fitted them with makeshift leads. He noticed the saddles tossed haphazardly into the grass and pressed his lips together. *If that's the worst thing right now, we're still doing okay.*

"All right. Let's go see the headmaster."

"I'm happy to show you to his office." Worley glanced at the rope leads in his hands and frowned. "But I'm not sure…"

"Hitch 'em up to the post, man." Ernie nodded. "They won't go anywhere."

"Is that right?"

"Teo and Calista are some of our best. We probably wouldn't have to tie 'em up at all, but that would bring a whole new wave of questions down on our heads and that's the last thing we need right now."

"Sure." The professor looked warily at the dragons and nodded. "Come on, you two. You heard the man."

"Indeed," Teo muttered.

Calista uttered a short rumble of amusement and they both followed him to the hitching post beside the stables. He snorted in disbelief and shook his head as he tied the ropes. "The best-trained dragons are tied to a post, and the one who almost didn't make it gets to roam around in the field."

"Leander isn't trained," Teo replied. "He is a mage's familiar."

Worley stepped away and met the silver dragon's gaze. "And that means something even to other dragons, huh?"

Teo and Calista exchanged a glance and neither of them moved despite the yards of slack lead coiled at their feet. She inclined her head. "It means something, yes."

CHAPTER TWENTY-FOUR

"Here we are." Worley stopped at the top of the tower staircase and knocked.

"Come in."

The giant familiar-training professor pulled gently on the iron ring and left the door open in the staircase. He entered Headmaster Flynn's office and stood aside while William and Ernie stepped into the room.

"Mr. Moss. And Mr. Moss." Flynn stood behind his desk and nodded at the dragon trainers. "Please. Have a seat."

Ernie strode briskly across the floor and William followed, gazing at the odd knickknacks on the shelves, the rotating orb of glass that spun in mid-air beside the wall, and all the books and gadgets and magical things he didn't understand. He was still staring when he took the empty chair next to his father on the other side of the desk.

"Headmaster."

Flynn looked at Worley and nodded. "That will be all for now, Professor Worley. Thank you."

"Right." The large man nodded and left the room, closing the door softly behind him.

"Thank you for coming to see me on such short notice," the headmaster began. "And so quickly."

"Well, we do have dragons," Ernie said with a thin smile.

"Yes, you do. And, I assume, connections with other trainers and riders who have their own dragons. Correct?"

William nodded. "Many connections. Yeah."

"Good. I may ask you to use those connections at the end of this conversation. And I'm sorry to say I must start with grim news."

"We know about Raven Alby," he said quickly and leaned forward in his chair. Flynn's eyes widened, and Ernie glanced at his son with a small frown. "Leander arrived at Moss Ranch early this morning—without her. He was scared and a little beat up, but he managed to tell me most of what happened. I think."

"Is that so?" The headmaster nodded and his gaze seemed fixed on the surface of his desk. "He was awfully loud and barely coherent when he arrived on school grounds at sunrise."

"Well, he'd probably had enough time for everything to sink in at that point."

"I see. Professor Worley has had quite a difficult time getting anything more out of Leander than bits and pieces. Mr. Moss, I would very much like to hear your version of what happened last night. Secondhand, of course. But right now, it's the best we have."

"Sure." William shifted in the chair and took a moment to collect his thoughts. *At least he's asking me to tell it. So far so good.* "Like I said, Leander came by the ranch about an hour before sunrise. He woke everyone up, including the dragons, and I went out to see what was going on. He and Raven were staying at the Haverson Ranch outside Dresdel. Well, he was there, but she was at the inn nearby."

Flynn took a deep breath. "Yes. Miss Alby contacted me yesterday evening and told me the same."

"Well, the Haverson Ranch caught fire last night. And not a barn or stable fire, either. The entire ranch. The way Leander told it made it seem like the fire was started on purpose—and not in any way a human or even a mage could start it, if you know what I mean."

"Dragon fire."

He ran a hand through his hair. "That was my first thought too. But Leander's convinced it wasn't a dragon. He said he could smell it there. Some…angry creature."

"Such as?"

"I don't know. But I'm more inclined to believe him than to jump to conclusions about a dragon starting that kind of fire."

The headmaster glanced at Ernie, who stared intently at the corner of the desk without saying a word. "Beyond the fact that you are close friends with Miss Alby and have spent considerably more time with Leander than anyone else in this room, why would calling it a dragon-started fire be jumping to conclusions?"

"Because whatever creature was there took Raven."

Ernie's head jerked up, and he gaped at his son as if waking from a dream. "What creature?"

Oh, no. Hold on, Dad. Come on. William clenched his jaw. "Again, we don't know. But as far as Leander could tell me, whatever it was knocked him out of the sky. Raven…fell and the monster carried her off before her dragon could get up and go after her."

"Monster." Ernie snorted. "You're a grown-ass man, Will. There's no such thing as monsters."

Ignore it. "Right now, we don't really have anything better to call it, do we?"

"I'm sorry, Headmaster." Ernie shook his head with a self-conscious smile. "My boy's spent too much time with his head in the clouds. Literally. If I'd known about any of this nonsense, I would've left him at the ranch and come here on my own."

"Dad—"

"I'm serious, son." The look he gave him held more condescension than he had seen since he was twelve. "We have a kidnapped girl and a mage-less dragon outside, and you're wasting everybody's time yappin' about *monsters.* That wasn't part of our conversation."

"We talked about this." *Please, stop talking. You're gonna blow it.*

"And we'll talk about it again when we get home. I don't know where this crazy idea came from, Will, but you're not helping anybody by making up stories when you should be—"

"Dad!" William spun sideways in his chair. "You were there with me. You heard everything Leander said."

"No, I was..." Ernie grimaced, frowned a little, then sank into his chair and looked away. "I was... This morning, I got up to..."

The young man gritted his teeth and clutched the armrests beneath his hands. *Well, now it's out. I can't let him flail like that.*

"Where was I this morning?" His father stared at nothing in particular and his lower lip trembled. "I can't..."

"It's okay, Dad." He smiled and caught his father's wrist gently. "It's okay. We can go over it again later."

"Sure. Sure." Ernie patted his hand and stared blankly across the room.

"William." Headmaster Flynn's voice was quiet enough to make the young dragon trainer look at him. "Did Leander tell you anything else about this creature?"

If he can pretend to ignore what happened, so can I. "No. But he described the Haverson Ranch well enough, and it's not the first time either of us have seen something...like that."

"Like what, Mr. Moss?"

"Scorched earth. Destruction for its own sake and gouges in the ground that could have been left by a dragon too. If it happened to be four times a dragon's natural size."

Flynn narrowed his eyes and stroked his beard before he gave it a little tug. "Where?"

"Up north in the mountains. The sanctuary for clipped dragons." William leaned back in his chair and held the armrests again. "Raven and I flew out there two days ago with Leander and Teo. The clipped dragons were as upset as Leander was when he came to see me this morning. We saw signs of a similar fire with huge scratches in the earth and even in part of the cliffside. Only whatever made a stop at the sanctuary tore a few dragons apart before it left."

"Tore them apart?"

"Like at the butcher's."

The headmaster looked at the wall above the door to his office and licked his lips. "Anything else?"

"Leander saw something before that, too. Or only its tail, at least. There's something out there, Headmaster, and I don't have any idea what it is."

"But it took Raven Alby out of the sky." The man swallowed. "We can't let this go."

"We won't."

"I would like you to reach out to your connections among the dragon riders and trainers, Mr. Moss. We need to mobilize as many—"

"We already did." William glanced at his father, who now leaned back in his chair with one ankle crossed over his knee, stroked his chin, and stared at the headmaster like he understood the entire conversation. "My dad and I rode out this morning after Leander left the ranch. We went to Nadine first, then a few of the other smaller towns around it with dragon ranches. Magnes Thell. Eidertown. Everyone knows and everyone's keeping an eye out. They're all waiting for me to tell them where she is and they'll be ready to come with us when I do."

"Well done, Mr. Moss. You and your father took action where action was needed. Had I known, I might have sent a few messages with you to reach out to my own contacts, but I'll connect with them in other ways. I suppose the only thing left to do is find where this…creature is keeping Miss Alby."

"Right. And as far as that goes, I don't even know where to start."

"I believe that's where it's most important for us to work together, Mr. Moss. Now, before we go any further, is this meeting of ours keeping you from any other important business today?"

William's laugh was completely humorless. "Even if it was, Raven's more important than all of it."

"Very good. So please, if you don't mind, tell me again what Leander told you. Perhaps we'll find something we missed the first time."

Behind the rear wall surrounding Fowler Academy, Bella, Murphy, and Henry huddled together in the wall's shadow.

"Try it again," Bella said. "But make sure you picture exactly who you're trying to reach."

Henry glanced at her in irritation and shook his head. "I almost passed out the last time. You want me to do it *again?*"

"Do you want to help Raven or not?"

"That's a stupid question. Jeez, maybe you should be a mage trainer once you graduate."

"You haven't watched Alessandra with war-mage training, have you? Trust me, she makes me look like a teddy bear."

With a snort, he glanced at Maxwell, who sat perfectly still in the grass beside Fritz. "Okay. One more time."

"You got it." Murphy gave him a reassuring smile.

"Yeah, sure. If I can keep from falling over." The young wizard pushed onto his knees and took a deep breath. He raised both hands and muttered, *"Loquimi magus."*

His hands shook and he gritted his teeth as the shimmering circle of light appeared in the air before him.

A second circle materialized in front of Bella, and when his face focused from blurry to crystal-clear, she grinned. "That's it, Derks."

Her voice echoed once from her own mouth and again from within Henry's magical window through his Full Appearance spell. He grunted and fell back to sit in the grass and hang his head between his bent knees. The action cut off the spell abruptly. "This is insane."

"But you did it." Murphy patted his shoulder. "That was really good."

"It actually was." Bella smirked. "It only took you, what? Seven tries to get an image that clear."

"I have a feeling that's too many times," he muttered.

"I heard most mages can't cast an image for weeks when they practice the Full Appearance."

He raised his head to look at Bella with a cocked eyebrow. "I feel like I've done this for weeks."

"Yeah, it's supposed to be draining too. But when you guys can use this, we'll be able to talk to Raven. Together." She leaned toward them and smiled. "We can talk to each other if we have to. No matter where we are."

"And this is the only time we're doing this on the school grounds," Murphy added.

"We already went through that, Murphy." The other girl waved her off. "You have to learn it in person. But I think you guys are getting it."

"Okay, Henry." Murphy nudged him gently. "Do the thing, then."

"The thing." With a sigh, he lowered his hands to the grass and cupped them. "Come on, Maxwell. Time for *the thing*."

The toad leapt twice and landed in his mage's hands. Henry lifted him to his lips and muttered, "*Sana vulnera.*" He kissed Maxwell's bumpy back and closed his eyes.

A warm wave of tingling magic spread from his lips, through his head, and into his core until his fingers and toes were tingling.

"Good work, buddy." He set his familiar down again and opened his eyes. "Still not a hundred-percent, but it works."

"You'll get better at that too." Bella nodded. "It only takes practice."

"You know what I don't get? How come the only helpful hint I get from an actual professor is to give the toad a good lick? And then you come along with this actual spell that does more for Maxwell's healing abilities than anything I've learned in the first year of school."

"I read it in another spellbook I've been studying." She shrugged. "And I happened to remember it."

He shook his finger at her with a little smirk. "You've been holding out on me, Chase."

"Don't call me that."

"Hey, fine."

Bella eyed him until she gave in to a tiny laugh. "Okay, Murphy. You're up again."

The girl folded her arms. "If you get to call me Murphy, he gets to call you Chase."

"What?" Bella shook her head and scoffed. "That's ridiculous. I—"

"No, Murphy has a point. If we're all in, we're all in. Chase." Henry grinned.

"Whatever. Do the spell." She gestured toward Murphy,

settled in the grass again, and folded her arms. The girls exchanged a knowing glance, and she couldn't help a little smile.

"All right. Here we go." Murphy shook her hands out and focused on the task at hand.

Unaware of the students hiding behind the wall to practice restricted and highly advanced magic, Professor Worley made his way through the stone archway and onto the field again. "Horses? No problem. Birds, reptiles. Hell, give me a pissed-off raccoon or the biggest alligator in the pond. I could handle a hippo. But dragons? *Three.* They want me to keep an eye on *three* dragons. There's a reason dragon training is its own—"

He stopped when he caught sight of the dragons spending the afternoon on the school grounds.

Teo and Calista had walked out onto the field as far as their leads would allow them to, which was much farther than he was comfortable with in the first place. The ropes drooped slightly from their necks, not quite stretched taught. Both dragons faced east, their heads raised toward something only a dragon could see. Between them lay Leander, curled in his usual tight ball and breathing calmly. The red male's eyes were closed but at this point, Worley knew better.

"Would you look at that." He scratched the side of his head and chuckled. "The dragon who won't listen to anyone but Raven Alby merely needed a few dragons to calm him. Sure. Why didn't I think of that?"

He shook his head and sighed. "He has a long few days ahead of him. We all do. It had better be long enough."

A screech echoed from overhead. Teo and Calista

looked up briefly before they returned to their posts. The professor gazed at Gresh wheeling above him and nodded. "Yeah, me too."

With his head down and his focus on other things, the bearded man trudged across the grass toward the forest surrounding Fowler Academy and disappeared quickly into the trees.

CHAPTER TWENTY-FIVE

"*Erigo.*" Raven's eyes widened as she watched the large stone elevating at her command toward the top of the pile. "Easy. Careful..."

Her hand shook a little as she levitated it to the very top. When she was sure it wouldn't go anywhere, she released her spell gently and held her breath. The stone remained perfectly still, and she pumped her fist.

"Yes! Now I only have..." She craned her neck to view the distance between her pile of rocks and the crevasse at the top of the cave. "Halfway to go. Right. You can do this, Raven. It's like rebuilding that tiny bridge but with more magic and in a cave that belongs to who knows what kind of creature. No pressure."

She centered her focus again, stretched toward another large hunk of stone on the cave floor and took a breath. "*Eri—*"

A thud and deafening scrabble like fifty blades on a whetstone stopped her. The cave trembled beneath a massive footstep...once, twice, three times. She whirled toward her makeshift escape ladder and extended both hands. "No, no, no!"

The top third of the stones she'd piled leaned sideways and fell and all the others beneath crumbled to fill the cave with the deafening rumble of falling rubble. The young mage leapt away and covered her face with both arms, waiting for the noise to stop.

When it did, she coughed, straightened, and waved a thick plume of dust out of her face. "You've gotta be kidding me. All this time trapped in here by myself and right when I'm starting to get somewhere, the whole thing is—"

She put a finger to her lips and turned slowly. A slanted shadow moved against the far wall of the cave, followed by the grinding of stone moving against stone. The shadow disappeared but the rumbling, earth-shaking footsteps resumed.

Raven stared at the end of the wide tunnel leading out of the massive cavern. *It looks like somebody came home to check on their next meal. They're not gonna like the way I taste.*

A black, shimmering thing peeked into the cavern and moved slowly. It looked like another shadow until an unexpected blast of hot air hurtled across the cavern and ruffled her hair. *Crap. That's only its snout?*

Massive claws clicked against the stone before they came into view, and the glistening black shape she'd seen grew bigger and bigger until one huge golden eye peered into the cavern and settled on her. The rest of the huge beast emerged slowly and its heavy body slid across the floor as it pulled itself fully into the chamber. It remained near the far wall but stared intently at the young mage on the other side.

The creature's entire body shimmered with black scales, each of them studded with sharp barbs and glistening points. A line of wicked-looking spikes rose from the back of its head and continued down to its curling tail. Sparks flew as these spikes brushed against the stone walls with screech after screech that set her teeth on edge. Finally, the beast stopped moving and gave her a little more time to take it all in.

This is like ten of Leander at least. Mixed with a porcupine.

It stared at her and the glowing golden eye was larger than her head. It snorted again and flurried a puff of dust and bones across the cavern. She coughed again and waved the dust out of her face.

If it looks like a dragon and snorts like a dragon, maybe it talks like one too.

"Are you the one who caught me?"

It was only a guess, but the fact that those gigantic black talons could fit around her entire body and looked like what she'd seen after falling made it a fairly educated guess.

The beast growled and lowered its head to the floor.

That head's as tall as Leander is when he's standing. Try again.

"I guess it doesn't really matter what I ask you if you can't understand me. So we'll start there." Raven raised her head and stepped forward. "Can you understand me?"

Huge black nostrils flared in and out with each breath, and the giant golden eyes flicked to study her from head to toe. "Yes."

It's voice cracked through the cavern, which made her jump and duck her head. *I'm gonna lose my hearing after five minutes of this.*

"Okay. That's a start." She rubbed her ear and forced her hand down against her side. "My name's Raven. What about you?"

The beast raised its head again and stretched it toward her by at least six feet. "I don't give my name to snacks."

Raven swallowed. "Yeah, I don't either. But that's the thing. I'm a mage. Not a snack."

"We shall see." As it coiled its head like a snake ready to strike, the creature rose to half its full height to get a better angle from above. "You smell like a dragon."

"Well, that's probably Leander." *I don't care how nuts this is. Don't look away from that eye.* "He *is* a dragon. And my friend. And he's terrified right now because someone knocked us out of the sky and brought me here without telling him where here is."

Another growl rose in the creature's throat. "You were interfering."

"With what?"

"None of your concern, mage snack." Still eyeing her warily, the great beast turned sinuously to walk in the opposite direction toward the corridor out of the cavern.

"You will stay here for now. Until I decide what to do with you. Perhaps we will keep you as bait."

Raven blinked. "*We?*"

"Five of us. We were driven out by the misuse of what you call magic. You know all about magic, don't you, tiny mage?"

Damn. Maybe I shouldn't have led with that. "I know about

it, yes. I don't know about a misuse of magic, though. Is that what brought you here?"

"We brought *ourselves* here," the creature hissed. It turned and paced along the wall again. "Something woke us from our slumber across the sea. Something stronger than any of us could contain. And we came to this land to find our brethren whittled away into nothing more than livestock. It pains me to call them my kin, mage. You and your kind have whipped the dragon right out of them, and nothing but shells and empty husks remain."

He's talking about trained dragons. That's what all this is about. The dragons.

"So tell me, tiny magical beast." The enormous creature snorted again and narrowed those golden eyes. "How do you come to call a sheep dressed as my kind a *friend?*"

"You don't know Leander," she replied and clenched her fists. "He's not a sheep."

"You rode upon his back!" Stones and a rain of dust shivered from the cavern ceiling as the creature's thundering voice shook the walls. "You have as much of a dragon's scent on you as a human's. What did you do?"

Raven steeled herself and raised her chin, ignoring the ringing in her ears. "I saved his life. And he's saved mine."

"That's all?"

The young mage thought she really was losing her hearing until she realized the gargantuan dragon from across the sea now hissed at her in laughter.

"You think saving someone's life isn't worth a friendship?" she called in response. "Or even trust?"

The hissing cut out abruptly. "I saved you from

breaking your body on the ground, dragon mage. Are we friends?"

She fought to not roll her eyes. *It's like starting with Leander all over again but with a much higher chance of death if I'm not careful.* "Not yet."

The onyx-black dragon's huge eyes widened. "But someday, hm? Perhaps when you find something from which to save *me*."

"Honestly, I doubt there's anything in Threndor you'd need saving from. Just by the looks of you."

With a snort, the creature reared and shook its head. "You're not even trying to impress me."

"I didn't know that was why I'm here." Raven shrugged and glanced around the cavern. "I'm not all that impressive when I've been dropped in the middle of a giant cave. Get me on Leander's back and it's a whole different story."

"You're exactly like the rest of them. Using the beasts because you can."

The young mage gritted her teeth. "No one uses him. And no one uses me, either. So if you're serious about keeping me here as bait, I'd reconsider. I may not be able to get out of here on my own, but I do have magic."

"Yes." The word hissed out of the monstrous dragon as it turned and resumed pacing again. It's barbed tail slid and scraped against the floor and walls and threw up billowing showers of sparks. "I smell that too. Tell me why we're here."

"I don't know."

"If you really have magic, tiny mage, use it to discover why it woke us from our slumber and brought us to this world. Tell me why we're here, if not to release our kind, and I may let you live. You'll have more than enough time to think about it."

The beast moved faster than seemed possible and darted across the cavern toward the corridor beyond in a flashing blur of black scales and sparks. Raven hurried after it but remained well behind the sparks.

I've gotta see how that thing got in here.

The cavern shuddered and trembled again, filled with the harsh rumble of grating stone. She thumped her hands against the rough walls for balance and stumbled down the corridor. One golden eye blinked at her from the other side before the rumbling started again. More dust and small pebbles dropped onto her head and back before what little sunlight had snuck into the corridor vanished completely with a resounding thud.

The young mage waited in the darkness and listened to the clatter of the last rocks that fell from the walls. Everything fell as still and silent again as when she'd woken and found herself in this mess.

"Oh, sure. Roll a huge rock in front of a giant hole and trap the mage inside. Exactly like every other gigantic dragon that wasn't supposed to exist." Raven tossed her hands in the air and let them fall against her thighs with a smack. Disgruntled, she sighed and turned to return to her satchel and the area that had become her own personal space.

"*Circum inlustro.*" A soft ball of light elevated from her finger and floated in front of her to illuminate the corridor until she stepped into the cavern. She looked up at the crack in the ceiling and the bright sunlight spilling through it. "He wants to know why five dragon monsters woke up across the sea. If Elizabeth hadn't read about that in books, I'm sure I won't find those answers anytime soon."

She stopped beside her satchel, pursed her lips, and sat beside it with her legs crossed. *I'd better come up with something, though. I don't think that beast had much patience to begin with.*

Raven waited until dark for the giant black dragon to reappear. When he didn't, she mustered what energy she had left and shook her hands out. "Okay. No problem. We can do this again."

Her stomach emitted a ferocious growl and sweat beaded at her hairline. *Well it's not like I'm too busy to eat. Ignore it.*

After a deep breath, she focused on Bella Chase's face. "*Loquimi magus.*"

The shimmering circle of light appeared instantly between her hands. Bella's face appeared a second later, and the dark-haired mage looked up from whatever she was doing. She seemed startled to see her face hovering in front of her.

"Raven! You're okay!"

"Yeah, so far. How's Leander?"

"Pissed. Scared."

"That sounds about right. Listen, I know a little more about the creatures that brought me here."

"*Creatures?*" The girl's eyes widened, and she looked over her shoulder before she leaned toward the Full Appearance spell that hovered over the desk in her room. "As in plural?"

"Yep. There are—"

"Wait, wait, hold on. Can you cast this spell again but with two other people?"

Raven rolled her eyes and swayed where she sat. "Bella, I haven't eaten in twenty-four hours. Probably not."

"Okay. That's okay. I'll do it."

She frowned when her arms started to burn. The image in her Full Appearance spell crackled. "What two other people?"

Bella grinned. "Murphy and Henry."

"*What?*"

"I taught them. Don't worry. They've actually picked it up really well. It's surprising, honestly. I didn't know either of them had the—"

"Bella. I didn't cast this spell for a friendly chat."

"Right. Sorry." The girl's smile faded, and she nodded in response. "I'll open the spell for all four of us from here. You just…don't wear yourself out, okay?"

"No problem. I don't have much to do here anyway but don't take too long."

Bella smirked. "Are you kidding?"

Raven lowered her hands and closed the spell. Her body tilted sideways, and she thrust her hand against the ground to keep herself upright. "Nope. You will *not* pass out, Raven Alby. Pull it together."

She glanced at the stone floor, rolled her eyes, and lowered herself slowly to lay on her back. *Just in case.*

Bright stars winked at her through the crevasse in the cavern ceiling. The pinpricks shivered and three patches of bright, wavering light appeared in the air above her. Bella's face was much closer than the others and her jaw worked as she strained to maintain the spell.

"Good work, Bella," Raven muttered.

"Almost. Murphy!"

Murphy's eyes flew open, and she bolted upright in her bed. Bella's Full Appearance spell moved when she did and angled itself to stay in front of her at all times. "Holy crap."

"I heard you did some training, Murph."

"Yeah, but I didn't expect this."

Raven smirked. "Henry. Henry Derks! Get up!"

He rolled over in his bed, scratched his armpit, and farted in his sleep.

"Oh, come on." Bella rolled her eyes. "Henry!"

He sat and flailed around in the sheets. "Who...what...you—ah!" The wizard thumped backward onto the floor, and the wavering circles of the girls' faces followed him. "Raven! Oh, man. I'm so happy to see you. Are you—"

"I'm okay. Really. We gotta make this quick, 'cause Bella's casting this spell and it's heavy."

"It really is," the girl added through clenched teeth.

"So just listen and don't ask me to explain something. I'm telling you everything I know." Raven pushed herself slowly to a seated position on the stone floor as she spoke. "The creature that took me is essentially a huge dragon—like, ten times as big as Leander. And...a little different but mostly dragon. There are five of them from somewhere across the sea. They're attacking all the dragon ranches in Lomberdoon because they think that's why they were awakened—a crusade to free all the dragons because magic has been misused, somehow. I don't know what that means, but my guess is these things are super-old and obviously super-dangerous. So far, they haven't tried to eat me, so that's a plus."

"Not funny." Murphy looked like she was about to cry.

"Hey, if we don't have humor, Murphy, what's left?" She glanced around the cavern. "I'm in the mountains somewhere—it's all rocks and cliffs—and I'm in a cave with a giant crack in the ceiling. I'm fairly sure it's somewhere near the valley of clipped dragons so if anyone happened to fly over it, they might see me waving at them."

"That's great! We can send someone to find you that way!"

"Not with five legendary beasts flying around, Henry. Sorry."

His smile faded and his shoulders slumped where he sat on his bedroom floor.

Raven sighed regretfully. "I'll try to find out as much as I can. These megadragons think mages have been misusing magic and totally destroyed what dragons are supposed to be, so they don't like any of us. If someone tries to come for me here, they need to know that."

"Someone's definitely coming," Murphy said with a nod. "We promise."

"I know, Murph. So I need you guys to get all this info to Leander, William, and Headmaster Flynn, okay? They need to know, and I'm sure they can think of something together."

"Yeah, we can do that."

"You got it, Alby."

Bella grunted. "I can't keep this up anymore."

"That's okay, Bella." Raven nodded at her. "You did great. I'll see you guys soon."

The wavering circles of light with each of her friends' faces rippled and disappeared. The young mage ran a hand over her hair and looked at the stars through the crack in the ceiling again. "But sooner rather than later would be really nice."

She stretched on the floor again, used her satchel as a pillow, and curled in a tight ball. Her stomach growled, and she brushed her fingers against her mother's pin on her jacket.

CHAPTER TWENTY-SIX

The next morning, Henry and Murphy met at their usual spot at the fountain in Brighton's town center on their way to school.

"How crazy was that last night, huh, Murph?" He nudged his fist playfully into her shoulder and grinned broadly. "That was *us*. Doing real high-level spells!"

"That was all Bella last night."

"Yeah, but it wouldn't have worked if we hadn't learned the Full Appearance in the first place. And Raven's okay. So far so good. We have a plan, and we have something to do about it. We'll have her back by the end of the day. I know it."

Murphy gave him a small, tired smile and glanced at Fritz, who darted between their feet. "You sound excited given that your best friend is locked in a giant dragon's cave."

"No, I'm excited because my best friend is locked in a giant dragon's cave and is *still alive*. There's a difference."

"As long as we get her message to the people who need to hear it."

They moved beyond the center of the town and walked silently down the road heading northeast toward Fowler Academy. "Murphy."

"Yeah."

"She's gonna be okay."

She shrugged. "I know. I keep thinking about what that must be like for her. All by herself. She's probably terrified."

"Nah. Raven Alby's not afraid of anything. She's careful, sometimes, sure. But that's it."

"I know I'd be terrified."

Henry nodded. "Yeah, me too. But I don't think she'd be able to cast a Full Appearance to anyone if she was really that scared. She's holding up. We have to do the same thing." He threw his arm around her shoulders and pulled her in for a sideways hug. When she didn't respond at all, he lowered his head to look at her and frowned. "You look like you're about to cry."

"No I don't." She sniffed and nudged him away so he had to pull his arm free. "You look like a crazy person, though. Smiling like that." They reached the end of the avenue of trees that shadowed the road to Fowler, and the huge clearing of the school grounds came into view. "Maybe *pretend* to still be sad, huh? If Flynn or any of the professors see you grinning and jumping around, they're gonna know something's up."

"Oh, yeah. I didn't think about that. How's this?" He stuck his bottom lip out in an exaggerated pout.

Murphy snorted and shoved him away. "That's even worse."

"All right. I'll take it down. I'm fairly sure I can— Woah." Both young mages stopped in the road outside the gates and stared at the gathering in the field. "That's more dragons than yesterday."

"That's more dragons than any day." Murphy tugged on his arm to pull him with her toward the front gates. "Come on. We need to stick to the plan."

"The plan didn't include a dozen dragons at our school, Murph."

"It doesn't matter." They stepped through the school's front gates and into the main courtyard that teemed with Fowler Academy students. Everyone was talking about the dragons in the field and jostled one another at the stone archway to get a better look.

"Why'd they bring so many?"

"I heard they're trying to stop another attack on the school."

"It's weird, right? Suddenly, there's all these dragons hanging around and Raven Alby's not even here to show off."

"That's Brighton's dragon trainer out there. The Moss guy."

"Wait a minute. What?" Murphy turned toward the second-year talking about the dragon trainer. "That's not supposed to happen."

"If William Moss is out there with all those other people, I guess sticking to the plan isn't really an option." Henry frowned.

She caught his arm again and pulled him through the

throng of curious, loud students. "We need to find Bella because she was supposed to be out there talking to—"

"Murphy! Henry!" The other girl pushed through the students. Circling above her, Wesley screeched in greeting. None of the other mage students seemed to notice.

"Do you know what's going on out there?" Murphy asked and gestured toward the growing crowd inside the stone archway.

Bella shrugged. "My guess is Flynn called in backup. I had a good look at who's out there."

"From here?" Henry frowned at the students pushing each other out of the way to peer through the archway. "That doesn't really seem doable right now."

"No, Wesley went to go check it out." Bella waved them off. "But we have to—"

"Wait, and he *showed* you?" Murphy's mouth dropped open.

"Yes, Wesley can now send me images like Professor Worley showed us. Hurray. Can we please focus on what actually matters right now?" Her companions nodded. "There's a change of plans. Headmaster Flynn's out there with the riders who came in from wherever. I saw two patches with Nadine's banner and a few others. So, Murphy, you won't find him in his office. And William Moss is out there too."

"Yeah, we heard the rumor—hey, watch it, Thomas." Henry rubbed his shoulder and glared at the other boy's back. "Put a few dragons out in the field and people lose their minds."

"We need to get out there." Bella gestured for them to follow her as she headed toward the front gates. "They have no idea where Raven is, and they can't leave without hearing what she told us last night."

"So you're suggesting…"

"That we run full-speed into a field full of dragons and tell everyone to stop what they're doing and listen to us." She peered around the corner of the wall surrounding the school and shrugged. "Unless you guys have a better idea."

"Not really…"

He smacked his forehead. "We're totally getting expelled."

"Not if you let me do the talking. Got it?"

Murphy nodded and Henry gestured toward the field. "Lead the way, Chase."

Bella rolled her eyes. "Keep up."

The three mages darted out into the field. They were halfway to the group of at least a dozen dragons gathered beside the stables before another student in the courtyard pointed them out. "Hey, look!"

Professor Gilliam shoved the students out of the archway and shouted, "Miss Chase! What do you think you're—Professor Worley."

Worley slipped under the archway and nodded. "They must have missed the memo. I'll bring 'em back." He hurried after the young mages, his teeth clenched.

"Headmaster Flynn!" Bella shouted. The dragon in front of her stretched her wings and staggered back. The surprise rippled through the others, and a few startled shrieks filled the air. "Headmaster!"

"Watch out!" Henry jerked her back with a handful of her shirt seconds before a silver dragon's head swung toward them.

Murphy went in a wide circle around the dragons and skirted the barn.

"What's going on over here?" A man in a navy flight suit raised his hands to pull one of the startled dragons down before his gaze settled on Henry and Bella. "Students aren't allowed out here this morning. Go on back to the courtyard."

"We have to speak to Headmaster Flynn." Bella ducked and tried to see through the milling dragons stretching their wings and walking across her view. "I know he's out there."

"Miss Chase. Mr. Murphy." Professor Worley came up behind them and folded his arms. "You might not have heard but the field's closed to students."

"Yeah, this guy told us." Henry gestured toward the man in the flight suit. "Whoever he is."

The man scowled. "Professor—"

"I got it. Thank you." The professor motioned for Henry and Murphy to come with him. "Right now. You're already in enough trouble running into a group of gathered dragons like this. Don't make it worse."

"We need to talk to Headmaster Flynn," Henry argued. "Seriously. Raven got—"

A piercing screech rang through the air, followed by a guttural bellow that made all the other visiting dragons fall still. Bella and Henry glanced at each other, then raced around the dragons to see Leander standing on the far side of the field.

The red dragon bucked his head up and down, his wings stretched wide. He flapped them once and blew

Murphy's hair away from her face as she stood directly in front of him with her hand outstretched.

"Miss Murphy!" Headmaster Flynn bellowed as he strode across the silent field toward her. "I must ask you to step away from Leander and join your fellow students in the—"

"They found her," the red dragon growled.

"They…" The man gaped in surprise when Bella and Henry came running around the edge of the field and stopped beside the girl. He turned to gesture for the other dragon riders to wait and approached the three young mages who stood in front of Raven Alby's familiar. "I made myself perfectly clear when I said the three of you were to have no part in this."

Henry stepped forward. "Right. But we—"

"We didn't do anything, Headmaster." Bella stepped closer to Flynn, and Henry shoved his hands in his pocket. "Raven contacted me again last night and told me more about where she is and what those creatures are."

Flynn pressed his lips together and studied the other two students. "What about you two?"

"Bella told us everything," Murphy lied. "We believe her."

"Yesterday, you had a hard enough time being in the same room together in my office." Flynn tugged his beard. "What changed?"

"Raven got taken," Henry muttered. "That's what changed. And that's the only thing that matters right now, don't you think?"

"Indeed, Mr. Derks." The headmaster looked at Leander hovering behind the students. "The riders Mr. Moss was diligent enough to round up for us were about to take off for a search party. I do sincerely hope you three have a good reason for delaying Raven's rescue."

"We might be delaying the search party," Bella said. "But it's because we know where she is. Relatively speaking."

"You want to hear this, Headmaster." Murphy crouched to scoop Fritz into her arms. "That search party won't make it very far if they don't hear what they're up against."

The man studied his students' eager faces. "You have ten minutes to convince me that they weren't ten minutes wasted."

"Thank you."

"Out near the stables, please. You'll say what you have to say to the entire fleet of riders who've set their own well-being aside to ensure Miss Alby's. Make it good." Flynn spun quickly and headed toward the stables.

"Whew." Murphy glanced at Henry and Bella. "I definitely liked our original plan more."

"Yeah, well, things change. Come on."

Henry stepped beside Murphy and leaned toward her. "What were you thinking going up to Leander like that? You've never been that close to him before, Murph. He could've broken you in half if he wanted—"

"That is not what I want, mage."

"Ah!" He leapt sideways and spun to see Leander walking behind them, his head almost over Murphy's shoulder. "Jeez! You can't sneak up on people like that, you...you *dragon*."

"Obviously, I can."

Henry gave Murphy and Leander a wide berth as they

passed the other gathered dragons and their riders. "I meant figuratively."

"And figuratively, Henry, I don't care about anything but finding Raven. I will hear you speak of what you know."

"Right."

Murphy slipped past the red dragon's lowered head to walk beside Henry. "That's how I got so close. We all want the same thing."

"Including not crapping our pants when a dragon sneaks up behind us." Henry shook his head and adjusted his shoulder bag with a grunt.

"Henry?" William Moss pushed through the gathered riders and headed toward them. "What's going on?"

"We got word from Raven last night."

"You heard from her?"

Murphy nudged Henry in the side. "Oh, uh…Bella Chase did. We're here for moral support, basically."

"What did she say? Is she all right?" William stepped in front of the mage students to block their path. "Seriously. If you guys know something, you have to—"

"That's what she's about to do," Henry said and pointed beyond the trainer's shoulder at Bella. "You're gonna want to hear this too."

William spun to face the girl, who stood beside Headmaster Flynn in front of the stables.

Flynn pointed at Henry and Murphy and crooked his finger. "A joint effort got you three into this. Only a joint effort will get you out of it."

"Great." Henry shoved his hands in his pockets and stepped forward.

"We got this, Henry."

"Yeah, as long as Bella does all the talking."

With the three young mages standing in a row in front of the gathering of out-of-town riders and their dragons, Headmaster Flynn swept his arm toward the group. "Miss Chase, Miss Murphy, and Mr. Derks have delayed our search to bring us important information about Raven Alby's disappearance. Her life may depend on what you're about to hear."

"It does," Bella added.

Flynn leaned toward her and raised an eyebrow before he muttered, "I certainly hope so, Miss Chase." He clasped his hands behind his back and stepped away from the students to listen.

She cleared her throat and Wesley swooped out of the sky to perch on her shoulder. "Raven contacted me last night with something basically like a calling potion."

The riders in the front of the group frowned or gave each other confused glances.

"Which…most of you don't even know about because that's magic. Okay. The how doesn't matter, but she told me as much as she could about where she is and what took her two nights ago. Raven and Leander were attacked by a dragon—"

"That's outrageous!"

"Headmaster Flynn, we don't have time for this."

"No trained dragon would deliberately knock another rider out of the sky. Not to mention abduct another rider."

Wesley screeched in a miniature version of a dragon's angry cry before he launched a huge ball of fire into the air. The agitated riders stopped talking.

"Please hear me out." Bella scanned their faces and took a deep breath. *This is what I was made to do. To talk sense into people and get things done. So do it.* "These aren't normal dragons we're dealing with. And I don't mean the wild ones with clipped wings or any of those that might still live off the ranches somewhere. These dragons came from across the sea—"

"Do we have to stand here and listen to this girl's wild fantasies?"

"There aren't any dragons across the sea. Everyone knows that."

"We need to fly—"

Leander uttered another earsplitting bellow, lowered his head, and swung it across the entire gathering as if spraying them with dragon fire instead. The other dragons shuffled nervously and tossed their heads, but everyone was silent again.

The red dragon lifted his head and seemed to grow an extra few feet. "Listen to the girl. If you think you know more than a mage who's spoken to Raven herself, go home."

Henry nodded at Leander with a crooked smile. "Okay. I like his style."

The dragon looked at Bella. "Speak, mage."

"Thank you. From what Raven said, these dragons are massive—bigger than anything I think any of us has seen—and there are five of them. They came from across the sea because they think it's their duty or something to...free the other dragons on Threndor."

Murmurs of surprise and concern floated amongst the

dozen riders. Their dragons shared silent glances but turned their attention quickly to the young mage.

"She said they have something against mages for some perceived misuse of magic. And these giant dragons are especially angry with dragon trainers. Probably riders too. If they see a group of dragons carrying humans to rescue her, I don't think they'll care about who makes it through that attempt."

"And we're supposed to believe the tale from a teenage girl who *claims* she spoke to Raven?" The man in the navy flight suit stepped forward, his dragon's harness hanging loosely in his hand. "I'm sorry, miss, but I can't afford to put my stock in hearsay. Not with someone's life on the line."

"She's telling the truth," Murphy shouted. "Why would she make this up? Why would *Raven* make any of this up?"

"Wait a minute." William Moss stepped beside the mage students and turned to face his fellow dragon trainers and the other riders who'd answered his call. "It makes sense."

"We followed you here, William," another rider shouted. "But you should let your father speak. He's the one representing Moss Ranch."

His gaze flicked toward Headmaster Flynn and he folded his arms. "My father, Roderick, has entrusted me with this gathering and to lead the fleet to find Raven Alby. I speak for both of us today. What we should focus on is everything Miss Chase told us. Raven and Leander were at the Haverson Ranch two nights ago when it burned to the ground. I know you've all heard of it. Some of you might have seen it. That's where she was taken. And four other dragon ranches have been destroyed in the same way in the last week. Sure, there was another fire out in Canterdown a few days ago, but so far, that's an outlier. And they all look the same. Not only burned buildings but complete demolition by dragon fire. Only not from *our* dragons."

"That hardly proves that a clan of gigantic dragons from across the sea have come to burn our ranches, Moss."

"True. But I saw the same thing at the sanctuary a few days ago too."

Another murmur of surprise rose from the riders. "The dragons we clipped and sent to that valley might have even been the first attack. Four dragons were dead and the valley had been scorched to ash. The others were terrified and angry, and they had no idea what had done this to them."

"They called it a monster," Leander added and raised his head.

"Yes, they did." William nodded at the red dragon. "And these monsters, even if they are enormous dragons, took Raven Alby, a mage with a dragon familiar. I'm sure I'm not the only one here who can see that Leander isn't like the rest of our dragons. He was never trained and was almost sent to the sanctuary himself before she stumbled upon him. Sometimes quite literally."

Leander snorted.

"I have no problem believing Miss Chase's story or that it came straight from Raven. I don't understand magic, but I know Raven Alby as well as I know myself." He swallowed and stared at the ground for a moment. "So I say we listen to these mages who risked more than we know to warn us of what we'd fly right into otherwise."

"We still don't know where she is, William."

"I don't buy it."

"We've wasted enough time already."

Leander screeched again. "Ask your dragons," he roared.

Every rider looked at the dragon beside them, and none of them knew what he meant.

"Truth," a silver dragon muttered.

A green female on the other side of the group raised her head. "Truth."

The other dragons quickly took up the one-word vow and their voices rose together. The riders were astonished but didn't interrupt.

Bella folded her arms and looked at William with a smirk. "Dragons can smell a lie."

He met her gaze and raised his eyebrows. "Yes, they can."

When the short chant was over, Headmaster Flynn cleared his throat. "Miss Chase, did Raven happen to give you a location of where she may be now?"

She nodded. "She thought she was somewhere in the mountains near the dragon sanctuary."

"In a cave," Henry shouted. "With a giant crack in the ceiling!"

Shooting the wizard a warning look, Bella muttered, "I was getting to that part."

"Right. I know you told me. I only wanted to make sure you...hadn't forgotten." He glanced quickly at Flynn and shrugged.

The headmaster raised his chin and stroked his thin gray beard. "Thank you, mages. I believe your ten minutes is up."

"You believe us, don't you?" Murphy asked, her eyes wide.

Flynn frowned. "Mr. Moss, I'll defer any other decision making to you."

William nodded and the headmaster turned away from the stables.

"Headmaster, wait!" Bella hurried after him, followed closely by Murphy and Henry. "You have to believe us. If the riders go in there looking for her and get too close, they'll be—"

"Mr. Moss is clearly on your side, Miss Chase. He will direct his fleet with a well-laid plan to ensure as few people get hurt as possible."

"What about the giant dragons, though?" Henry asked. "We're not making that up."

He ignored his students and stopped in front of Raven Alby's large red dragon. "Leander. I would very much like to hear your thoughts on the subject of enormous dragons from across the sea. If you would be so kind as to share them with me, of course."

Leander pawed the ground and raised his head toward the sky with a growl. "I saw something in the sky. It was like a dragon and nothing like a dragon, but it was enormous. The fire felt like dragon fire, but it smelled like rage. I do not know what these creatures are." He lowered his head to fix the headmaster within his glowing yellow gaze. "But I believe they have Raven Alby. I believe they think they know what's coming to save her. And I believe they're wrong."

"Thank you." Flynn bowed his head, and Leander waited until the man looked up again to do the same.

"There's only one more thing to settle, then, and this is something I would never have asked if the circumstances weren't so severe."

The dragon snorted. "Ask, mage."

"I believe the same as you. I also believe I have certain skills with magic that are starkly lacking among the riders Mr. Moss has gathered this morning. What I lack, Leander, is my dragon. Neither of us can replace what we've lost and I will do everything in my power to return Raven to you. I'm asking your permission to fly with you into the mountains to bring her home safely."

Henry's mouth fell open. "Did he ask to ride Leander?"

Murphy covered her mouth with both hands and nodded.

"I didn't even know it was possible." Bella looked at them with wide eyes. "Is it possible?"

Leander studied the headmaster of Fowler Academy and the dragon-rider veteran of the Great War. Finally, he lowered his head and closed his eyes. "For Raven's sake and so we can get her back."

"And he said yes." Henry clamped his head between both hands and shook it. "Is this real."

"It's real." Bella still seemed bemused. "Now, there's nothing else we can do."

CHAPTER TWENTY-SEVEN

"One thousand two hundred and eighty-eight." Raven lay on her back in the cavern and flicked her finger at the ball of magical light so it bounced a foot above her before it floating down slowly. "One thousand two hundred and eight-nine."

A shimmering oval of light opened in the air above her. The magical glow fell through it and onto her face but disappeared instantly. Bella Chase's face stared at her from the newly cast Full Appearance.

"Raven."

"Hey." She swallowed and gave her friend a weak smile. "How'd it go?"

"Well…" The girl glanced over her shoulder and shrugged. "We encountered a few roadblocks—"

"But we busted right through 'em, Alby." Henry's face appeared in the spellcast window, and he flashed her a thumbs-up before his grin faded. "Woah. You don't look so great."

"Good to see you too, Derks." She blinked and forced her eyes to open again.

Murphy squeezed in on the other side of Bella and tried to smile reassuringly. "They're on their way toward the sanctuary, Raven. They're coming."

A flash of excitement and concern burst through her veins. "You told them about the megadragons, right? That they can't simply fly here and expect to get me out of here by force."

"We told them everything," Bella said, her lips tight as she focused on holding the Full Appearance open as long as possible.

"Except for the fact that Murphy and I know this spell too," Henry added. "You know. Trying to save you and not get expelled in the process."

Raven managed a small chuckle. "I appreciate it. Is Leander coming too?"

"Oh, yeah. He's—"

The grating of stone on stone rose from the other side of the cavern, shook the walls, and reigniting her fierce headache.

"What's that sound?"

"A visitor." She frowned. "I have to go. You guys worked fast. Thank you."

"We all want you back and safe, Raven," Murphy said. "You'll be—"

She waved her hand over the Full Appearance and muttered, *"Finis magus."*

The shimmering circle of light vanished and her hand flopped onto the cold stone floor. *Sorry, guys. I can't take any chances.*

The screech of the monstrous dragon's spine-riddled side and tail against the cavern wall echoed around her. More sparks lit up patches of the darkness on the other side of the chamber, even with sunlight spilling through the crack in the ceiling.

He stopped in his usual place and sniffed the air. "What's wrong with you?"

Raven sighed and ignored her pounding head and the black hole in her belly. "That's a very long list right now."

"You look sick. Why do you look sick?"

Is that a hint of concern? I guess I'm not a snack today, either.

Slowly, she pushed herself off the floor to shift slowly and face the massive beast. She crossed her legs beneath her and shrugged. "Oh, I don't know. Maybe it's because I've been stuck in a cave with no food or fresh air for the last two days."

"That's not very long."

She snorted. "Humans generally eat three times a day. Or, according to my best friend, twice that at least. Merely a minor oversight on your part."

"I see." The gigantic black dragon curled his body to turn back toward the corridor and sank onto his belly. "I can change that."

"That would be very much appreciated."

"Tell me what you've discovered."

Licking her lips, Raven stared at the crack in the ceiling. "That it's really not as easy as I thought to discover the mysteries of magic waking ancient dragons with no food, water, or fresh air for two days."

The dragon growled. "Do not test my patience, mage."

"I can't help it. We call it being hangry." The dragon stared at her and she leaned forward. "You know, hungry and—forget it. I'm talking to a giant dragon from across the sea named... Oh. You never told me that part."

Golden eyes narrowed beneath the glinting black ridges of the creature's scales. "If you must have a name, you may call me Po."

She stared at him and couldn't help a smile. "Po? Does that mean something?"

"What I am called cannot be translated to the human tongue."

"So you went with Po. Wow. Personally, I would have gone with something a little more intimidating, you know? Like Smaug or...give me a minute. I'll come up with a better—"

A sharp hiss issued from the other end of the tunnel leading out of the cavern. Po lifted his head and stared at the entrance, and Raven watched the shadow moving along the wall. *Great. Now, it's a party.*

"This has gone on long enough." The new voice was all hissing and grating timbres. "You were wrong."

"I have not decided," Po growled.

"So let me decide for you." A second ancient dragon not quite as large as Po stepped into view. His barbed scales and massive spikes along his spine were exactly the same, only the new creature was a vibrant, glittering emerald-green. Eyes of the same color flickered around the cavern and finally settled on Raven. "This? This is what you've made us wait for?"

"This one is different."

"You cannot read the signs!" The green dragon lurched

toward the larger black beast and hissed angrily. "The rest of us see right through your lies. I will not defy our calling because you wait for a snack to decide our fate."

"Now, hold on." Raven raised her hand and let it slap against her thigh. "We've been over this already. I'm not a snack, I'm—"

"Finished." The emerald beast reared and opened his terrifyingly huge mouth. The glow of dragon fire illuminated in the back of his throat as the rumble filled the cavern.

Shit. Here it comes. Raven clenched her fists and waited for the two seconds that felt like two hours.

The black dragon roared as the other unleashed a column of churning flame at the young mage seated cross-legged across the chamber.

"*Sequantur flamma!*" she screamed and extended both hands. Her spell and the force of the great beast's attack met each other with a crack of power. She threw her arms up and the flames hurtled up and away from her to direct the entire conflagration toward the crevasse in the stone ceiling. Fire burst from the mountainside along the northern peaks of the Mountains of Jared and seconds later, everything fell still.

When all the flames were gone, her exhausted arms dropped and her hands fell into her lap. Her head drooped to her chest as she swayed over her crossed legs. Beads of sweat rolled down her forehead, cheeks, and the bridge of her nose before they dropped into her palms. *I'll take care of that later.*

"*What?*" The green dragon hissed again, and the black beast behind him rumbled in amusement. "This can't be."

"It can," Raven muttered. "It is. Look, if you guys want to keep me around to find your answers, I'm gonna need food. Water, at the very least." She pushed to her feet and stumbled a little before she regained her balance. Then, she spread her arms and sighed. "So how about it, Po? You feed me, and I'll...well, I won't feed *you*. But I'll help with your magical questions."

"You little—" The green dragon skittered toward her and scattered sparks in all directions as his massive claws and spikes dragged across the stone.

"*Ecflicto!*" The white light burst from her hand and struck the creature dead-center in its snout.

He skidded to a stop with a nerve-racking shriek like steel on stone and snorted a billowing cloud of thick black smoke. His green eyes rolled, and he shook his head vigorously before he stretched his neck to tower over the young mage. Nostrils she could've climbed into flared as he sniffed her and snorted again.

The force of his breath made Raven stagger and she pointed at him and glared into one large emerald eye because she couldn't look at both of them at the same time. "Do you want another one?"

"Enough," Po rumbled. "I have seen enough. Get out."

The green dragon swiveled his head slowly to look at Po, then snorted again and stalked out of the cavern. His massive spiked tail pounded against the wall beside Po's head. The black beast didn't react at all to the explosion of sparks and the crumbling stone at his brethren's disgruntled warning.

"For a mage who looks as ill as you do, that magic was more than powerful enough to find the answers I seek."

Raven's legs trembled, but she raised her chin and clenched her fists. *I'm gonna have to bluff my way through the rest of this. Only until backup arrives.* "Those were all simple spells. They don't take much focus or energy, so…"

"Hmm. Come with me, tiny mage. We will set you right. And then you can commune with magic for my answers."

"Sounds good to me." She scooped her satchel up and almost toppled forward. Her teeth gritted, she slung it over her shoulders and moved as fast as she could across the cavern while she avoided the showers of sparks Po left in his wake. *Commune with magic? These old dragons really have no idea how this works. I can't simply toss a coin in and ask a question.*

When her guide vanished from the tunnel entrance, she took a deep breath and squared her shoulders. *Here we go. Be ready for anything.*

The gust of wind when she stepped out of the tunnel almost knocked her over. Po turned his massive body to block the wind and stared at her from his looming height.

"Wow." Raven gazed at the enormous valley of jagged stone and craggy cliff faces, all of it as sharp and cold and unforgiving as her hosts. *How far into the mountains are we?*

A shriek from behind made her jump, and she turned to gape at a massive silver dragon, this one with spikes lining the back of her head to look like a dragon's crown. A pure-white dragon clutched one of the stone spires poking through the valley, his tail wound around the base. The spikes punctured the stone itself with the force of his grasp. He echoed the shriek, and a shadow passed over the valley before a gargantuan dragon with golden scales landed on the edge of a cliff to her right.

That one's as big as Po. And they're all staring at me.

"We are the five," Po said, his voice strong enough to punch through the wind howling through the stone valley. "My brethren do not believe you are of much use to us at all, tiny mage."

Raven glanced at the dragons surrounding her. The emerald beast crouched yards away on the wide ledge and watched her intently. "Well, I guess that depends on what you want me to do."

"You may start," the silver female above her snarled, "by telling us why we should believe anything you have to say."

"Besides the fact that I really like being alive?" Despite her situation, she chuckled. "I guess the main reason would be that if I jerked you around and made all kinds of things up, you'd all know. Dragons can smell the truth. Or a lie."

The five watched her silently. Then, the white one stretched his neck out from behind the spire of stone. "But the truth and what you believe may be very different things."

"True. I'm not sure I could pick out those instances for you. That doesn't make for very strong belief, does it?"

"This one is part of the problem too," the green male spat.

"What problem is that, exactly?" Raven turned toward him and tilted her head. "The part where you tried to fry me and eat me? Or the part where I stopped you?"

The green beast's wings shivered and stretched halfway from his back as he lowered his head and glared at her. "You think you're here to control us. All our kind. To pit a dragon against themselves to forget their own will and answer only to yours."

"Okay, I don't know where you got that idea, but that's not the way it works."

"Then explain," Po added and bent his neck in a massive U to look at her while his body faced the jagged stone valley below.

"I can't speak for the dragon trainers themselves because that's not what I am. But I can tell you about mages and dragons." She took a deep breath and glanced from one looming ancient dragon to the next. "We've worked together for centuries. Not every mage has a dragon, and not every dragon has a mage. But my grandfather did. He had the same connection with his dragon that I have with mine. And that's what I was made to do too. Yes, there might be a few dragons who didn't have the best trainers and that definitely needs to change. But those are the exception. Most trainers do a great job of forming relationships. Everyone knows you can't tell a dragon what to do and even asking politely isn't enough without building trust first. Believe me, I learned that the hard way."

"Did you train this dragon?" The female voice came from the golden dragon perched on the cliffside.

Raven looked at her and shook her head. "Not really. Leander's my familiar."

"Familiar what?" the silver female asked.

Pinching the bridge of her nose, she sighed. "No, that's what it's called. Every mage has one. Like a partner. They help us with our magic and we help them grow stronger. It's a win-win for everyone and my familiar happens to be a dragon."

"That's no different than lashing a beast with a whip

until he moves the way you want," the green dragon snarled. "A *partnership*."

"No, it's not." A wave of dizziness washed over the young mage, and she closed her eyes again and shook her head. *Hold on.* "Leander and I have an even stronger connection because he's my familiar. We can sense each other. Almost like sharing thoughts—" She stopped and looked across the valley. *Careful. Can't give too much away.*

"This is absurd," the white dragon growled. "This human may have an abnormal fondness for that runt of hers, but this changes nothing."

"We should fly tonight," the silver beast rumbled. "Attack again—"

"No." Po looked at her and snorted. "We wait." His massive head tilted slightly so he could fix an eye on the tiny mage beside him. "This one and I will speak of that... connection between a mage and a dragon familiar. I would hear more of that, mage."

"Sure. I could talk about Leander all day." Raven shrugged. "And I will as soon as I eat something."

"Yes." Po's rumble of amusement echoed between the spires of stone and the jagged peaks. He glanced at the green beast. "Bring this snack a snack."

The emerald one snorted and turned in a tight circle on the jutting precipice before he vanished into an over-hanging cave.

Finally. Let's hope whatever it is, I can keep it down.

A minute later, the dragon returned and lifted one enormous forepaw to toss a hunk of charred meat at her. It thumped across the ledge and rolled itself in a fine coating of dust and small pebbles. Raven stooped to pick it up and held it out in front of her. "Out of curiosity, what is it? Not that matters. I'm merely…curious."

"Cattle," the green beast spat.

"Okay… It's the biggest steak I've ever seen." She did her best to brush the dirt off the outside of the charred chunk, lifted it to her mouth in both hands, and ripped off a huge chunk with her teeth. "Not bad. It could use a little salt, though."

Po snorted, and the other five stared at her with vengeful disdain.

Raven spat a pebble out and swallowed. "Thank you."

"When you are finished, we will talk."

"You got it, Po. I will uphold my end of this bargain." She bit into the meat again and moved to sit on the rocky ledge and cross her legs as she chewed slowly. *At least I have his attention now. I'm sure I can talk my way out of this. Or at least talk myself out of being ripped apart before help gets here.*

CHAPTER TWENTY-EIGHT

With a full belly and feeling strangely energized, Raven followed Po through the tunnel into the cavern and told him everything she knew about mages and their familiars, specifically of the dragon variety. She was careful to make a point of saying that most familiars couldn't go very far from their mages and that communicating with images took considerable time and practice. He didn't ask if she'd reached that point with Leander so she fortunately didn't have to lie.

"What else?" he asked once she'd stopped talking.

"Um...that's it, really. Unless you have any questions." She tried not to cringe as he stared at her. *Why did I open that door?*

"I will think on this, tiny mage. And I will return when I am ready to proceed."

"By all means." She spread her arms and gave him a flippant bow, but the black beast didn't pick up on the sarcasm. *He's definitely not like the dragon I know.*

"I still owe you one of your demands." The huge dragon

headed toward the very back of the sealed-in cave, opened the immense claws that had snatched her from the sky, and drew them down the back of the wall. The sound grated so harshly, she clapped her hands over her ears and grimaced. Sparks exploded at the back of the cave, followed by chunks of wall that crumbled away as if the beast had clawed at cheese instead. "The mountain bleeds here, little mage. Now you have everything you need to fulfill your promise."

With a final intense stare that lasted five seconds—she counted—Po snorted and turned to leave the cavern in a burst of echoing screeches on stone and flurried sparks. The chamber filled with the roaring grumble of the ancient dragon sealing her in with what she assumed was a giant rock before everything fell silent.

Raven sighed wearily and wiped a sheen of sweat from her forehead. *I didn't promise anything. But I didn't not promise anything, either.*

Licking her lips, she peered at the back of the cave and frowned. "The mountain bleeds?"

When the sound of trickling, dripping water reached her, she leapt forward. "Oh!"

Sure enough, the trenches the great dragon had carve into the cavern wall now glistened with thin streams of water. Quickly, she cupped her hands beneath the section of wall that released a tiny stream of cool water, and when that wasn't fast enough, she knelt and opened her mouth beneath it.

She knelt there beneath the stream for a long time before she finally stood, her knees damp, and wiped her mouth. "Po dug me my own drinking fountain. How nice."

Turning, she surveyed the cavern and the crevasse in the ceiling. *In the mountains, in some kind of stone valley, near a river. Keep narrowing it down.*

With her thirst assuaged, she stretched the crick in her neck out and returned to her satchel. Crossing her legs beneath her on the stone, she settled her hands on her thighs and closed her eyes. *We all thought Alessandra's meditations were a waste of time. It might be the only thing that saves me now.*

Pulling up the memory of the stone valley outside and all the ancient dragons staring at her from their perches, she focused intently and reached out with her mind and her heart for Leander. *A mage can communicate to her familiar. I simply gotta find the sweet spot.*

The sun passed over the cave as Raven sat and meditated and tried to send Leander an image of where she was. She got up twice for more water and went right back to work. By the time the light falling through the crevasse in the ceiling faded into the muted gold of sunset, her growling stomach was too loud and painful to ignore.

She opened her eyes and sighed. "This isn't gonna work. He's too far away. Not even an all-day meditation session is enough to—"

An image entered her mind in a flash—a bird's-eye view of the Mountains of Jared's southern range and a feeling of urgency.

"No way." She froze and broke into a huge grin. "I did it! He saw my thoughts. Or at least I connected with him somehow."

Raven closed her eyes again and tried to settle the

butterflies in her stomach. *One more time to make sure he sees it all.*

Two minutes later, Leander sent her another image. In her mind, she saw a fleet of dragons of every color streaking through the sky with their riders. William and Teo were among them, but she didn't recognize the others. Leander had, however, made sure to include what he saw when he turned his head on his long neck to look behind him.

Headmaster Flynn sat astride her dragon familiar, his fingers loose around the harness where they rested on the pommel of his black saddle from his days as a dragon rider.

"Ha!" Her voice cracked through the cavern and echoed to her. She clamped both hands over her mouth and stared at the far side of the cave. *They did it! They're coming! And he actually let Flynn—*

She blinked away the tears forming in her eyes and focused on steadying her breathing. *Don't freak out, mage. There's still too much to do before you're out of here.*

Despite her impatience, she waited until nightfall, when the stars came out and filled the crevasse in the ceiling with twinkling lights. She summoned all her energy and raised her hands. *I seriously hope he knows this one.*

"*Loquimi magus.*" The light of the Full Appearance bloomed between her hands and the strong magic tingled up her fingertips and into her arms. She held steady and waited for the image to focus.

Headmaster Flynn looked up from the table in his room at the inn and the quill dropped from his fingers onto the wood. "Raven."

"Headmaster." She grinned. "I have to say I'm *very* glad you know this spell."

He cleared his throat and focused on her. "So am I. How did you—"

"You can thank Alessandra's master training techniques for this one." He didn't echo her joking smile and she glanced quickly at the tunnel out of the cave. "I don't know how much time I have, but I wanted you to know that I—"

"Managed to get through to Leander. Yes, I am aware. He told us the second we landed outside Morningstar City."

"Oh. Good. That's…really far north."

"So is Windroot Pass. Based on what Leander and your friends have told us, that's where we think you are. We should reach you at some point tomorrow."

She sighed with relief and couldn't keep the smile off her face. "Thank you."

"There's no need."

"Did he tell you about the dragons?"

Flynn frowned. "He tried. I imagine it's difficult to accurately describe an image in one's mind, no matter how clear. He said they were huge."

"That's something of an understatement. Listen, I couldn't send Leander information beyond what I could see, so that's why I connected with you. The five dragons keeping me here are—"

"From across the sea. Your friends explained a fair amount yesterday before we left. They believe they were awakened from some form of slumber because magic has been misused and they have convinced themselves it is their duty to free the dragons of Lomberdoon from apparent mistreatment. Focusing on the dragon ranches first."

"Wow, they really did tell you everything."

"We put a few of the pieces together ourselves as well. Mostly, that was your friend William Moss."

"Leander showed me he was with you." Raven's heart fluttered in her chest. "I found out a few more things today. They feel like the most important."

"I'm listening."

"I have running water here, so wherever I am, there's water close by. A river or a lake or something. And the black dragon here—I think he's their leader— was *very* interested in what I had to say about mages and dragons working together. Especially as familiars."

Headmaster Flynn's eyes widened. "Go on."

"The others don't want to hear any of it but this one does. He thinks I can commune with magic to discover why they were...called across the sea, I guess but he wanted to know more about the connection Leander and I have. I don't know why, but when you and the others reach the valley here, don't send riders. You probably shouldn't come either, Headmaster. No offense."

"None taken, Miss Alby."

"But send a few dragons. I think we can talk our way out of this. The black dragon is curious enough to hear us out. Leander and Teo will know what to do. Teo and William have a great relationship. That might be a plus for defending the dragon trainers and their ranches, at least, and Leander and I can show these other dragons what we can do together. That way, they'll see I'm not his master, only his friend."

The man nodded. "I will talk to them all in the morning and we will form a plan to incorporate what you've told me."

"Okay. I—" Raven gritted her teeth and glanced at her shaking hands.

"End the spell, Miss Alby." The headmaster lowered his head. "It's all right. You've done very well."

She smiled weakly at him. "See you soon."

As soon as she disconnected the Full Appearance, she slumped over her crossed legs, completely exhausted. Once she regained enough strength to move, she lowered herself slowly to the cold stone floor and curled around her satchel. *We did it. They're coming. I gotta be extra careful from here on out.*

The young mage closed her eyes and let her exhaustion pull her into sleep.

In the secret, dusty room of the king's fortress in Havendom, Connor Alby leaned forward over the table and widened his eyes at the woman seated across the table. "What have you heard from the other kingdoms?"

War Mage Kyree Athena took a deep breath. *He'll like what I have to say as much as he did the last time we met.* "Only rumors. An overturned cart or a split tree, none of which are exactly unnatural occurrences."

He thumped back in his chair and grunted. "That can't be all, Kyree. I refuse to believe Lomberdoon is the only kingdom on the continent with visible changes."

"Visible only to people looking for them." She shook

her head. "We're leaving no stone unturned, Connor. I assure you. But the process to find this kind of information isn't exactly something that's been tested and laid out for us. There's no precedent for this."

"We're *creating* the precedent!" The man thumped his fist onto the table with a puff of layered dust. "That's why we have to do this right. We must build the foundation now so that when the time comes, this kingdom doesn't descend into terror and chaos. Because it will be terrifying. Believe me. I've seen what happens when those with magic can't control it."

She waited for his outburst to end and stared solemnly at the man who'd put more effort into this search than she'd expected of him in the beginning. *We're both full of surprises, aren't we?* "Are you finished?"

Connor cleared his throat. "Yes. I apologize."

"I'll accept your apology on the condition that you don't raise your voice to me again."

"That's a fair request." The man swallowed and sighed heavily. "I'm tired, Kyree. I put my entire life aside—the life I built for myself and my granddaughter—to follow this wild goose chase. Although I know it's not only a chase."

"I agree. There is an answer."

"And I intend to find it. With your help, I really do believe we can do this."

She inclined her head toward him and her blonde bob framed her face. "So do I. These things take time and patience."

"I'm very much aware of that, thank you."

Kyree smirked as the veteran dragon rider folded his arms and scowled at the table. "I do have something that may interest you very much. The Consortium won't take this as proof, I'm sure, but it's proof enough for me."

He looked impatiently at her. "What is it?"

"You said your magic returned to you years after you believed you were spent."

"I did."

Kyree raised one hand over the table, her fingers pointed at the ceiling. "Do you know why I wear these gloves?"

The man's lips twitched into the ghost of a smile. "There was hardly enough information to find on your background or your status with the Consortium. It didn't include your wardrobe choices."

She chuckled wryly and grasped the fingertips of her black leather glove with the other hand. "I was badly injured during the Great War. I was sixteen at the time, the same age as your granddaughter, I believe. So of course, I didn't fight in the true battles. But when the Swarm attacked Sethvarin, the people there turned to using what weapons we did have. Burning pitch was one of them. The city panicked. I panicked and I paid a high price for it. I started wearing these gloves halfway through my first year of school at Mandrose Academy, mainly to keep the other young mages from staring."

"I'm sorry to hear that," he said softly. "And I'm glad to know it didn't stop you from becoming what you are today. But I don't see how that—"

Kyree stared at him and slipped her hand out of the long leather glove that reached all the way to her elbow. Then, she thumped that elbow on the table and twisted her hand and wrist under the low light in the dusty abandoned room so he could get a better look.

"No…" He frowned and leaned forward to stare at the smooth, unmarred skin of the woman's forearm, wrist, and hand. "Is it—"

"Not an illusion." She extended her hand so he could take it, he ran his fingers quickly along her smooth skin before he leaned back in his chair with wide eyes. "For almost two-thirds of my life I've worn gloves like these. I'd given up trying to find a spell that would rid me of the scars and the phantom pain. A month ago, they were no longer necessary and I can't tell you why."

Connor rubbed his mouth and met her gaze again. "But you suspect."

"I suspect my scars were healed in the same way that magic returned to a spent wizard living out the rest of his days as a reclusive goat-rancher with his granddaughter."

"Who have you told?"

"No one. And I don't plan to until we've made a strong enough case to take to the Consortium. We'll reveal everything we've found at that time, including this." She raised her hand before she slid it back into the black leather glove. "This is about timing as much as it is about proof."

"I know that." He tapped a finger against his lips and stared at her gloved hands again. She rested them in her lap. "I've arranged a visit with—"

He frowned and leaned back when a shimmering circle of light wavered into existence in front of him and hovered over the table.

"It looks like someone's trying to reach you."

The man licked his lips. "I haven't seen this in quite some time."

"I'll leave you to it, then. Wait for my next message. I'll let you know when it's safe to meet again." Kyree stood and her chair scooted back with a muffled sound across the dust-layered floor.

"Connor." The man's voice that came from the other side of the Full Appearance spell sounded urgent and slightly unsure.

"What's going on?" he asked.

Kyree slipped through the door and into the dark hall but not before she caught a glimpse of the man who'd cast the spell to speak to Connor Alby. *It looks like the past is catching up with all of us.*

CHAPTER TWENTY-NINE

Raven was jerked awake the next morning by the sound of the massive boulder outside the cave being rolled aside once more. The screech of Po's claws and spines scraping against the walls preceded him before his gargantuan head appeared at the end of the tunnel.

"Outside, tiny mage. You may take your meal and then, we will speak."

She pushed off the stone and rubbed the back of her neck with a grimace. "I'm coming."

A short stop at the trickling water for a drink and to splash her face woke her fully. She slung her satchel over her shoulder and headed toward the bright light that spilled through the mouth of the tunnel.

Po sat in his usual place to her right and shielded her from the buffeting wind that howled through the stone valley below them. He'd already prepared her breakfast which fortunately, hadn't been rolled in dust and pebbles this time.

Raven picked it up and almost dropped it again in

surprise. *It's still warm.* She looked at the black dragon and smiled politely. "Thank you."

"Eat. We have much to discuss."

She glanced around the desolate landscape and gnawed on whatever part of whatever animal the beast had cooked for her. "Where are the others?"

"They do not wish to be seen. But they are here."

Great. I seriously hope these aren't giant, ancient dragons who can also make themselves invisible. That might be more than we can handle.

At Sunrush Dragon Ranch outside Morningstar City, Headmaster Flynn and William Moss gathered with the fleet of riders and dragon trainers to discuss the slight change in plans. Flynn relayed what Raven had told him the night before and more than a few options were discussed as to how they could succeed with this rescue.

When the details of the final plan were set, the headmaster of Fowler Academy turned toward Leander and Teo and inclined his head. "Is this something you two are willing to do?"

"You know where I stand, mage," Leander replied.

"Indeed. Teo?"

The green dragon studied the veteran dragon rider and narrowed his silver eyes. "I am willing. For Raven."

"Excellent. I want to thank you both, although I know you're not doing it for me."

The dragons lowered their heads in solemn bows. Flynn walked away to approach a handful of other riders who thought their dragons could handle what was being asked of them.

With a gentle tug on Teo's harness, William led his dragon away from the fleet for a private conversation. "Flynn asked you before I even had the chance. I know you're willing, Teo. And I know I don't have to question your loyalty to me. But I can't help but wonder—"

"If a trained dragon without a rider or a mage to direct him can fly alone to save a girl from monsters?" He focused his gaze on his trainer and snorted.

"Well, yeah…I guess." William chuckled. "When you put it like that, it seems simple."

"I believe it will be simple, William. And I believe I can do it. I will follow Leander and that should be enough."

"Good." He turned to study the other trainers and riders as they saddled their dragons and made last-minute preparations before the fleet began the journey farther north into the mountains. "What about the others?"

"I cannot speak for the others but they know what's at stake. I think they will try."

"Yeah, that's the most we can ask of anyone here, isn't it?"

Teo lowered his head again. "Indeed."

"But promise me one thing." William looked at his dragon and patted the sinuous silver neck. "You get out of there at the first sign of trouble. Got it? There's a time for being heroic but taking on a beast ten times your size and who knows how old is plain stupid."

"I am not a war dragon, William."

The trainer smiled. "I know. But promise me."

"As you wish. You have my word."

"Thank you."

When Headmaster Flynn finished his conversation with the other riders and their dragons who had volunteered, he returned to Leander and bowed slightly at the waist. The dragon acknowledged him politely. "Are you ready?"

"Always."

"Good. Then would you be so kind as to—"

Leander lowered himself onto his belly so the headmaster could climb into the stirrup.

He chuckled. "I know you're not my dragon or my familiar, but I can't help the feeling that you can read my mind."

The dragon snorted. "You're not the first. Get on, mage."

Still smiling, the headmaster stepped into the stirrup and swung his leg over the black dragon saddle he hadn't ridden in fifty years. He adjusted his seat, gazed at the gathered fleet of dragons, and whistled loudly. "Mount up, riders. It's time to bring Raven Alby home."

Riders stepped into saddles and within minutes, the fleet of over a dozen dragons took to the sky outside Morningstar City, led by Leander with the headmaster of Fowler Academy on his back. Flynn left the harness wrapped around the pommel of the saddle and didn't touch it at all.

"Now tell me, tiny mage. How does a familiar benefit from accepting such a position?" Po had lowered himself onto his belly on the protruding ledge outside the cave and even lying down, he was large enough to block the buffeting wind.

"Well, companionship, first of all." Raven leaned back and propped herself up with her hands on the cool stone. "I told you Leander and I are friends. And that's—" She belched and followed it with a surprised chuckle. "Excuse me."

"Continue."

She darted the huge black dragon a sidelong glance. *He's not offended by burping after breakfast so ancient-dragon etiquette only goes so far.* "A familiar forms a special bond with their mage. Not as a pet or a mount or a work animal but more like equals."

"But a familiar cannot practice magic."

"Well...no." She squinted at the rocky valley. "Mainly because they're animals, I think. And dragons, of course. Only humans have magic, and not all of us. But every familiar has some kind of magical property. It's inherent in them, even without bonding with a mage. The mage merely...brings it out."

"And what does the mage receive in return?"

The girl opened her mouth to answer but another image from Leander burst into her mind. He was in the air again and wheeled to show her the view of most of the fleet settled on a rocky ledge below a massive ridge of sharp, jutting stone. William, Headmaster Flynn, and three other riders stood on the ground and looked at Leander. Teo and three other dragons, their saddles and harnesses removed, soared toward the ridge above the fleet in tight formation.

They're here.

Raven's heart fluttered and she straightened over her crossed legs.

"I asked you a question," Po growled.

"Sorry." She thumped a fist against her chest and shrugged, burped again, and sighed. "There it is."

I can't keep counting on coincidence and I can't keep lying. Things are about to get intense.

"What a mage gets from their familiar," she mused. "Well, first, a familiar helps to focus their mage's abilities. It takes tremendous concentration to cast any kind of spell at first, when you're starting out. Building a bond with a familiar helps kickstart that, in a way."

"And what of mages who already understand their own potential?" He watched her with one golden eye, which flicked up and down by centimeters to take in her entire body.

"Well, the last part's still true. Familiars help their mage focus, even an experienced mage. They add power and force to a mage's magic. So a spell cast with a familiar's added intention is much better than without it."

Leander sent her another image of the five dragons reaching the top peak of the ridge. *Almost.*

"That hardly interests me." Po snorted and a spray of dust and small rocks hurtle over the edge of the precipice. "What else?"

Raven pushed to her feet and turned her face to the small gusts of wind that streamed over the ancient black dragon's hide. "My favorite part, so far, is that a mage and her familiar can communicate with each other across distances—almost like reading minds."

His eye widened and he glanced at the five comparatively tiny dragons who glided over the highest edge of the valley behind them. He screeched and a heavy shower of large rocks tumbling from the walls beside the cave entrance. "What is this?"

"Do you see that red one?" She looked at him with quiet pride, her affection for Leander bright in her eyes. "That's my familiar."

Two more earsplitting shrieks rose from opposite ends of the valley. The monstrous gold dragon emerged first and her scales glinted in the sunlight. Moments later, the white male appeared out of another cave below and stretched his neck toward the five dragons circling in the valley.

"Why are they here?" Po demanded quickly and stood with a growl.

"For me. Nothing comes between a mage and her dragon, Po. Didn't I tell you that?"

Right on cue, Leander swooped down and landed on the wide ledge on the other side of the cave. He kept his wings spread wide with sufficient room and lowered his head toward the massive black beast that could have eaten him in one bite. "She's mine."

With a shout of relief, Raven ran toward him. She barreled into his broad chest and wrapped her arms around the base of his neck. "You're here!"

"Of course I'm here. Are you all right?"

She released him and stepped back as she wiped the tears from the corners of her eyes. "I'm fine. But we have to—"

"Stop!" Po roared. The other ancient dragons bellowed

in response seconds before Teo and the three riderless dragons landed on the ledge beside Leander.

Behind them, the emerald-green beast emerged slowly and sniffed the air. "They smell like humans." He opened his huge jaws to expose the flaring light of dragon fire glowing in the back of his throat.

The black dragon snarled. "I will rip you to pieces, brother. Hold!"

The green male snapped his jaws shut with a deafening crack and a puff of smoke.

"We will hear from the mage and this dragon familiar," Po shouted. "Then I will decide."

The silver dragon leered at them across the valley beside the white male and hissed. "That is not your decision to—"

"It is *always* my decision," he roared. "Be silent!" After ensuring that his brethren wouldn't challenge him further, the beast lowered his head and fixed his huge golden eyes on the five dragons and the young redheaded mage. "I have heard interesting details from the tiny mage. You will tell me, red one, of being a dragon familiar."

Leander lowered his head until it hovered over Raven's shoulder and muttered, "What does he want to hear?"

"The truth, Leander. That's the only thing that's gonna get us out of here."

He stepped forward and brushed her gently behind him with a twitch of his wing. "I could take her right now and be gone."

"You could not." Po's rumble amusement made her head vibrate. "I swatted you from the sky like an insect, red one. If you deceive me, I will know. If you try to escape without telling me what I wish to hear, I will know. And none of you will leave this valley alive."

Leander growled and stood his ground. "Raven Alby is my mage. And my friend."

"So I've heard." The black dragon sat on his haunches and lowered his massive head. "Continue."

"I would have been one of those flightless dragons you tore apart if it weren't for her."

"Abominations!" the silver female shrieked.

"They have shamed themselves," the green male hissed.

"No." Leander stared at Po, but his voice carried across the valley. "Those were the dragons who refused to be trained, knowing full well what would become of them if they did not relent. I was the same until Raven showed me another way."

"As her familiar," Po rumbled.

"Yes. She broke the ways of training dragons and let me choose who I wanted to be. In return, I chose to be her familiar and I wouldn't change a thing."

Behind him, Raven folded her arms and smiled. *He's got this.*

"And what of these other dragons?" The black dragon sniffed the air and studied Teo and the three others who'd come to negotiate with the monstrous beasts from across the sea. "They are trained."

"We are." Teo stepped forward slowly, his silver eyes wide. "I cannot remember the last time I flew beyond the ranch I call home without my rider. Most of us never do."

"Imprisoned!" the gold female shrieked.

"Never." Teo turned his head to focus on the female, his confidence unwavering. "William Moss is his name. He has no magic and I am not a familiar but I call him my friend as well. He provides everything I need. Food, shelter, and space to roam with my clan. I allow him to put a saddle on my back and fly with me in return."

"And you...enjoy this arrangement?" Po's voice was much softer now and openly curious.

"It is a good life. Yes."

The brown dragon beside him nodded. "My trainer's name is Katerina Daverin. I hatched with a deformed paw, but she treated me no differently than the other dragons in my clan. No one believed I would be of much use. I now fly with the second-in-command of the kingdom's military fleet in Delton's Crossing. I have everything I need and more."

Raven glanced at the brown female with wide eyes and the dragon nodded and fell silent.

Po snorted. "You did not bring your riders. Why?"

"To show you that we've come for Raven Alby," Teo replied. "To take her home. Nothing more."

"You would do this for a mage who is not your own?"

"We do it for her," a gray dragon on the other side of Teo answered. "For our riders, too, and for the dragons who've lost the good lives they've had to destruction."

Raven grimaced. *Don't blame the monster holding me captive.*

"I see." Po stood to his full height and stretched his long neck toward the sky. "Have you heard?"

The other four dragons raised their heads and screeched.

"I have decided, tiny mage." The black beast lowered his head toward Raven and the five much smaller dragons. "I believe the testimony of these dragons. I believe your familiar. But I wish to know once more—"

"Lies!" The emerald-green male jerked his head up and hissed. "Look at what they bring while they deceive you?"

Every head looked up to see another dragon circling toward the valley from the northeast. This one was fully saddled and carried two riders on her back.

She swallowed. "Oh, no."

"You." Po glared at her and exhaled two massive clouds of black smoke.

"I don't know who that is," she replied and curled her hands into fists. "No one else was supposed to come."

The green dragon opened his mouth and launched a column of fire into the sky as the dragon with two riders passed overhead and soared over the top of the highest valley ridge behind the cave. The dragon screeched and barely escaped the flames.

"You dare to think you can distract us while you bring more mages here?" The black dragon dug his claws into the ledge beneath him and threw up showers of sparks and pieces of stone as the other four dragons bellowed in anger. "More humans on another beast of burden?"

"No!" Raven stepped forward and shook her head. "That's not—"

"Stand back, Raven." Leander lowered his head in front of her to stop her. "And be ready."

Po snorted more clouds of black smoke and roared. "You are nothing like you claim, tiny mage. And the rest of you runts are traitors to your entire kind. You let your-selves be used for this—"

"Go!" Leander shouted. Teo and the three riderless

dragons vaulted skyward and darted toward the ridge to swoop down to safety.

The white dragon screeched and leapt from his perch in the valley. His massive shadow blocked out all light on the ledge where Raven stood as he unleashed more fire at the retreating dragons. Steel-like claws shrieked against the top of the ledge when he landed above her and Leander to peer after the escapees.

A massive boulder broke free and tumbled down the side of the ledge. Leander shoved his head into her back and threw her forward. They both escaped the rock that hurtled toward them before it bounced and toppled over the ledge.

The white beast snarled. "There are more!"

"*What?*"

"Dragons and riders below. You've been eating lies, brother."

"Impossible!"

Raven pushed herself off her knees as Leander nudged her shoulder in concern. "Are you hurt?"

She turned and caught his muzzle with both hands. "No. You?"

"I'm fine."

"You will never leave this valley, human," Po declared. "I will finally enjoy that snack."

To steady herself, she looked into Leander's glowing yellow eyes and swallowed. "We're not giving up now, right?"

"Never."

The black dragon reared and opened his mouth. Fire built in his throat with a hiss.

"Okay. On three. One…" She let go and nodded. "Two…"

"*Verecundia!*" The voice resounded over the valley, and a bolt of blue light crackled from behind Po's head all the way to the jagged cliffs on the other side.

The black dragon's jaw snapped shut, and as he whirled to face the source, his barbed scales scraped against the stone wall and sparked.

"*Absolutio lychnus!*" The blue light crackled toward the valley floor, and while he lowered his head to follow its descent, a shower of small pebbles fell from another narrow shelf above the black beast. The falling rubble came closer and closer toward her and the soles of black boots appeared at the edge of the stone ledge. "*Erigo.*"

The boots illuminated with white light before someone leapt over the edge, and a man in a dark cloak surrounded by the light of his own levitation spell descended to the stone between Raven Alby and her infuriated captor.

CHAPTER THIRTY

When the blinding light faded, Raven gasped and lurched forward. "Grandpa!"

Connor Alby turned and the edges of his cloak whipped in the buffeting wind. He held a hand out for her to wait. "Almost, Raven. Be ready."

"What is this?" Po spun again, scraped against the walls, and released huge showers of sparks.

The old man didn't even flinch. "My name is Connor Alby, mage and dragon rider. I've come to speak to you in person, great one, and to take Raven and Leander home."

The dragon snorted and his black, scaly lips glistened as they peeled back to expose teeth almost as long as the man who stood before him. "You would risk yourself here for this hatchling?"

With a thin smile, the man tilted his head and stared at the black beast. "That hatchling is my granddaughter. And at this point, she is all I have left to lose. If you want the truth about what mages and dragons have accomplished together, let me show you."

The white dragon perched on top of the ridge shifted to turn and more loose boulders tumbled down the mountain on both sides. "More deception."

"Enough." Po looked at him and snarled. "A mage who came here willingly must have something to say. I will listen."

With a screech, the white dragon launched from the ridge and swooped across the valley to return to his roost, hissing until he disappeared inside another huge cave.

Raven and Leander stepped toward the other side of the tunnel entrance. "What does he mean?" he asked

The young mage shook her head. "I have no idea."

"What have you come to show me, mage?" Po rumbled.

Connor gestured with both hands. "Everything I know."

With a snort, the dragon narrowed his huge golden eyes and lowered his head slowly. "If you lie—"

"You'll smell it. Yes. I came to bring you the truth, dragon. Do you want it or not?"

"Show me." The black beast's nostrils flared as he lowered his head all the way to Connor's outstretched hands. Mage and ancient dragon touched and the entire valley fell still.

A glowing orb of opalescent light erupted where his hands touched Po's snout. It bloomed in shimmering, rippling colors until it formed a dome over them and held them within the mage's immense magic and his ability to commune with a beast from across the sea.

He focused his entire being on the memories of his time spent training to become a mage. The images flashed in his mind as he shared them with Po—sparring in the field at Fowler Academy, meeting his dull-yellow dragon Honalei at a ranch outside Havendom, his first flight upon her back, and the bond they shared when he was still young and capable of anything he wished. The memories expanded to the rest of Lomberdoon to show military fleets of dragons training with their riders, laughing, and enjoying each other's company. He thought of patrols, of dragons soaring in droves with their mages and riders to fight the Swarm in the Great War and of dragons helping to build the wall around the kingdom for protection and peace.

Something else flashed through Connor Alby's mind—a memory he did not recognize. The kingdom of Lomberdoon in the beginning, when all but the capital city had yet to be established. Dragons roosted along the fortress walls that now housed King Vaughn. There had been dragons then too.

I knew this would happen.

When he finished, the man removed his hands from the ancient beast's black scaly snout and stepped back, breathing heavily.

The dome of powerful magic winked out, and Po took a deep, hissed breath. He'd closed his eyes when Connor's mind had touched his, and he kept them closed as he lowered himself to the ground and settled his mighty head on the stone in front of the veteran dragon rider.

Raven's mouth had run dry, and she shut it slowly and frowned at her grandfather. "Did he…"

"I believe he did." Leander tilted his head and peered at Connor and the huge black beast lying like a trained dog at the man's feet. "His familiar was a dragon, was she not?"

"Yeah. He never told me he could do that."

"Now you know what we can do."

She set a hand on her dragon's shoulder to steady herself and to gain comfort from a friend.

Finally, Po opened his golden eyes and stared intently at the man. "I do not understand."

"It was plain enough," he replied. He swayed, shook his head, and sat to keep from falling. "Ask, and I will explain as best I can."

"Dragons and humans...and *mages*..." The golden eyes narrowed. "If they are so connected as you've shown me, why were we awakened? Why were my brethren and I called from across the sea if not to right the wrongs against our own kind?"

"Ah. I'm sorry. That question has an answer I simply can't give you. But I have a theory."

"Give it, mage."

"I believe that magic as we've known it and used it for hundreds of years is...changing. It's returning to the way it once was before it became a tool only for witches and wizards with magic in their blood. Magic is slowly seeping back into the world, and while I don't yet know why, I intend to find out. Maybe that's what woke you and your kind in the first place. It could be that the magic in Threndor and the dragons here who are such an integral part of our lives called you to us."

"A theory." The black dragon growled softly.

"Yes. I've been looking for my own answers, very much like you have. If we can form a truce, great one—the five from across the sea and the kingdom of Lomberdoon as one—I will tell you everything I know as soon as I discover it."

"You would return?"

"I *will* return. I can't say when, but I give you my word."

Po sucked in another sibilant breath and raised his head up from the ground. "We lived for centuries and slept for longer, mage. We will wait."

"This only works if you stop the attacks on the dragon ranches and farms across the kingdom. No hunting, either. You may stay in these mountains, if you like. There are no towns or villages nearby. And of course, the lands beyond the wall encircling Lomberdoon belong to no one, although I have to include any manmade property raising livestock beyond the wall."

"There are plenty of other creatures to meet our needs." The massive beast turned his head to face the valley and the four ancient dragons watching the exchange. "I accept such a truce, mage. And I hold you to your word."

"As I hold you to yours." Connor pushed to his feet and brushed his cloak and pantlegs off. "Now, I would very much like to take my granddaughter and her dragon home."

"Go. I no longer need her."

The other massive dragons screeched and bellowed around the valley as Connor returned to Raven. He stumbled once and she raced toward him before he wrapped her in a crushing hug.

"That was incredible!"

"Was it?" He chuckled weakly. "I hardly noticed."

"It's so good to see you. How did you know where I was? How did you even get here—"

"Later, girl." He cupped her cheek and nodded, his blue eyes sparkling. "Right now, we need to leave."

"Right. Leander?"

"I have carried two before." The dragon lowered himself to his belly and winked at Connor. "It will be fun."

The veteran dragon rider eyed his glistening red back with hesitation. "You have no saddle."

"That's been a thing for a while, Grandpa. Come on." Raven took his hand and led him toward Leander's tail. "Do what I do." The mage stepped as high as she could onto Leander's tail and walked swiftly up the ridges of his long back until she reached his shoulders. "It's okay."

"My word." Connor swept his gaze over the expanse of dragon he was about to walk on. "All right." He stepped up with a grunt, his arms held out at his sides, and walked slowly up Leander's spine. "Incredible."

"Yep." She glanced away from him and saw the emerald-green dragon watching them from his cavern on the other side of the wide ridge. The beast's huge nostrils flared as his shimmering green eyes narrowed. "I think we should hurry."

"It's a little…" The old man finally reached her, and they crouched to straddle Leander's back where a saddle should have been. "There's nothing to hold onto, Raven."

She patted her thighs and gave him a reassuring smile over her shoulder. "Just squeeze."

"Ha. Simple, is it?"

Leander rose gently to his feet, and Connor clamped his hands on his granddaughter's shoulders.

"It's okay, Grandpa. You'll be fine."

The dragon turned his head as far as he could on his long neck and muttered, "They're very quiet."

"I know." Raven glanced around the valley. Po stared

blankly at the ledge and seemed to be considering everything he'd learned. The other ancient dragons continued to stare at the young mage and her dragon. "I don't think they like the deal you made, Grandpa."

"Hmm." Connor raised his head toward Po. "You've given us leave to fly, great one. I hope your kin will agree."

Po's eyes darted toward the small red dragon and the two riders. "If they do not, they will still obey. Go."

Leander headed swiftly toward the edge of the stone shelf and spread his wings. "Hold on."

"To *what?*" the old man shouted as the red dragon leapt from the precipice and took flight.

They wheeled up and around the valley to pass over the highest ridge. The ancient dragons shrieked and bellowed.

"No truce with traitors!" the emerald male screamed and slithered from his hole in the mountainside with a burst of sparks.

"Hold!" Po roared.

The dragon didn't listen. He rocketed into the sky after Leander with a snarl and dislodged an overhanging ledge from the rock wall with the force of his wingbeats and his claws scrabbling to kick off from the mountain.

The gold, silver, and white beasts launched from their perches after him with rage-fueled screeches and roared. They separated and went in different directions to circle the valley to position themselves for a multi-sided attack.

The emerald male behind them snapped his mighty jaws at Leander's tail. The dragon familiar dove—which elicited a shout of surprise from Connor—and narrowly avoided losing the end of his tail.

"That wasn't supposed to happen!" Raven shouted.

"I know." Her grandfather turned to look over his shoulder as the four dragons headed toward them.

Po bellowed and leapt atop the highest ridge to watch the chase.

"I knew it felt too easy."

"What do we do?"

"Leander," Connor shouted. "Lead them away from the fleet. Flynn and the others need time to get away."

The red dragon banked and turned right and away from the dozen dragons and their riders gathered on a rocky slat outside the valley. The green beast darted after them, and the white one headed directly to the fleet.

"No!"

The attacker opened his mouth and unleashed a massive column of fire at the gathered dragons on the ground.

Leander turned back so swiftly, Connor shifted sideways and clamped his arms around Raven's waist as she extended her hand and shouted, *"Sequantur flamma!"*

The fire stopped mere yards above the startled fleet and splashed against her magic. The red dragon banked around the fleet and roared, "Get out!"

Her arms shook as she held the fire at bay. Then, she pushed with all her strength and the churning column of flames streaked into the sky and engulfed the ancient silver dragon. She screeched and faltered, losing height as she struggled to right her wings. The silver beast barely escaped impact with the mountainside, but she broke off a huge chunk of stone from the ridge that towered over the valley before she disappeared over the other side.

"Verecundia!" Connor shouted. The blue lightning bolt

launched from his hands and caught the underside of the white male's throat.

He screamed and followed it with a choked cough and a puff of smoke. Enraged, he banked toward Leander and shook his head.

The golden female dove toward the last of the riders still mounting their dragons. Leander swung toward her and unleashed a burst of flame at her head.

"*Sequantur flamma!*" Raven directed his attack into a pinpoint of flame toward the gold dragon's eye.

The female screeched as she flapped and fluttered to slow her descent with massive, deadly wingbeats. Once stable, she focused on Leander.

Raven's dragon familiar released another fiery attack, and she directed it again, this time toward the ancient beast's open mouth. His flames didn't stop, and she screamed in an effort to retain control as the golden dragon beat steadily toward them. The flames she held grew brighter as they shifted from orange to yellow, to white, and finally, a crackling blue.

Seconds before they would have collided, the golden female screamed and descended while Leander elevated. Raven and Connor leaned forward as far as they could, the man's cheek pressed against her satchel while the red dragon climbed into the sky. A massive thud and the scrabble of claws on stone rose below them, and when he leveled out, they saw the golden female scramble to her feet, shake her head, and snort.

"What was that?" Connor shouted.

"Something awesome," Raven replied. *Exactly like when we destroyed that Skiffling skull and buried the Swarm.*

Their attacker tossed her golden head before she became airborne again. This time, however, she retreated up and over the ridge to take shelter in the stone valley.

"You scared off a beast like that," the old man muttered.

Raven peered at him over her shoulder as Leander circled to continue his attempt to draw the ancient beasts away from the retreating fleet of Lomberdoon's dragons. "We've been busy while you were gone, Grandpa."

"Yes, I can see that—look out!"

The huge white male hurtled toward them from below. Leander dove out of the way, turned, and almost flew sideways to avoid the ancient dragon's beating wings. Fortunately, the male dragon apparently only intended to return to the valley. He landed on the highest ridge beside the section that had been demolished by one of his brethren's flailing bodies. The white beast raised his head to the sky, his massive wings outstretched, and uttered a shuddering bellow.

The mountain pass fell silent after that. Raven, Connor, and Leander scanned the cliffs below in search of the fleet.

"They got away," she muttered.

"Well done." Her grandfather wiped the sweat building above his brow and sighed heavily. "I think it's time we follow."

"Two more," Leander growled.

"What?"

"The green and the black."

"Po gave us his word." She scanned the mountains, searching for giant dragons too big to hide in the open. "He wouldn't go back on it. A dragon doesn't—"

A huge shadow passed over them and blotted out the

midday sun. The three looked up slowly to see the emerald-green dragon soaring above, his lips pulled back in a deadly dragon's grin. In the next moment, he opened his mouth and dove.

"Leander!" Raven screamed. "We—"

A black shadow streaked toward them out of nowhere and struck the attacker in the side. The emerald dragon screeched and tumbled to the stony shelf outside the valley to land amidst a spray of boulders and shards of shale in every direction. Leander dove again to escape the worst of it, then Po landed on top of his green counterpart and caught the male's neck between his massive jaws. The black beast whipped his head from side to side, the green dragon screamed, and Po stomped a forepaw on the other beast's shoulder and with a spray of sparks, turned his opponent onto his back. "You will *obey!*"

The aggressor fell still, his sides heaving and green eyes clenched shut. Despite no blood being drawn, the winner was clear.

"They *will* listen, mage," Po shouted after Leander and his riders. "Return before the frost!"

"Let's go." Raven patted her dragon's neck and stared over her shoulder at the ancient black monster who returned her look implacably.

Leander snorted and pushed even harder to leave the stone valley in the Windroot Pass behind. Raven stared ahead, her jaw set firmly after such a close call.

Behind her, Connor Alby didn't try to stop his granddaughter's bright red hair from whipping against his face as their flight continued. Nor did he raise a hand to wipe the tears carried away by the wind.

CHAPTER THIRTY-ONE

They met the rest of the dragon rescue fleet outside the small town of Parslen. The field was far enough from the road to not draw undue attention, and every rider was accounted for when Leander landed beyond the trees.

Raven slid from her dragon's back and draped her arms around his broad shoulder as far as she could. "You were amazing, Leander."

He swiveled his head toward her and rested the side of his muzzle against her back. "Yes, we were."

Connor grunted and swung his leg over Leander's back before he dropped onto the grass. "I understand the thrill, girl, but I still say a dragon rider needs a saddle." He rubbed the inside of his thighs and grimaced. "This is not for me."

She turned to face him and grinned. "Maybe you spent too much time *not* riding."

He straightened, met her gaze, and drew his brows together as he flashed her a pained smile.

Damn. This is not the right time to bring his dragon up. "I'm sorry. I didn't mean to—"

"No, you're absolutely right. It has been too long. And I rode two dragons today. I shouldn't complain." He pulled her in for another hug and buried his face in her red hair that fell over her shoulder. "I am so proud of you."

"Thank you." She pulled away and chuckled. "Mostly for coming to get us out of there. How did you know?"

"Connor!" Headmaster Flynn strode briskly toward them, his eyes wide. The expression accentuated the long scar down the side of his face before it was lost beneath his beard. "You made it."

The men embraced and clapped each other on the back. "Thanks to you. Plus Rider Bentler and Abigail, of course." Connor nodded at the rider in a smart flight uniform with a silver lapel and his dragon of such a dark-blue, she was almost black.

"Wait, you knew he was coming?" Raven asked Flynn.

The headmaster nodded with a small smile. "I'd be in trouble, otherwise, Miss Alby. I'm the one who called him."

Her grandfather smirked. "That's one hell of a way to show your headmaster that you've learned the Full Appearance."

Raven grinned.

"And that she learned it far quicker than either of us did," Flynn added. "I was really quite impressed."

"Thanks. I had more than enough time in that cave to practice."

"Among other things, I'm sure." He tugged his beard and glanced at Leander. "I used the same spell last night to contact your grandfather, Miss Alby. There's unspoken knowledge between mages that the Full Appearance is used for emergencies."

"You guys have obviously already used it together."

"Once or twice." Connor nodded. "Many years ago."

"Raven!" William pushed through the gathered riders and ran toward her.

"Hey. You—"

He wrapped her in his arms, lifted her off her feet, and spun her in his excitement while everyone watched. She laughed when he set her down again. "Sorry. I'm sorry. You just—" He held her face between his hands and studied her from forehead to chin and back again. "I was so worried. I know you told me not to be, but this was different and I— Are you okay? Did they hurt you?"

"Um… William?"

"Yeah." He stared into her eyes, his brows raised as he waited for her to share bad news.

"I'm fine." She glanced at Connor and Headmaster Flynn beside them and chuckled. "I can tell you about everything later, okay?"

Leander rumbled in amusement.

Her grandfather cleared his throat, and the young trainer removed his hands instantly from her cheeks. "Right. Yeah, later." He ran a hand through his hair with a self-conscious chuckle, caught sight of Connor, and jumped. "Mr. Alby!"

"William. I have to say, I wasn't nearly as worried about how we'd pull this off when I heard you were riding with this fleet."

"Thank you, sir."

The two older men exchanged a knowing glance, and the headmaster inclined his head. "I told you."

"Always modest." Connor slapped a hand on William's

shoulder and gave him a quick shake. "I also heard you're the one who put the fleet together in the first place. And you didn't correct me."

"I didn't even think about it." William grinned and nodded at Raven. "The only thing that matters is that Raven's safe."

"That is the most important thing, yes." He removed his hand from the younger man's shoulder and glanced at Headmaster Flynn. "But there's more we need to discuss before we start south again."

"You're coming back with us?" Raven asked.

"For the night, Raven. We'll part ways again in the morning, but we'll discuss that later as well. Right now, we need to make sure everyone's on the same page. Riders!" Connor clapped and stepped toward the fleet.

"Connor!"

"It's Connor Alby."

"He didn't leave Brighton with us."

"I heard he never leaves Brighton."

Her grandfather raised his hands, nodded, and gestured for the riders to settle. "You did very well in coming together for this mission. So first, I want to extend my deepest gratitude to each and every one of you for risking your own safety to ensure my granddaughter's. Headmaster Flynn contacted me last night and explained the situation, so I also want to thank Rider Bentler and his dragon Abigail for setting aside their duties at the capital so I could join you.

"Yes, five enormous dragons are roosting in the valley east of Windroot Pass. Yes, they are ancient and powerful, as you all are quite aware. And yes, I spoke to them. Those dragons and I, on behalf of Lomberdoon, agreed to a truce. They will not touch another dragon ranch or farm within the great wall while they reside in that valley. The attacks over the last few days are extremely unfortunate, but they will not continue.

"But it's imperative that we leave them alone. Do not target them or seek to drive them out. I need as many riders as possible who can still head out today to spread the word across the kingdom. The capital will draw up warnings to post but for now, word of mouth flying in on dragons' wings is where we start. The Windroot Pass and especially the eastern valley beyond is forbidden to everyone. There will be fines, I imagine, for trespassers. At least, for those who manage to avoid being captured by the dragons who've agreed to this arrangement. No one is to approach Windroot Pass unless otherwise stated. The people need to know."

"I can leave now," one rider shouted.

"So can I."

"Us too."

"Thank you." Connor put a hand over his heart and nodded. "I'll leave it in your hands to decide the routes. Expect to hear from the capital. Your actions today won't go unseen."

The man turned and headed to Raven, Flynn, and William.

She stared at her grandfather. *This is Rider Alby. I've only known the rancher.*

"Now." The old man smiled at them. "I think it's best if we head as far south as we can for the next few hours and find a stable with enough space and an inn nearby. I imagine my granddaughter would enjoy a full meal and a soft bed."

Raven snorted. "You have no idea."

He gave her shoulder a reassuring squeeze. "And the four of us will have a chance to discuss the future in more detail."

"Did you find something?" Flynn asked.

"Almost. Dinner first." Connor pointed at the rider who'd brought him in from Havendom. "Rider Bentler will stay with us until they take me back in the morning. I'm quite sure he knows of the best place to stop for the night."

"We'll follow you." William nodded. "Headmaster, you're welcome to fly with Teo and me."

"Thank you, Mr. Moss." Flynn turned toward Leander with a smirk. "No offense."

The dragon snorted. "Raven's a better rider, anyway."

"Ha. I have no doubt." The man gave her a wink before he followed William to prepare Teo for two passengers and an extra saddle.

"Grandpa."

Connor paused and favored her with a gentle smile.

Raven approached him and lowered her voice. "Why didn't you tell the riders about the other part of your deal with Po?"

"With whom?"

"Oh. The giant black one."

"That's his name?"

"It's the one he gave me."

Her grandfather looked nonplussed for a moment before he fought back a laugh. "First of all, Raven, my business right now is none of anyone else's. I did not tell them because they simply don't need to know. Because now, we have ancient dragons from across the sea and magic is most certainly changing."

The Benicio Dragon Ranch was smaller than the others Raven and Leander had visited, but the owners were more than happy to accept coin for stabling three dragons overnight and lodging five travelers at the inn located on the ranch.

The party received the keys to their rooms and were shown out to the large side porch overlooking the ranch. Mr. Benicio's wife served them a full meal of spring vegetables, chicken pot pies, and berries with cream for dessert. Raven laughed when she'd cleared her plate and had a second helping of berries.

Seated beside her, William leaned over his plate and chuckled. "What?"

"I'm so glad beef wasn't on the menu tonight."

He frowned over a confused smile, and she laughed again.

"Giant dragon monsters aren't really the best cooks."

"They fed you beef?"

She shrugged. "I think so. Honestly, it was kind of hard to tell but it's not like I had any other options."

Shaking his head, he stared at the table. "I can't believe you were in a cave with those beasts for two days."

"Two and a half, really. And I was alone most of the time, so it wasn't as bad as it could've been." She grinned at him, but the dragon trainer didn't find it funny. "Hey. I'm okay. Thanks to you."

"You can forget about it just like that, huh?"

"There's no use in dwelling on it." She shrugged and picked her tin cup of water up. "I think I did well in there, all things considered.

He laughed when she lifted the cup toward him in a toast, then picked his up and clinked it against hers.

Connor watched them with a knowing smile and cleared his throat. "Now that dinner's out of the way and we're all fed… Unless you want more, Raven?" He gestured toward the berries.

"No. Definitely not."

"All right. There isn't much I can tell you all without making things even more complicated and confusing. We simply don't have the time before I return to the capital in the morning. But I will say this. I'm much closer than I was a few months ago to finding hard proof of magic's return. Not only to spent mages, mind you, but to people who haven't had magic in their family for years."

"Have you found anyone else who suspects the same?" Flynn asked.

Connor's face lit up as he looked at his old dragon-rider friend. "As a matter of fact, I've made contact several times with War Mage Athena. We're working together on this, although it's of a sensitive nature more along the lines of what she's used to dealing with."

"I see. And she agrees with you?"

"She does. I'm also quite certain she'll agree with me when I tell her of this situation with the very old, very large dragons taking residence at Windroot Pass."

"That magic woke them and brought them here, right?" William asked.

"Or that magic's return woke them indirectly and the creatures manufactured a purpose and a reason for something they couldn't explain. Whatever the answer is, I believe it lies somewhere along those lines, yes."

Raven set her cup down. "Who's War Mage Athena?"

"A friend. I hope. And that's as much as I can tell you for now, Raven. It took me long enough to find her myself." He turned to Headmaster Flynn again and leaned back in his chair. "It's been a bumpy road and we're not finished. Aiden, I may need Raven and Leander's help with this in the future."

"That's something you'll have to take up with them, Connor." Flynn raised his hands. "I merely run the school."

The men chuckled before Connor placed a hand on the table beside Raven's. "Would you be up for it? If I sent for you?"

Her eyes widened. "I don't know. Is it gonna mess with my finals?"

"Hmm...probably not. I expect to be at this for another month at least before being able to take any real action. So until then, the rest of your year at Fowler shouldn't be interrupted by anything else."

She snorted. "I wouldn't be so sure of that. It's already been more interrupted than I thought was possible."

"Yes. I've heard what you and that dragon have been up to, Raven."

"You have?"

Connor nodded and drained the last of his water. "Word travels fast, girl. It's hard not to hear something about the young mage Raven Alby and her dragon familiar Leander. Even in the capital."

She brushed the loose hair away from her face and smiled. "Wow."

"Wow is right." Her grandfather leaned toward her and grasped her wrist to give it a little squeeze. "I am *so* proud of you."

"Well." Headmaster Flynn pushed himself away from the table. "I think I'll turn in early tonight. There's been a marked lack of sleep all around. Good night."

"Good night, Headmaster." Raven and William nodded as the man stepped around the table and headed into the inn.

"I think that's the best thing for me now too." Connor stood as well and waited for her to join him. "I may not see you in the morning before we leave—"

"You'd better. I don't care if you have to wake up the whole inn banging on my door. You can't leave without saying goodbye."

He wrapped his granddaughter in another massive hug and squeezed her tightly. "Then I'll wake you if you haven't yet outgrown the habit of waking up before dawn."

"Not yet." Raven pulled away and held his shoulders. "I love you, Grandpa."

"I love you more, girl. Keep doing what you're doing. Except for being abducted by monsters." They both laughed and released each other. "Enjoy the rest of your evening. Mr. Moss."

"Good night, sir." William extended his hand and Connor grasped it firmly before he pulled the dragon trainer in for a firm hug.

"You've done very well too, William. Your father should be incredibly proud. Give him my best, will you?"

The young man bit his lip and nodded. The frown that flicked across his brow disappeared almost as quickly as it arrived. "I will."

With another smile and nod, Connor Alby turned and disappeared off the side porch into the inn.

CHAPTER THIRTY-TWO

"Wow." Raven wiped her forehead and drained the last of her water. "The last few days, huh?"

"And to think you were jumping off my roof five days ago."

Raven snorted and walked around the table to stand at the edge of the porch. The dragon ranch glowed with brilliant hues of orange, pink, and yellow as the sun set across the valley. Benicio Ranch only had about a dozen dragons in their paddock, all of whom still roamed freely out in the enclosure three-quarters of the size of Moss Ranch's field. "It doesn't matter how many dragons are around, does it? These are still happy."

"Looks like it, yeah." William joined her as she sat on the edge of the porch and dangled her feet over the edge. "It's a tricky thing to get right. You know, what makes a dragon happy. But once you do, it doesn't take much to keep it going."

"So I've noticed."

Leander trotted along the fence around the paddock, tossed his head, and spread his wings while a smaller light-brown male swatted playfully at him.

"He's become much better at making friends, hasn't he?"

Raven gave him a sidelong glance and smirked. "It depends on who those friends are and where he finds them. Haverson Ranch outside Dresdel is really—*was* really good for him. He was stuck there all day while I waited in a lobby and he didn't even notice. That's how much fun he had out there."

William chuckled. "What were you doing in a lobby?"

"Waiting for a meeting." The young mage rolled her eyes. "I spent five hours sitting in a chair to meet with an apparently super-important man. Only for two minutes in a room with him to deliver a letter."

"How did that go?"

"How do you think?" They shared a laugh and she leaned forward, her fingers curled over the edge of the porch. "It was awful. At least I'm absolutely sure now that I'm not cut out to be some kind of emissary mage once I graduate."

"I didn't know that was a thing."

"It is. We saw a few in Azerad. Bella would be way better at it than I would."

"Do mages ever get any assignments with dragons?"

Raven shrugged. "I don't know. You mean like at the ranches?"

"Or anywhere a dragon shows up." William chuckled and leaned toward her to bump his shoulder against hers.

"If you had that kind of assignment, Raven, you could come to Moss Ranch. Then it'd be your job to do what you do all the time anyway."

"Right. That sounds an awful lot like a secret ploy to get me to stick around after I graduate."

The dragon trainer watched the dragons roaming in the field and shrugged. "Maybe it is. It wouldn't be such a bad thing for you to stick around. Maybe I *want* you to stick around."

"Really?" She smirked at him and shook her head playfully. "I'm not sure you could handle me jumping off your roof every day of the week."

"Well, hopefully, you won't have to do that after you graduate. That should be far behind you by then, right?"

Raven laughed. "I hope so. But I think you're onto something about sending a mage out for dragon assignments."

"Oh, good. When that's your new thing, you can credit me and tell everyone that Moss Ranch is your number-one recommendation."

"I would anyway. If it ever came up in conversation."

In the field, Teo uttered a cry of excitement and bounded toward Leander and the other smaller dragon to join the fun.

"On a serious note, though, someone really does need to look into those dragon trainers and the handlers and riders in Azerad. That's probably not the only place it exists, but it's a start."

"Were they really that bad?"

"It wasn't the dragons' fault, William."

"I meant the trainers."

Raven closed her eyes. "Right. I didn't see anyone mistreating a dragon, if that's what you mean. But there was clearly something going on. Leander could feel it. *I* could feel it after a while. You said there were some trainers out there with a heavy hand. I'm starting to think it might be a little worse than that. Did your dad say anything more about it?"

"No." William grimaced and looked a little sheepish. "I barely had the time to bring it up. But I will."

"Okay. Let me know when you do. I'm not a graduated mage from Fowler Academy yet, so I can't exactly put my own assignment together and lead this myself. But I know I can do something as long as I know who to talk to and where to go. No one should abuse dragons, period. But I have a feeling those megadragons had some suspicions of their own about how dragons are treated these days."

"The...megadragons said that?"

"Not directly. Actually, they thought all humans were bad. Trainers were the real problems, obviously, but once I told them about how mages can work with dragons as familiars, things got a little dicey."

"Raven..."

She looked at him with a crooked smile. "What?"

"I'm so sorry."

A small laughed escaped her. "You didn't do anything. And I'm fine."

"I know you're fine. I'm glad you're okay." William shrugged quickly and turned away from her, pretending to watch the dragons.

Why won't he look at me? "So why do you look so upset?"

He swallowed loudly and released a deep sigh. "Honestly, I'm not sure if *I'm* okay."

"Oh. Then I'm sorry too."

"No, don't be." He turned quickly to look at her, and she froze when she saw tears swimming in his eyes. "You have absolutely nothing to be sorry about. You... I mean, look at you. You did more as a monster's prisoner than most people can even comprehend when they're going through their normal, daily lives. It's amazing that you kept it together so well. I don't think I would."

Raven bit her lip with a sympathetic frown. "It looks like you're doing a good job to me."

"I don't know. There's so much happening these days, you know? And since the day you came by the ranch and heard what Leander was up against if he didn't pass the dragon trials... I don't know." He shrugged. "Having you around has been the one thing that makes all the other stuff melt away. Even when you scare the hell out of me with your tricks."

She laughed, and it finally brought a small smile to the dragon trainer's face.

He leaned toward her a little more and met her gaze. "Jumping off roofs and flying bareback on a dragon are scary things to watch. I'll give you that. But none of it even came close to how terrified I was that we might not be able to get you back. And if that had happened, I don't—"

"It's okay." She nodded and studied his blue eyes that still swam with tears before she caught his hand and held it in both of hers. "You don't have to worry about me. I mean *really* worry, not like the scary little tricks."

After a glance at their hands, William licked his lips and

looked at her. "I know. But that's all that was in my head over the last few days, and I couldn't get it out. If something happened to you... Raven, I don't know if I could keep going the same way."

She froze and he squeezed her hand. *This is actually happening right now.* "What way is that?"

"Having something to look forward to every day." His other hand came up and brushed aside the lock of hair hanging loose beside her temple. "Like this."

William's warm hand settled against her cheek and he leaned slowly toward her. Raven closed her eyes and raised her chin.

"Raven!"

"*What?*" She and William jerked away from each other. Hovering between them was the circle of shimmering light opened by a Full Appearance.

"You did it!" Bella grinned despite the need to concentrate to keep the spell open. Henry and Murphy's faces appeared in the circle and both of them smirked.

"We're so glad you're okay," Murphy said.

"I...yeah." Raven laughed and glanced at William to mouth, "Sorry."

He chuckled and shrugged.

"So, since no one else is gonna call it, Alby, let me say that your face when Bella opened this spell looked an awful lot like you were about to—"

"Where are you guys?" Raven stood from the edge of the porch and made sure not to turn so her friends wouldn't see William Moss seated on the edge of the porch with her. *It's none of their business, even with an interruption.*

"Still on the grounds," Bella said.

"We waited after class," Murphy added. "Gilliam told us she was waiting to hear from Flynn about how everything went. As soon as she told us, Bella cast the spell."

"And I did not want to try opening it four ways again," Bella added.

She nodded and folded her arms. "Yeah, good call."

"Seriously, Alby, who's there with you?"

She ignored Henry. "Hey, thank you for everything, guys. I wouldn't be standing here right now without you."

"Which is where, exactly? Ow!" He flinched and chuckled when Murphy elbowed him in the ribs. "You're not curious about this?"

"Now we're crossing our fingers that Flynn won't expel us for helping," Murphy added.

"What?"

"That was kind of the deal." The girl shrugged.

Henry scoffed. "Yeah, which none of us actually agreed to."

"He can't expel any of you." Raven shook her head. "I'm sure he's obligated to give you guys some kind of medal or something. You know, as heroes of Lomberdoon and all that."

"Sounds nice." Murphy grinned.

"Or *maybe* we won't have to take our finals and it's an automatic in for the rest of our training at Fowler!" Henry spread his arms dramatically and opened his mouth in excitement.

"You have the right attitude, Derks." She laughed. "I'll tell you guys all about what happened when we get back to Brighton tomorrow."

"Oh, yeah. Good idea." He patted Bella's shoulder and

she squinted through the open window of the spell. "We don't wanna waste all Bella's magic with this if we don't have to."

The girl rolled her eyes. "We only wanted to see you. Now that we know you're okay, we can wait a little longer to hear the rest."

"Sounds good. I'll see you guys tomorrow."

"Wait!" Henry shouted. "Give us a tiny hint about—"

Bella cut the spell off, and the young mages' faces disappeared with the shimmering light.

Raven chuckled and shook her head. "I'm sorry."

William looked at her from the edge of the porch. "I thought I told you not to be."

"Still. That was a poorly timed…surprise."

"Nah, don't worry about it. Your friends deserve to know you're okay and back to civilization. If I had magic like that, I would've used it a long time ago to check on you."

She bit her lip through a smile. "Well, thanks."

He leapt to his feet and headed across the porch toward her. "I'm gonna turn in, anyway. Flynn wasn't kidding about a lack of sleep all around."

"Okay." *Well, there went that moment.*

The dragon trainer opened his arms and pulled her in for a long, tight hug. She slid her arms around him and closed her eyes. He took a deep breath and muttered in her ear, "I'm really glad you're okay."

"Me too."

When he released her, he didn't pull away very far to meet her gaze. "Goodnight, Raven."

"Night."

William pressed his lips against her forehead, slipped through the door into the Benicio Inn, and left her alone on the side porch.

With a sigh, she shuffled to the chair at the head of the table and slumped into it. *Maybe it's a good thing we were interrupted. I need less complicated right now, not more. But that was—*

An image from Leander entered her mind—his view from the dragon paddock of Raven and William leaning toward each other, one of his hands in hers and the other cupping her cheek.

When it faded, she leaned forward in her chair and searched for her dragon among the others. He stood right at the fence, his head weaving from side to side. "You were spying on us, huh?"

His hissing laughter traveled the short distance from the paddock to the porch.

Raven rolled her eyes playfully. "Okay. Get out of my head for a little while, dragon. I like my own memories, thank you very much."

He stretched his wings and looked at the sky glowing with sunset. When he screeched, a few other dragons in the paddock echoed it.

"Yeah, I'm happy too." She slid her hand into her pocket and pulled out the key to her room for the night.

A bed sounds really nice right now. And getting back to normal life tomorrow to put this completely behind me. Even if I still have to wait a little longer for Grandpa to come home.

Standing from the chair, she gave her dragon a goofy

little salute, turned, and headed inside to sleep on a mattress with sheets instead of the cold stone floor of a dragon's cave.

I'd better make sure that's never an option again.

CHAPTER THIRTY-THREE

A cross the unclaimed lands beyond the wall surrounding Lomberdoon, a young man named Cadmus Vudro stumbled through the slanted front door of the tiny hut he shared with his mother and father. Their raised voices followed him outside into the evening light, and he gritted his teeth against the anger that rose within him.

The view of their neighbors' rundown huts with makeshift roofs and the refuse and junk scattered about the tiny yards of the destitute village all but forgotten by the king and queen of Sterlin Velt only fueled his rage. He stalked down the trampled road that was little more than a well-worn footpath. His bare feet were covered in calluses from a lifetime of only wearing shoes when his parents took him to the temple to pay tribute to the old gods. Even those had had holes in them for the last three years.

They can't stop me from trying. I don't care if I have to steal everything I see to get us out of this hellhole. I won't work myself to the bone for scraps. Not anymore.

"This is the lot we were handed by Old Skybrow himself," Cadmus' father had told him. "We make do with what we have, and if we've satisfied the gods by our deeds in this life, we'll return for another life with much more at our disposal to help us improve."

Bullshit. He kicked a clod of dirt and it puffed into a spray of dust as he stormed down the path. *Pleasing the gods is a coward's excuse. Just because I was born to cowards doesn't mean that's what I have to be.*

His rage fumed within him until his arms tingled with a warm itch, almost like the pins and needles of a sleeping limb returned to life but not quite.

The young man—who was old enough to have already passed through at least one year of magic school if he'd been born to different parents in a different kingdom— glanced at his clenched fists. The tingling in his arms spread to his hands and he opened them slowly. *My arms can't fall asleep from making a fist.*

Shaking his hands, he stopped at the huge oak tree that had died three years before, although no one had bothered to cut it down.

"No one ever bothers to improve anything around here," he seethed. "They simply work themselves to death, keep their heads down, and constantly pray and pay tribute while they wait for damned gods to give them a pat on the back. Old Skybrow can rot for all I care. And take every single one of the other gods with him. They're all useless!"

Cadmus thrust his hand toward the dead oak tree as if he'd held something to throw at it. The warm tingle flared in his chest now and seared down his arms. Before he knew what was happening, a black burst of energy streaked from his open hand and struck the center of the tree.

The dead oak cracked and split and the hollow wood splintered down the middle before the bare branches tilted sideways. The top half of the tree landed with a resounding crunch and bounced, while broken branches scattered in every direction like poorly carved arrows.

The young man raised his arms to shield his face and head from the worst of it, and when he lowered them, his mouth fell open.

Shouts of surprise and alarm came from the other villagers, and his mother screamed his name as her bare feet pounded down the footpath toward him.

He stared at his open palm and forced his mouth shut. *I did that. It came from me.*

"Cadmus!" His mother reached him, threw her arms around his broad shoulders, and pressed her head against his shoulder because that was as high as it would reach. Her hands roved over the back of his head, desperately smoothing his hair. "What happened? Are you all right? That was the most horrible sound. I thought the Hangman had split the ground to take us with him..."

None of her babbling penetrated his awareness. His body rocked as she hugged him again, but the young man could only stare at his hand. It didn't shake in the least, nor was there any pain. In fact, it felt strong despite the absence of the tingling warmth he hadn't recognized.

He felt strong.

A small smile flickered at the corner of his mouth. *Curse the lot we've been handed. In this life, I mean to take what I deserve. And everyone will know what I can do.*

The End

While Raven Alby prepares for her final exams as a first-year mage in training at Fowler Academy, she finally discovers the truth behind her parents' deaths. Was it really an accident? Is the Order of War Mage keeping secrets, hidden from two entire kingdoms? Get ready for the revelations behind the history of where Raven Alby comes from and the sacrifices that were made for the safety of Lomberdoon's people. But with magic returning in unexpectedly dangerous ways, will the secrets drive a misinformed young man with powerful magic of his own to seek a mistaken revenge on all mages? Will her mother's sacrifice be for nothing? Find out in WarMage: Unleashed!

Get sneak peeks, exclusive giveaways, behind the scenes content, and more.
PLUS you'll be notified of special **one day only fan pricing** on new releases.

Sign up today to get free stories.

CLICK HERE

or visit: https://marthacarr.com/read-free-stories/

Have you started the Goth Drow series from Martha and Michael? Book one is Once Upon A Midnight Drow and it's available now through Amazon and Kindle Unlimited.

I'm not Goth to hide my Drow heritage, I'm Goth because I'm not a quitter.

My name is Cheyenne Summerlin, remember that name. Somebody should…

The world can't know I'm a Drow halfling. Not yet. I

barely have these powers under my control, but time's up. I'm about to take magic for a test drive. Want to come along?

The black ops government group believe they can run my life... But I have plans of my own.

Watch out magical evil doers – I'm about to crash your party.

But will my training be enough?

Grab your copy today from Amazon or Kindle Unlimited.

Michael Anderle likes to say I sometimes author note block him with my stories. I take it as a compliment. Here's another good one.

If you've been coming to the Adult Story Time on Facebook Live (Monday through Friday at 1 pm CT – right now it's WarMage Book 01) you've heard the good dog Lois Lane in the background barking at the window in her deep baritone. She could give any police dog a run for their money. She was born deaf and half the time she's running to the front window already barking, hoping something is going on but a lot of the time there's nothing.

She's squirmy, loves to run zoomies, sheds fur like it's a superpower, leans against people with all 90 pounds when she wants her back rubbed and unfortunately eats poop – and I adore her. We first met at a Christmas parade when she was just 11 months old. The local animal shelter was holding an adoption booth. I wanted a dog – I was a first-time homeowner and wanted to complete the picture. My choices were between a small thirty-pound dog that was described as a 'busy bee' and Lois Lane, who was deaf. She stood very still and didn't react to noises around her. I thought she'd be quiet and easy to manage.

But, what I wasn't really getting at the time was that Lois Lane hadn't really discovered how to live, yet. She had spent all 11 months of her life – minus the 30 days in the shelter – locked in a crate and never, not ever, let out. To this day I never put her in a crate or confine her in a small room. It's too much for her.

What I discovered was that for her grass was a new experience, a couch was a new thrill, a dog bed was something wondrous and other dogs were a mystery. She had no experience with toys and would often fall asleep standing up with her head crouched down, like she was still in that confined space. And sweet Lois had terrible separation anxiety (deaf dogs are often referred to as Velcro dogs – they typically stay near you but hers took it a few more steps). It took a year of trying every trick and lots of training and finally lots of doggie day care but eventually she figured out, I always return. Along the way a lot of things got chewed up, including the frame around the door I always left by, but that's okay. Wood gets replaced. And who knew that a door mat when carefully shredded could look like brown puffy clouds in the backyard.

At daycare, where they loved her, she learned how to play and that's when we all discovered she's endlessly curious and somewhat mischievous. They spotted her getting a dog to help her untie a sun sail and for a while she liked to take off other dog's collars and play keep-away.

We also discovered she's endlessly kind. In fact, Lois Lane got to pay it forward in a way every time there was a new dog who had come from a similar situation, cowering in a corner, not sure how to play. Lois would teach them the ropes.

Lois is only six years old at this point and still runs like a puppy (looks more like a horse) and I have a thousand stories about her at this point – like the time she scooped up a baby bird in her mouth and I was yelling at her to drop it. She sheepishly opened her mouth and just let the unharmed bird roll to the ground. It got up squawking mad and wet and strode away while Lois looked at me with her big eyes. Anyway, by the time she's old, I will be too and along the way there will be so many more goofy stories and probably a lot more very loud barking. (All the neighbors seem to know where my house is…) I'm glad I picked Lois Lane that day, even if I didn't know what I was getting into because it turned out to be a lot more than I could have ever hoped for. More adventures to follow.

BOOKS BY MARTHA CARR

Series in the Oriceran Universe:

SCHOOL OF NECESSARY MAGIC
SCHOOL OF NECESSARY MAGIC: RAINE CAMPBELL
ALISON BROWNSTONE
THE DANIEL CODEX SERIES
THE LEIRA CHRONICLES
I FEAR NO EVIL
FEDERAL AGENTS OF MAGIC
SCIONS OF MAGIC
THE UNBELIEVABLE MR. BROWNSTONE
REWRITING JUSTICE
THE KACY CHRONICLES
MIDWEST MAGIC CHRONICLES
SOUL STONE MAGE
THE FAIRHAVEN CHRONICLES

Series in The Terranavis Universe:

The Adventures of Maggie Parker Series
The Adventures of Finnegan Dragonbender
The Witches of Pressler Street

OTHER BOOKS BY JUDITH BERENS

OTHER BOOKS BY MARTHA CARR